ROSINA

A NOVEL

ROSINA

A NOVEL

MIRIAM POLLI

SERVING HOUSE BOOKS

Paperback ISBN: 978-1-947175-85-3
Hardcover ISBN: 9781947175860
Library of Congress Control Number: 2024950513

Cover art by Bella Agostino
Cover design by Jacob Arms

Printed in the United States
Published by Serving House Books
Lawrence Landing Company
Raleigh, North Carolina 27609

www.servinghousebooks.com

Serving House Books is a proud member of:

Independent Book Publishers Association
 and

Community of Literary Magazines and Presses

SERVING HOUSE BOOKS

FOR MY FATHER, ROMEO,
WHO LIVED A LIFE OF DESPAIR

Even God cannot change the past.
—Agathon (447-401 BC)

1

On a sun-sharp, cold afternoon at the end of March in 1913, some twenty-five miles south of Boston, Rosina stretches out on her bed and catches a whiff of sweet carrots and sage simmering in the veal stew she had prepared. The walls of the room had given up their chill to the assurance of spring. Yet, she feels the ache of more snow to come in the bareness of her feet. She reaches for the pink and gray blanket she crocheted years before: uneven, loopy stitches, enough for a toe or elbow to poke through, yet still cozy and familiar enough to soothe and cover her protruding belly. This baby takes more energy than she thought possible. A tiny foot pushes against her ribcage, and she touches the spot. It jabs into the concave of her palm. *Presto, amore mio*, she says. Soon, my love.

Floating on the edge of a daydream, she is startled by a loud crashing sound. Through the sheers of the third-floor window, past the iron ribs of the fire escape, she recognizes the black woolen cap of the landlord as he wrestles his way up the steps, carting yet another pigeon cage to the rooftop. Lowering the shade, her elbow bumps against the industrial-sized soup can, heavy with the coins they collected for the victims' families. Taped to the can is a faded photo of the eleven-year-old girl crushed when the factory ceiling fell as she worked at her sewing machine. Under her picture, the words—NEVER AGAIN.

It's too difficult for Rosina to imagine the child's death. She cups her swollen breast and wonders how a mother survives. The factories, the sweatshops, someone *must pay*, and then she turns to the coins. *What good is this money doing sitting on their desk?* She can't believe they haven't had the time to distribute it. Pamphlets scattered next to the soup can need to be folded for tonight's meeting. Three weeks since the tragedy and the work stoppage at the Silk Mill, and although she has learned there is much to be afraid of in this world, she has made up her mind not to allow fear to own her.

She gathers a lapful of pamphlets into her apron, brings them to the bed, and begins folding them into threes. Bomb violence was never her choice, yet the handout before her instructs the reader on how to assemble and detonate a homemade bomb. The front fold now reads in large black print:

CAPITALISM IS FABLED FREEDOM.
A DEVICE TO DOMINATE.
SOME GIVE ORDERS,
WHILE OTHERS TAKE THEM, DIVIDING US.

The flyers are disturbing, but revolutionists cannot sit by and do nothing. Something stirs inside her—the idea of bloodshed. Blood on blood never works. She wonders if Nicola has read the brochure.

A gulping sound comes from the small fish tank on their dresser. The goldfish glide, left, right—a metered tempo. Mesmerized by the simplicity of their monotonous rhythm, Rosina's thoughts shift to home: Italy, Lago di Garda, those years spent in the convent. How enchanting it suddenly seems against the noise of her current city life. The low *Italia* sun hid behind the trees cut sharply through the tall timbered pines as she'd run down to the lake after lessons and chores. She sighs, yearning to swim in that lake again, especially now, heavy with a baby. She imagines the pleasure, floating, buoyant, soft freshwater licking, ruffling over her skin until she's whisked back by the creak of the front door and her husband Nicola calling.

"Dove sei? Where are you? *Cara mia, dove sei?"*

Nicola kisses her fully on the mouth. He smells of new, raw leather. Oily. Stronger than usual. Having recently constructed his first pair of women's shoes, his self-belief is poised in his facial expression. He is now that expert shoemaker he so wanted to be.

"How is my son?" His hand, brown leather-stained fingertips, as if he were a chain smoker, glide over her stomach.

Pregnancy has heightened her sense of smell. Her sensitivity to leather is sickening. Bloody skins of animals are what she smells. A scent she can't get out of her nostrils or share with Nicola. "Wash, *amore*," she says. "We don't have much time before the meeting."

Nicola puts his arm around her lower back and helps her into a sitting position, his eyes adoring, unguarded, a trusting look he shares with everyone. She knows his generosity towards others and finds herself envious at times; his trusting nature borders on naiveté. Her jealousy towards the attention he gives others seems more profound now, another absurd notion of pregnancy. Also, she is acutely aware, and more sensitive to the sights and sounds of their life. She smiles when she hears her husband singing "*L'idea,*" a song they've been practicing.

She sighs deeply once again and thinks of how much she misses the Italian rural life and yet is drawn back to all that makes this her home: A basket of assorted material swatches in the corner, sock darner, pin cushion stuck with needles and straight pins, a shoebox filled with colored spools of thread. The cracked mirror they found at the street curb, gifting her with streaks of copper hair, hangs idly over the heavily grained oak dresser with its gilded frame. Secure in her environment, she can tell time by the comings and goings of neighbors, by the wheels of the fish peddler's cart rolling on the cobblestone street in front of their apartment house. She is attached to sounds–the creak, and the floorboards cracking when Nicola walks across the room.

There is more. On the kitchen table, straw-covered wine bottles with ribbons of wax cascading down the sides hold candle wax from the day they married over a year ago. The colander swings on a loose hook and clangs when she opens the cupboard door. Sounds and sights make her feel safe, rooted in time, unlike the uncharted months ahead, with no one to help or show her the way with a newborn. She had found a little lithographed illustrated book about nursing at the library. It wasn't shelved or cataloged, merely laid out casually on a table near the exit. An offering, she felt. A few pages bonded together. The author-artist signed her first name, Carolina. On the cover is a sketch of an infant nursing on an exposed breast. Someone had covered the nipple and baby's mouth with a square of gray electrical tape, then rubber-stamped over the tape: Stoughton Massachusetts Library.

At dinner, Nicola places the anarchist newsletter, *Cronaca Sovversiva,* aside and reaches for a piece of bread. "Did you read any of this yet?" he asks.

"No," Rosina says. "Just the pamphlets."

"Luigi Galleani is just the leader we need."

"Hmm, we'll see." After all the times Nicola praised this man, he will be speaking tonight. Their excitement has been building all week.

"Read the story about the Mexican, Emiliano Zapata," Nicola says and swallows his last bite. He taps the article with the end of his fork. "He's doing good work in Mexico. So much resistance."

She quips, "Anarchy and resistance, they come together." She pours a small glass of red homemade wine one of their comrades gifted to Nicola. "Would love to have some vino," she says.

"Have some. It will be good for you and the baby."

She knows the effects of drink make her too relaxed, affecting her sensibility. It's foolish, but she worries the baby might experience what she experiences.

"I'll wait," she says. "We have to leave in fifteen minutes." She reaches for Nicola's plate and hers and takes them from the table.

Ironically, the meeting is held at the Knights of Columbus Hall. Rosina can only assume that the Knights, who are heavily connected to the church, don't know of their ideology, their agenda against government. They arrive at the hall just after eight o'clock, and eighty or more men are already crowded into the small room. Like Nicola, the men are all dressed in dark suits with dark overcoats, well-groomed with clean white shirts. Some with ties, others with unbuttoned collars. Rosina was only recently aware of how American men and women dress, with their choices far more colorful and varied in style. As if they somehow knew something Italian immigrants, like herself, would never grasp. She spots a woman across the room, the only other female in the hall. She wears a brooch on her hat that sparkles from the low ceiling lights. Her own brown maternity dress and plain felt coat suddenly become drab.

Biscotti is passed around, and at a corner table, a man with a large, dented pot pours out one cup of coffee after another. They sit on black folding chairs. Written on the back of the seats in gold-rimmed plaques are the words, "Donated by Giuseppe Salvemini Funeral Home."

"Last week, the hall wasn't half as crowded," Nicola says. Leaning in, Rosina strains to hear him over the chatter. "*Uno momento,*" he says.

Nicola lifts the shopping bags of pamphlets, carries them to the front of the room and places them next to a podium. A group of men near the podium in serious conversation ask Nicola to join them. Rosina grins at how different they were when it came to meeting new people; he, open to everyone and everything. The Nuns and Mother Superior had nicknamed her *La ragazza timida.* After a while, they called her plain, *La timida.* The truth was, she wasn't timid. She felt browbeaten by their rules, worn by their silent control and angry her parents left her behind to find their way in America. The two-and-a-half years she spent at the convent, before her parents sent for her, stripped her of belief in God; the very opposite of what her mother and father intended.

Even as a young child, when visiting the riches of Vatican City with her parents, knowing of the Roman Catholic vow of poverty, Rosina felt an incredulous irony toward those who believed. Since she had read Tolstoy's *Anna Karenina* and the poems of Giacomo da Lentini, she felt betrayed by the Church. The only book she ever encountered at the convent was, sadly, the Bible. The Sisters' world ruled by the Bible seemed very small to her. Even at eleven years old, she felt a sense of superiority. Snobbishness led her away from most, allowing her to sink into her solitary world. Now she felt blessed to have Nicola in her life. He filled the spaces in her, gave her what she herself didn't possess. Besides, he was the hardest working man she had ever known.

Two men sit a few chairs away from Rosina, they tap their feet impatiently and hold their hats on their laps. Their glances are on her. Each time she looks at them, they are staring. She wants to stand and remove her brown wool coat to show how ridiculous their attention is. Instead, she smiles to herself, reminding herself of the foolishness of many Italian men.

A stout man from the front of the room shouts. "*Signori, prego siedano, per.* Please sit." The woman with the hat moves to the row in front of Rosina, nods, and smiles as Nicola weaves his way to his seat.

When Luigi Galleani appears, the room explodes with shouts and applause. He is tall and thin, and his coarse beard is grown in a wiry wooly "V," while the ends of his mustache are curled tightly. *He looks more like a Russian Tsar*, Rosina thinks, like one she saw in a history book. Triumphantly he pumps both fists in the air as the shouts persist.

He has a handsome, kind face, bluish-gray irises, the lightest eyes Rosina has ever seen. It is rumored while in prison in Italy, he somehow managed to persuade the wife of the prison warden of his revolutionary ideas and ended up bringing her with him to the United States.

"I welcome all my friends here."

Nicola squeezes her hand excitedly.

"A dear friend of ours once said, 'Government is an association of men who do violence to the rest of us.' Tolstoy, a great man, knew this years ago. Like Gandhi, he surrendered to pacifist beliefs. We now see the results or the non-results of the nonviolent approach. They refused physical violence. Why?"

One could hardly hear him over the shouts of approval.

"We are called anarchists. What is anarchy?" He pauses and scans the crowd. The audience begins to quiet. And in the silence of that moment, Galleani's eyes watch her, or perhaps on the woman in front of her. The baby kicks; pushing against her sitting bones. She wants to stand, doesn't want to call attention to herself, so instead, she repositions her weight.

"We are visionaries who believe in human nature. We envision a free society that allows all human beings to realize their full potential. Freedom from formal education. Our children's appetites for learning are based on need and want. We are opposed to domination—such simple needs, yet!"

Shrieks of encouragement and gratifying "*Si`. Si`*s" fill the room as Luigi Galleani continues to speak.

A chill of excitement crawls over Rosina's skin; is she truly in the right place at the right time? Nicola squeezes her hand; his lips brush her ear. "We are damned fortunate to be part of history."

Was a false sense of achievement consuming them? Were they all mad? Too idealistic?

Still, pride consumes her; her individuality—her need to live by the truth—to build a better world. Although having found her cause years before, she never felt it more than now in this room filled with strangers.

Galleani motions for the crowd to sit. "We are considered disruptive because we see government and the state as an ultimate expression of organized violence." He stops speaking and looks around the room. "Yes, my friends, what does the state equal?" Now walking back and forth in front of the podium, "State equals legalized aggression." His left fist lands in his right hand. "Slavery, right here under our noses." Another fist into his hand. "Mass murder, war, and the soldier, a hired assassin." Another punch. The clamor of the crowd grows louder. "We've tried passive resistance in the past, and civil disobedience during the strikes, and boycotts, and have had peaceful demonstrations, only to have our people beaten with police sticks and end up in jail. Let us not forget the executions of innocent men from Barcelona. We are being killed from Spain to Mexico, to Italy and France," Galleani says with fervor, both arms in the air. He again signals the group to sit down.

Nicola whispers, pointing to a man in the second row, "That fellow over there, the one with the bow tie, told me once you hear Galleani speak, you're ready to go out and shoot the first police officer you see." Still applauding, Nicola laughs. Rosina, caught up in the excitement, never felt so welded to a community of like-minded people.

"My philosophy, my belief, was and still is the greatest bomb we could possibly make is made of the written word. This is why I will continue to print the chronicle, *Cronaca Sovversiva.*"

He waved the newspaper. "They've closed me down repeatedly, but they cannot stop the written word. Emile Zola says, 'Truth marches on, and nothing will stop it.' And so will *Cronaca Sovversiva.*"

The crowd grew louder in agreement. Galleani motions to quiet the room. "Sadly, there are those who do not read, who do not understand, who do not want to know because it is easier for them to be told what to do. Like the sheep who follow the sheep, they believe they are safe until they reach the guillotine. And then it is too late." He coughs and takes a drink of water from the glass on the podium.

"He is so like my brother," Nicola says.

Rosina remembers when Nicola came to say he wanted to take his brother's name. She recalls meeting his brother. His unrestrained manner and bold enthusiasm were traits her husband interpreted as courage. Be it courage or foolishness, Rosina still wasn't sure where all this would lead, but her resolve, their resolve, to help change the world for better was strong.

Luigi clears his throat, "This is not an American problem. This is a world problem."

She leans to her husband's ear, and whispers, "Isn't that why we left Italy? Poverty, chaos. The same greed as in America."

"Everywhere there are masters and servants, oppressors and oppressed, rich and poor. Never has the world been so blindly united in suffering. Yes, the proletariat came to this country only to find all nations resemble one another."

While Galleani pauses for a moment to accept pamphlets handed to him by an associate, Nicola writes the word, "Proletariat" on a piece of paper. His habit of searching for words in the dictionary, to learn as many as possible, had recently developed.

A man in the audience shouts, "*Ma cosa possiamo fare*?"

"*Aspetate, per favore*," Galleani says with a halting hand gesture.

"We've all come here, to the land of plenty, only to be stricken down. To be discriminated against, to be denied work, to be arrested for an opinion." He waves one of the pamphlets Rosina had folded in the air. "The gentleman just asked, 'what can we do?' I offer you this knowledge. If you choose to use it. Look over the information here. In the future, we may be destined to enforce it."

He thumps his chest with his fist, "*Amici miei, con amore. Viva L'idea!*."

Everyone stands and shouts, "*Viva L'idea!*"

Luigi Galleani tries to speak over the howling, then waves to two men who walk to the front with their mandolins. "Listen to Mario and..." He laughs, trying to be heard through the standing ovation. "...sing original songs for 'the idea,' for all of humanity."

Nicola embraces Rosina from behind, and sways to the music and hums along. The songs bring tears to Rosina. Lyrics speak of universal love, of workers stricken with oppression and the hope for a freer new world in America. Chairs are folded and then moved aside as some begin to dance.

The woman in front of Rosina turns to her, "My name is Susan. I'm so happy to find another woman here."

Rosina takes her hand in hers, they have a good firm grip, equal to each other. "My name is Rosa, and this is my husband, Nick."

Susan's blue eyes study her face, "I remember you," she says, "Aren't you the woman who was voted 'most beautiful working girl in Massachusetts?' When was it? Two years ago?"

Rosina blushes. "It's no fault of mine. Someone entered my picture. *Fault,* is right word?"

"Fault?" Susan says, "It's an honor!"

"My wife doesn't take credit for her beauty," Nicola shouts over the music. "She says it's purely an accident of birth."

Rosina tries to recall if Susan was one of the women in her row of sewing machines. Number 19 "sleeve" machine pops into her mind. She hadn't thought of the sweatshop for some time. One afternoon, Bianca, the girl who was on the "collar" machine, number 22, had sneaked her husband in through the side door, while the foreman was on his lunch break. Bianca's husband had a new camera that came from France and was practicing being a photographer for weddings and baptisms. He snapped pictures of all the girls.

"Were you on piece work too?" Rosina asks.

"Oh, no. Not at all. I can't sew a straight line." Susan laughs. "I was one of the people who organized the demonstrations outside the factory. For a couple of weeks there, I remember seeing your photograph posted on the outside of the building. Even a larger one on the trolley I took going home each night. I never forget a face."

Rosina is flushed with embarrassment. She hates this kind of attention. "Are you still picketing there?" A dumb question.

"No. We moved on. I go where I'm needed. When are you due?"

Rosina is distracted as a man hands a newspaper article to Nicola, and they begin protesting the unlawful deportations.

"It'll be another five weeks or so. I hope no longer."

"Well, good luck to you," Susan says as she finishes buttoning her coat. "Perhaps we'll see each other again at one of these meetings. I'll be going down to Washington in two months for the Suffrage March." Glancing at Rosina's stomach, she says, "I guess that leaves you out."

Something about this woman makes Rosina feel comfortable. The skin on her face glows. Light rouge on her high cheekbones. If her eyes were darker and her hair reddish-brown instead of blond, they would've looked like sisters; they were also the same height and build.

"*Si*," Rosina says. "Come to my house when you can, and I'll make you a cup of black coffee."

Rosina begins to write their address on the back of a pamphlet.

"Oh, I'd love to. The friends I have serve only tea."

"I can make you tea if you'd like."

Susan laughs, "No, please. It's just what I don't want."

2

Rosina was barely thirteen years old when her parents summoned her by telegram to come to America.

Mother Superior sat behind her desk and read the telegram to her as though Rosina was incapable of reading. Pacing in front of her, she waved the caramel-colored paper nervously: "America is not a place for young girls who don't know how to care for themselves." Her oval-shaped face, framed by her black habit, flushed. "Not for the puny and the shy." The white band pressed against the doughy flesh of her forehead. "You have the good fortune to go where there is much opportunity." She stopped pacing and bent before her. Rosina caught the odor of her familiar sour breath. "Say your prayers twice a day and think of those who aren't as fortunate as you." Her voice rose angrily on the word "you."

Mother Superior's envy was gratuitous. God, her husband, her warrior, seemingly included her in the "less fortunate." For a moment, the divine teachings of the church allowed Rosina to fall upon compassion. Mother Superior had given so much, and yet at that moment, the threads of abandonment consumed her entire being.

The telegram had said Arturo Puccinelli, a longtime family friend, would escort her on the journey. Arturo was a large man with straight black hair parted neatly down the center and, apparently, pockets padded with lire. She recalled the evening he had his driver carry a round mahogany drum into their parlor with a wide-mouth brass trumpet-shaped horn bulging from its center. He and her father would crank the handle on the side of the gramophone and listen to Puccini and Wagner while moving chess pieces on the game board. He always wore a long cape, and his shoes were highly shined with black polish. He had a strange speaking voice, which rose a couple of octaves higher than expected, taking anyone within hearing distance by surprise.

The day they sailed on the Citta di Milano; Rosina never looked back. She tried to focus on the adventure ahead. As they walked up the gangplank to the ship's opening, Arturo said, "We're fortunate because this ship is fairly new, and the accommodations are modern."

As it turned out, Rosina slept on a bunk in the bowels of the ship with other women and children, while Arturo, four floors above her, shared a three-bed suite and enjoyed a porthole overlooking the ocean.

Days of seasickness blended into nights of lethargic sleep. Wild dreams filled her nights. She rode the backs of strange, grotesque animals in flight, gliding like the seabirds she had seen as the ship moved from the dock. Wide, swooping movements, to and fro like waves on the ocean. Wonderment enveloped her until a cold sweat woke her, and she reached for the pail near her bedside. On the sixth day, nausea began to subside, allowing her to move about. And to eat. She ate a bowl of pasta with ragù sauce, and it tasted like heaven.

A few nights before arriving in Boston harbor, she couldn't sleep. Two heavyset women slept on both sides of her cot. They snorted and yelped like donkeys did when they ate prickly pears. As she slipped quietly between the bunks passing the warning sign, "WOMEN MUST BE ACCOMPANIED AT ALL TIMES WHILE ON DECK," the stench from her underarms, muddied by sweat and an unwashed body, was foul. She climbed the steps to the upper deck where the ocean and sky were black, and the stars glowed like fireflies. Thousands blinking, sparkling, with unexpected clarity. It brought to mind her father, reading aloud to her from Galileo's "great" book. Cloudy masses, constellations, and the boggling distance of light-years all came flooding back. When her parents left her at the convent, her father gave her his book; now lodged somewhere in her suitcase. Rosina had become fascinated with the life of Galileo, especially when she learned of his house arrest at the age of seventy, lasting through his death. This great physicist condemned for his core beliefs was beyond her grasp. It wasn't long after reading of his struggles, and his intolerance towards hypocrisy, her own views and passion for social justice emerged. So, early on, a pattern had formed. Knitted to the outrage she felt toward class and discrimination, it seemed her life would be devoted to ending man's cruelties towards man. If someone would have asked her what she wanted to do, she wouldn't have been able to verbalize this powerful feeling.

On the ship's topside, Rosina wrapped her green woolen sweater around her torso and sat on the slotted wooden bench bolted to the deck. The rhythmic shish of the ship rising and the repetitive pistons of the steam engine slapping the ocean's surface shot her with tranquility. Above her, stars were alarmingly close, a ceiling of lights. She felt weightless, as though she were hovering among the stars. Her thoughts drifted back to the nuns and their confinement.

Sister Cristina: happy, ample and plump, with her quick small steps, called out with a joyous singsong tone, "*Eccoti, bambina mia! Dov'eri?.*" Sister Cristina was always in trouble with the other sisters for being loud. Suora Cristina would've loved this, Rosina thought. She saw the monastery, the rococo corridor with its high, gold-leafed arch. The faded fresco on the ceiling of Jesus and his followers, and at the end of the hall, a brutal, life-sized sculpture of Christ was pinned to the cross. Heavy wooden doors echoed through the hallways, leading to the vaulted refectory where they took their meals. The long plain benches, cool to the touch, and holy water in the marble bowl that somehow always seemed pleasantly scented was an odor she could never forget.

It wasn't the monastic silence, the severe cloistered life that unsettled her, or the persistent community prayers every three hours in the chapel, nor the required private time in your own prayer cell, with the threat of a nun stationed outside your door, her ear to the keyhole to be sure you were saying your penance; none of this plagued her. It was when the priest came, with his miasma of perfume swallowing up the air, his manufactured falsehoods. The priest whispering in her ear, the *Padre himself appointed me, to absolve you of sin, so you may enter heaven, clean and pure. You must always obey. Without my assistance, you cannot enjoy the favor of God.* His thin gray hair was greased to his pink scalp. "You are a disciple, a follower of Jesus. As you grow, it is even more important you obey. Refusing a priest any request is sinful." *Father, Son, and the Holy Ghost...* "A priest knows, knows what is in your heart, and if you don't speak the truth to him, you will burn in purgatory for eternity." ...*Father, Son, and the Holy Ghost.* His large hand on the top of her head, he forced her to her knees. "Now, kiss the ground before me." Her lips pressed tightly together, she pretended to kiss the marble floor. When she rose, "Good girl," he said, and ran his arthritic fingers down the length of her small arm, gripping it so tightly, he trembled. His bloodshot gaze lingered on in her long after she turned away from him.

Now so far from convent life, the nuns, that world, no longer seems real. She now questions the reality of another life. Seeing her parents after two years. How much will they have changed? How have they all changed?

She had dozed off on the bench. Uncertain how long she had slept, she heard noises coming from under the stairwell. A woman moaned, and the gruff of another voice muffled. She moved close to the area where the sound came from. Huge drums with thick roping wound around them, like giant spools of thread. At least twelve or more were stationed in the area of the stern. Tracing the sounds, it took Rosina a few moments to adjust to the available light from a single muted ship's bulb. Periodic spurts of laughter and moans led her to the place where giant spools of rope lay. There she saw a man and a woman coupled on the floor between two bobbins of cable. The man was on top, the woman's legs spread around his back, her shoes, the highest heels she had ever seen, pressed against his long black cape. Recognizing Arturo, she held her breath and backed against the steel wall. Arturo began to move faster. The faster he moved, the more inarticulate sounds he made, and then he screamed out as if in pain, and the woman began to laugh once again. Her voice deep and husky, more pleasing to the ear than his, she laughed until he rolled over to her side.

Back in her sleeping quarters, it was another restless night, unhinged by what she had witnessed. She thought of the convent, those nights exploring her own body. She was irked by the thought of a baby coming from such a small place. She was confused by the woman's laughter. Was she mocking him? Was she happy it was over?

She didn't see Arturo again until the day they disembarked, and then she couldn't look him straight in the eyes; she was haunted by his eerie moans. Upon leaving the ship, they were ordered to separate into two lines, males and females. After hours of questions and medical and eye examinations and stamped documentation, Rosina found Arturo waiting for her at the end of her line.

Rosina squinted in the bright sunlight. Sharp angled shadows awaited them at the end of the long pier. They walked from the dock area towards a group of buildings, which looked abandoned. It was a different atmosphere. The air in America was clean, more filtered, she thought. No smell of trees or flowers or dust of earth, no terra firma to cloud the senses. Her lungs took in the harsh reality of sharp concrete and steel. Here she was close to the ocean, but no longer smelled the sea. Her legs were uncoordinated, wobbly, as though she was still in the middle of the Atlantic.

Hundreds of people were waiting and waving behind a roped-off area. Amazingly, Rosina spotted her parents among what could've been a restless mob if they weren't there to greet a loved one.

She lifted her voice, "There, there they are."

Rosina was convinced her childhood years were over; the abandonment and loneliness which consumed her at the convent forced her to harden, or so she thought. Now with each step closer to her parents, she became that young Rosa, melting back into her father's embrace, and sensing her mother's unease—all knotted into her clenched fists.

She was shocked to see her father thinner and smaller than she remembered, and the lines around her mother's mouth deepen. She had envisioned her parents for so long, made a pact with herself to not cry. After all, they were the ones who abandoned her. They deserved to suffer as much as she had. Her father clutched her hand, and she thought to snatch it away, but his touch brought tears. As he pulled her into his arms, she was unable to keep from crying.

A man selling chestnuts pushed his way through the crowd. Amid his shouts she heard her mother talking with Arturo. Her tone, sharp, precise, and wooden. Shielding emotions. When she finally bent to kiss Rosina on both cheeks and asked how the trip was, she found her mother's eyes watery, but no tears, reminding her of her mother's expectations of order and refinement. So, out of an old habit, she reverted back to the child in "public" and replied, "It was fine."

Her mother placed her hand on her shoulder and let out a sigh of disbelief; how she'd grown.

"*Sei cresciuto un bel po*," she said. A familiar, tight grip was on her shoulder, and she squirmed. She knew it was one of affection, yet it never failed to make her feel on some level it was a kind of warning, an expectation she could never accord her mother.

Vibrations of the ship's engine still in her ears, Rosina walked into her new life in a dress she had washed and ironed so many times it showed thin and shiny on the elbows and collar, dragging all her possessions in a square valise secured with a thick rope.

3

In the claustrophobic three-room railroad flat, there is no privacy. Poor, working-class families occupy the three-story building. Her mother does not associate with any of them.

"*Calabresi*," her mother says, "all lower class."

Rosina spends her days taking sewing lessons from her mother, hemming, cuffing, and the great and famous buttonhole. She had already learned to sew hemlines at the age of seven, but her mother, an expert seamstress, tolerates nothing less than perfection.

"Easier making buttonhole by hand. You have more control but takes too much time." Her mother's calloused fingertips, especially her pointer fingers where she guides the material near the pulsing needle has hardened, yellowish like the outer skin of popcorn.

"In America, time is money," she says with authority. "The fabric must be pulled at just the right tension, or the edging of the buttonhole will pucker, making an unsightly garment."

The fleshy part of Rosina's fingertips are sore and scraped from the near misses of the needle. She must get it right. She doesn't want hands, fingers like her mother's. This is a temporary world, she keeps telling herself, not knowing what she wants to do, yet knowing this wasn't it.

In the small alcove where she sleeps, statues of saints are lined up on a shelf that is bound with a scalloped oil cloth. Saint Catherine of Siena, her mother's most revered saint, is at the forefront. She recalls her mother's oration: "Santa Caterina was the purist. She first saw Christ at the age of five. She married him when she was just twelve. No one, not even her parents believed her. She shaved all the hair off her head, slept on the floor, and starved herself until they allowed her to go to the monastery to be one with God. She had the "gifts." Sacrificed all to help others. No one else was ever allowed such a vision."

No one else was allowed such a vision. Gifts? In another world, she would be condemned, locked up in a mental institution, yet if she helped others, then good was there.

Turning off the lamp, Rosina remembers her dream the night before. Walking down long, dark corridors of the convent. Surrounded by locked rooms with heavy wooden doors opening one by one as she passed, afraid to look, sensing something menacing, something evil waiting inside the rooms. She had woken in a sweat. She hasn't prayed since she's been home, maybe she should? God is now merely a superstition...*Our father who art in heaven, hallowed be thy name...*

Her father brings home a remnant of cloth, a new material that has some give to it. Her mother says it is called jersey. Rosina laughs and says they should've called it New Jersey. Neither of her parents laugh. After months of practice, Rosina finds herself working in the same factory where her father oils and repairs sewing machines. The factory smells of dyes and musky fabrics. Her first day, she sits at a machine making buttonholes for twelve hours. The next day when Rosina goes to the washroom, she finds herself cornered by two women—backed against the sink. "I work here ten years," the woman with the bleached red hair says, "you come one day and take my job from me."

The other woman whose machine is next to Rosina's keeps poking her finger into Rosina's shoulder. "She waits to get this job. More money. You give her back the work."

Rosina is stunned. She had no idea she was being treated in any special way, earning more money than these women who worked here.

That evening on the trolley ride home with her father, she says, "I don't want to do the buttonhole machine anymore."

"*Perché bambina?*" He still calls her baby whenever he sees she's troubled.

"I just don't like it," she says.

At home, she hears her mother and father quarreling in the kitchen. Her father speaking for her, "Maybe it's too hard work for a young girl." There are no words between her and her mother until she starts to place the dinner plates on the table. Her mother is banging pots, then stops to call out to Rosina and turning from the steam of the pasta, she says, "What kind of nonsense is this?"

Rosina knows her mother will call her a moron for worrying about the other women, so she lies. "I don't want to make buttonholes all day. I'll do anything else."

"You make good money with the buttonhole. What's wrong with you?" Her mother's temper shows in her clenched mouth. "We work hard for this. Without money, you have nothing in America." She slams the pot of sauce on the gas burner. "*Stupida ragazza*," her mother says with the harshness of the nuns who raised her in the convent.

On the way to work the next day, Rosina tries to explain to her father, "It isn't fair. The woman was in line for the job. She's worked there for ten years."

"I know," he says, with a downcast expression. "But this is America. You have opportunity, you take it." Her father's downtrodden expression, more than his passivity, suddenly revolts her.

At the factory, sitting at the sewing machine, although nervous she might lose her job, she decides to not line up the bottom holes on the shirts. Instead, she makes irregular holes. The next morning, she finds her ploy has worked when the floor supervisor instructs her to go to the hemming machine. "This is your machine, from now on. Too young, much to learn. Thank God for your father, or you'd be living in the street."

A few days later, when Rosina passes the red-haired woman, the woman looks up from her buttonhole machine with a hardened smile and says, "*Grazie, piccolo. Grazie.*"

Rosina feels blessed at this moment. She has done good. Both for the woman and herself. She is proud of her convictions. She is not impotent like her father. It is the first time she fully knows the circuit of love moving through her. She will be fine. She is strong. This love will come with a price, but it is a price she can bear. Her mother's anger comes out in her paycheck; but Rosina doesn't care. Because each payday her father slips her a nickel, and she is still able to buy an occasional soda pop.

4

One of Rosina's coworkers tells her of an Italian American woman who is giving free English lessons at the library. After work, on Monday and Thursday evenings, Rosina walks to the library, stopping by a street cart to buy a piece of fruit to take to class.

The library is dimly lit with a familiar musty odor. The dark wood walls remind her of the convent, but here she enjoys the aroma of paper and glue and anything else that binds the pages together; perhaps the unaired odor of thousands of shelved books is what she smells. Some of them unmoved for years, she supposes. Her amazement is palpable. *All these words waiting to be read.*

The teacher is a middle-aged woman. Attractive, with a flair for hats with feathers and heavy shawls, which look like they came from exotic parts of the world. Rosina is one of three women taking lessons. After four weeks, she realizes she is ahead of the others. She's excited by the idea. Soon, some of these books will be open to her. At night she dreams of English words: bus-car-train-boat. Simple words, some of which she already knows: *Arancio*, orange. *Uva*, grapes. *Lattuga*, lettuce. Stopping at the fruit cart on her way to the library, she practices her English. "May I have an apple, please?"

Joe, the fruit peddler, has two fingers missing from his right hand, his pointer and ring fingers, but it doesn't stop him from making fun of her. He laughs, "Why you speak American? We Italians."

His remaining fingers, thick like short sausages, show his hands in such an odd asymmetry. Rosina wants to ask how he lost his fingers. It doesn't seem possible his middle finger, or for that matter, his chunky pinky was saved. Yet, his distorted hand doesn't stop him from being a know-it-all.

"American. They want to learn American." He makes a barking sound and spits up phlegm.

Lately, Rosina is less tolerant of this kind of ignorance.

"I'm learning English," she says. "American is not a language."

He dismisses her by waving his disfigured hand at her.

Walking away from the fruit peddler, satisfaction washes over her; she relishes learning and to be able to use the information she acquires. *No one can take this away from me,* she thinks.

The library begins to live inside her. Comfortable and warm. *Like home. No. Better than home.*

Mrs. Voltino says, "When you learn to read, everything and anything is possible." These words give Rosina hope. She is capable of so much! Such life teems and brims at the library. Knowledge. Ideas. The world.

When they're on a break, Rosina leafs through various magazines or simply browses the shelves, running her fingers along the bindings as she walks the aisles. She adores the children's books, with their colorful illustrations, further inspired by her ability to read them. She is intrigued and excited continuously by every new thing. It seems she will never get enough. Each week Mrs. Voltino brings in copies of the Italian newspapers. She says she wants them to learn English yet feels it's essential to not forget the homeland. Rosina becomes interested in *Il Proletario* and reads the weekly columns written by the editor.

This week a massive strike of textile workers, most of them women and children, have formed in the nearby textile town of Lawrence, where the mills are located. She is moved by a story of a young mother who worked more than fifty-six hours a week and died of malnutrition, leaving two babies behind. Apparently, there have been others; the workers live on a diet of molasses, bread, and beans. Their life span is only twenty-two years of age. Rosina places the newspaper on her lap and takes a deep breath. *Only four years older than me,* she thinks. Each week, Rosina rushes to class early so she can find the time to read Arturo Giovannitti's column, and with each column she finds the situation heightened, growing more intense; more workers fall ill, mostly children. She must try to find a way to travel the twenty miles to Lawrence, to help stand for the workers.

The library is thick with heat this evening. Rosina removes her scarf and unbuttons her high neck blouse. Mrs. Voltino unfastens her shawl and says something has gone wrong in the boiler room. It will be fixed shortly. Rosina worries about the books—she visualizes melted glue on the shelves. As soon as they open their notepads, two young men walk into the room. Mrs. Voltino speaks with them a few moments, and then introduces them as the Sacco brothers. The older one is tall, named Nicola. His brother, Ferdinando, has a pleasant, open face. He smiles a lot and tips his hat before removing it. Better dressed than his brother; he wears a white shirt with a gray woolen vest that holds his pen along with a pocket watch. Nicola's white shirt collar is open, his hair, tousled in black curls. While the teacher speaks to one of the other women, Rosina senses Nicola staring. She tries not to look at him, but when she does, he places his pointer finger to his cheek and twirls it, a gesture she had witnessed growing up, indicating a man wanted a woman. Turning away, she then hears his brother speak to him in a low voice. They converse in a dialect that is hard for her to understand, but she can tell it's a confrontation of sorts by the tone of their voices.

When class is over, Ferdinando smiles at Rosina, nods his head goodnight.

The next week, on one of their five-minute breaks, Ferdinando approaches her as she sits alone, going over her lessons. "Your English is mostly perfect," he says.

He sits across from her at the library table, under the dim light, his eyes directed at her. No one had ever looked at her in this way. It is as if the heat in the library is off kilter once again. Her body is on fire.

Late at night, as she tries to sleep. She sees his eyes, *nero come il cioccolato*. His deeply brazen expression, consuming her; owning her, the heat of him as though he is near her, so much so that she feels ecstatic.

Ferdinando soon begins to walk her home in the evenings. On one of those nights, he asks her out for *qualcosa per cena*.

The plan is to skip the Thursday night class and go to dinner.

Ferdinando meets her outside of the library. His hair is combed back sharply. He wears a light black long overcoat. Rosina didn't want to go home, have to explain to her mother she had a date, so she wore her navy corduroy skirt with a long-sleeved, high collared pink blouse, and her mother's tan raincoat. "I came straight from work," she apologizes.

He reaches for her hand and says, "You are always perfect." His touch makes her weak, silly, giddy. Her flesh suddenly feels alive. She recalls the triteness of the romance books she read when younger—the way she'd laugh with her schoolmates when the hero bent to put his lips against the heroine's, his hand brushing against her breast. Her curiosity and desire always peaked in the corniness of those moments.

"There's a family restaurant over on Highland Street, about seven blocks from here. *Mio Fratello.* Nicola, and I ate there once. Would this be okay?" His voice rises over the passing trolley car coming to a complete stop, blowing its whistle.

They rush across the brick-lined street, over the trolley tracks to where there is no construction. Passing a tobacco shop with its door wide open, they make their way through a sharp pungent smell of burnt chestnuts. Heightened awareness ensues as she looks through the plate glass window of the colorful, lively bakery. *Cannolis,* Napoleons, along with Sicilian *cassata* swollen with cream. She wants to say, I'd be happy just to have a pastry and coffee but doesn't.

"We should come back here, after dinner," Ferdinando says, his voice elated. "Have you ever been to the north side? The best *pasticcerias,* almost like home. One day we'll go."

On Tremont Street, they pass Wolff's Men's Clothing store. A man stands outside with slacks folded over one of his arms. In the other, he holds a man's black suit on a hanger.

"C'mon, fifty percent off. Come feel the material." He rushes in front of them, blocking them from moving forward. "Maybe, your wife would like to touch. Feel it," coaxing Rosina. "You won't get any bargain like this in all of Massachusetts."

"No. Thank you, thank you," she says. Ferdinando laughs and politely guides them past him. Rosina loves the kind, authoritative way he treats the man. *Is this what happiness is?*

The restaurant has six or seven wooden tables and chairs in the dining room. An empty bottle of wine with a candle in the center is on each table. The walls are painted a deep brick color with mustard-colored woodwork. Opposite where they sit is a painting, a scene much like *Lago Di Largo*; lush, green hillsides with a deep silver-blue lake. The only painting on the walls.

"It reminds me of home." Rosina says, indicating the canvas.

Ferdinando turns to look, "It could also be *Torremaggiore*, my village, as well. The lake areas are so alike."

A young woman with the same elongated nose as the woman who seated them comes to the table to take their order. Red vino, pasta *Ortolano*, together with a shared whole fish. The girl is efficient, yet extremely shy; all the while, she avoids eye contact. Rosina knows this girl. Too young to break out—doing what her family wants her to do—not what she wants to do.

A group of people enters the restaurant with a ruckus. Tapping their feet, shaking the water from their clothes while closing umbrellas.

"It's raining out," Rosina says. "My father always says rain is happiness." Rosina is surprised by her willingness to talk about her parents; "My mother has what some would call, a stone heart. Kind of ironic for an Italian mother, yes? Usually, they are on pedestals."

"Your mother might be a victim of our materialistic world. The lira, the dollar rules most likely. Unfortunately...."

The girl appears again, interrupts them by placing bread on the table. Ferdinando orders a bottle of *aqua minerale frizzante*.

"My whole life, I've felt sorry for my father," Rosina continues. "He's such a calm man, always wants to keep the peace. I'm afraid he hasn't really lived a full life."

"Sometimes, we look for something in others that's not there. Maybe your papa is happy this way. Maybe this is the life he's made for."

Ferdinando simplifies things, and somehow makes it easy for her to talk and reveal her passions and ideas.

He is learning the shoe trade. "I don't want to be merely a *creatore di scarpa*. I want to design shoes for the worker, as well for the aristocrats. Shoes that will last and be comfortable. When the leather is soft, pliable, it feels so good in my hands." He laughs. "I even love the oily smell." Soon, he is talking about his ten brothers. "My brothers always teased me. They're all in construction, and me being the youngest, well, they tease me. I am too delicate to put a nail in a wall or lay bricks. They used to call me 'the poet.' a chuckle. "I never once wrote a poem, but I always write down my ideas."

Loud talking, laughter, wild shouts come from the table where the group sits. Apparently, two of the young children squabble over something, and the girl begins to cry. The father takes the boy by his arm, moves him to the other side of the table.

The rain rumbles heavily on the restaurant's roof. Rosina and Ferdinando find themselves lifting their voices to be heard. She envies Ferdinando being raised in a large family. Growing up, she had wallowed in the idea of having sisters or brothers. She recalls asking her mother for a baby sister and the incredulous way her mother frowned and said, "We don't talk about those things."

"If I had siblings, my life would've been fuller, much better. Maybe then they wouldn't have sent me to the convent." Drinking the sparkling water, Rosina delights by the bubbles dancing on her tongue. She recalls the Sunday special treat of *aqua minerale frizzanti*, at the convent, something she hadn't appreciated at the time.

"I studied Catholicism, the Bible, plus attended more funerals in one year than the average person must attend in a lifetime. Nuns, along with priests, people I never knew." She smiles. "They lived long lives, and yet someone was always dying."

Behind them, a man enters the restaurant, apparently to get out of the rain, then uncovers a mandolin. He begins to strum, tuning the instrument.

They continue to talk about God, religion, the lack of it in their lives. They agree on the spiritual. That invisible energy dominating them from time to time. Rosina knows no one had ever, or would ever again, listen to her with this kind of attention.

"I believe in angels," Rosina says, "Not ones with wings and halos, but human angels."

"We have the same soul." One side of his mouth lifts to a smile. "Maybe we've been brushed by the wings of one of those angels," he says playfully.

She wants to answer, *yes*, and say, *You, you are the angel who has touched me*; instead, she quiets to the hum that inhabits her body; lets the pleading cry of the mandolin fill her.

Ferdinando tastes the pasta and says, "This is what Nicola had the last time we were here. He says it was wonderful." He takes another bite. "My brother, he is leaving for Italy in a few days. It makes me sad. He doesn't like it here. He says why work in America for slave wages when he can go home and help his own country to improve. He'll go home and start trouble again." He chuckles.

Ferdinando's expressions are animated, going from gloomy to bubbly.

"What kind of trouble?" Rosina asks.

"My brother, he goes beyond being an activist, he's a true vigilante. Truth is, he's my hero. Did you hear about the strikers over in Lawrence? We went there a few times to help out." Ferdinando sips his wine.

"I read about the water baths with the fire hose. I've wanted to go and help also." Rosina says.

"We were there, at the plant that day the police drenched us with fire hoses." His wide-eyed expression shows excitement. "We all ran onto the rooftops of the buildings, so you can imagine the force of the water we were hit with. Nicola saved two children from being hurt. Covering them with his body." The red wine reflects a hint of deep purple as he brings it to his lips. "Now that Nicola's leaving, there should be room in the van for one more. Will you come this weekend?" He reaches for her hand, holding it assuredly. His virile strength races through her. "*Giovannitti*, the editor of *Il Proletario,* who is also known as a poet," he chuckles, "...and a friend of his from New York. Ettor, the head man from the Industrial Workers of the World, has organized food stations. They need people to handle them."

"I didn't hear about this."

Ferdinando explodes with excitement. "Rosina, there are 25,000 workers on strike, from all the textile mills in the area." His enthusiasm is infectious; it thrills her. She wonders how this can be.

"Nothing like this has ever happened before! What a great idea to have men meld together for one purpose—such power." He reaches for her hand.

The man with the mandolin slowly walks around the room, playing familiar peasant music, holding out his dented cup between songs.

Ferdinando tightens his hand on hers. She's exhilarated, as though she has broken free. "If only people would stand together like this always, oppressive governments would never survive," Rosina says.

The girl brings the fish to the table—translucent well-done skin, crispier on the tail. Knife and fork in hand, Ferdinando begins to filet the fish. The fish, soft and succulent, melts in Rosina's mouth. Ferdinando asks for more lemon, squeezes two pieces of lemon on his portion, then adds salt.

In a burst of energy, Rosina says, "My mother always says never salt fish."

"Oh, she doesn't know what she's missing," he says. He doesn't take her mother's rules seriously. How refreshing to hear him dismiss her so quickly. She's compelled to lift the saltshaker, and sprinkle a little on her fish, but decides against it since she already enjoyed its salty taste.

"Even with all the anger I have for my mother, I know I'll cry harder for her when she dies. She has lived as such an unhappy person."

Ferdinando leans his fork and knife at the edge of his plate. Elbows on the table, he shakes his head yes, and clasps his hands in thought.

"Nicola." He takes a deep breath. "He's been at the Altar for closing down factories that are dangerous for workers. He's a very courageous man. He's built a coalition of men who embrace the worker, fight the corrupted system. Besides, he also has a couple of lovely women waiting for him."

"The Altar?" Rosina asks, visualizing the small, pristine shiny marble at the convent lit with candles. Frescoes of Joseph, Mary, and the apostles on the ceilings and the walls. "What altar?"

Ferdinando laughs. "I'm sorry, I'm so used to hearing the expression, I sometimes forget. That's what Nicola and his *compagni* call prison. They're always joking. So the term began because when a man is sent to prison, he finds himself praying more than ever. They joke among themselves, but of course, I imagine only when they have their freedom. 'You'll end up at the Altar.' 'I'm going to the Altar.' *Ancora e ancora.* It's almost like they're not afraid, but of course, again, this is only when they have their freedom."

He looks beyond Rosina as though contemplating their fearlessness in the brick-painted wall beyond. "I tend to follow the rules more than Nicola. Being behind bars is not for me."

Rosina smiles at the absurdity of prison equaling an altar. She delights in the image. In her mind, they are very nearly the same. Her aunt, Erminia, comes to mind. Having lost her son at the age of ten to a fever that never broke. Her mother had taken her to the church with

Erminia, to speak to the priest. Her aunt fell onto her knees, begging him for an answer: *Why would God take my innocent Ignazio.* Rosina, only eight at the time, remembers how her mother held on to her sister's shoulders. The priest put his hand on her head as though forcing her into a prostrate position, and said, "God took your son because he was a good boy. He needed another angel. You should consider it an honor; your child is blessed. Our Gracious Lord's compassion is great."

Aunt Erminia, overcome with grief and anger, stood with the help of her sister. Her whole body shook as she spat at the feet of the priest, and cried out,

"*Compassione?*" she shrieked, "So why didn't he just make another boy? He's God, isn't he?"

The truth of this statement resonated throughout Rosina's childhood. If there were a God, couldn't he do anything he wanted?

Isn't this what a God does?

"More vino?" Ferdinando asks, holding an almost empty wine bottle.

"Enough for me." Rosina says, "There's work tomorrow."

Unknown to him, his gaze swallows her whole as he reaches across the table, past the wine glasses, and fish bones left in their plates. He kisses the inside of her palm.

"We are so lucky to have found each other," he says.

The mandolin player approaches their table, plucking away at a repetitious tune. Ferdinando pats Rosina's hand, "don't move." She wouldn't or couldn't. He searches his pocket for a coin, then waves the musician away. Reaching for her hand once again, he says, "This...my incredible, crazy dream, to find a woman like you. Someone who understands me. To share values and ideas. "*Vi ameró per sempre.* I feel we are like one."

Rosina wasn't a romantic. She didn't believe in love at first sight, but she did believe in the visceral, in her gut—her instincts. Was she being transformed? She, too, suddenly no longer felt alone. Sensing happy days ahead with Ferdinando, she fills with a warm light.

-

5

The day Ferdinando comes to ask for her hand in marriage, Rosina is in the kitchen, helping her mother prepare a *frittata*. Her pulses thrum, knowing any minute the doorbell will ring. "Slice the onion thinner," her mother says. "Keep them all the same size." Rosina's eyes burn as she hurries. The loud buzzer makes her jump. She needs to wash her eyes with fresh water. She drops the knife, then rushes off to the bathroom.

In the kitchen, Ferdinando sits at the table. He has a wide-eyed expression, more alert than usual, and stands when Rosina enters. He reeks of protocol. Once they all sit, Ferdinando doesn't waste time. "I've come to officially ask for the hand of your lovely Rosina." Her parents' glance at each other. "I have worked as a shoemaker. I will eventually make more money when I become a foreman. And Rosina has agreed to marry me."

Her father shakes his head, "Too young. Too soon, we hardly know you! How do we know you're not a thief, a criminal?" he says.

"Papa...I know he's not. He's a good, kind man, *un uomo buon e gentile*. He works hard for all the good in this world. And I love him."

Her mother's silence is unusual. She folds the edge of her apron over and over, releasing it only to fold again.

"*Amore*? What do you know of love at your age? *Amore adolescenziale!*" He waves his arm at her. *Tu non-capisci.*"

"Signor Zambelli. We do not have puppy love, and we do understand about love. *Rispettosamente.*" Ferdinando is not taking chances. He speaks with tradition, a respect for his elders.

Her mother stands, looking at her father. "*Ne dobbiamo parlare. Scusateci un momento,*" her mother says to Ferdinando, ushering her father by the elbow as they walk into the back room.

Ferdinando takes her hand, "Don't worry, *Bella*. It will be okay."

How can he be so positive? If her mother says no, that will be it. *No matter*, she thinks, *I will love him and still be with him.*

Rosina only now notices the boutique of dahlias he had brought for her mother. Still wrapped in their paper, they lay in the center of the table. A short while later, her parents return. Her mother clasps her arms together under her bosom, the same way she does when she's finished a task, and says, "You have our blessings. You can marry Rosina." Contentment washes over her mother's expression. She is proud, it seems. Rosina is thrilled to have their support, but when she sees the frown, the dark appearance on her father's face, even though he is shaking hands with Ferdinando, she is repulsed by how easily her father is swayed. *No one should have so much power over another.*

6

Two months before their marriage, Rosina enters the narrow hallway at the factory where she works and is about to clock out when the timekeeper says in his Sicilian dialect, "This kid here wants to give you something."

A young boy with a news cap on backward hands her a folded piece of paper. She is about to read it, when the timekeeper calls out in his raspy voice, "No, first you give me your time."

Once outside, Rosina unfolds the note. "*Mia cara, mio fratello,* Matteo, in Italy, ask that I pick up a telegram from him on Saturday. Come with me to the city to Copley Square. This will be our opportunity to dress up and celebrate."

She breathes in a sigh of joy. *Finally, I'm going to Boston.*

At the bus stop, Rosina is usually tired, but this evening she floats to her seat on the bus.

At home, Rosina's mother is already preparing her bridal trousseau. Her father had protested over Ferdinando's radical views: "He was probably a troublemaker in Italy too, that's why he's in America," he said.

To that, Rosina had added, "He believes in brotherhood, in human rights. There is no law against that."

Although she loves her father dearly, his parochial-conservative views cannot sway her. She will make her own life in her own way. This is what she's learned being in the convent for two-and-a-half years.

Rosina searches her closet. Nothing dressy enough. She settles on a black skirt and begins looking for a blouse when her mother enters her room carrying a dress she had just put the finishing touches on. The dress is made of black rayon, a new fabric, silky to the touch. Her mother went to the trouble to make modern puffed sleeves that narrow down the forearm, tight at the twelve-buttoned wrist with a white lace collar bib spreading along the shoulders.

"Notice the tiny buttonholes I made. It's not easy," she bellows. Her mother cannot help but lecture but when Rosina sees the beautiful dress, she realizes it's a small price to pay. "When you practice, become expert, you owe no one. You can stand proud of your achievements."

On Saturday, Rosina feels strangely adorned in her new dress and a hat made by a friend of her mother's. The fuchsia felt hat is trimmed in a black bow, which hugs the right side of her face. Since their announcement, Rosina senses her mother's contentment about her leaving home. Now she knew. The truth had taken flight. Her family home was her mother's territory, and her mother preferred her to be gone from the house. And it was not just her mother. Apparently, her leaving home was a relief to her father as well. She did learn something from the nuns after all. There are some things you cannot change.

When Ferdinando comes to the door, Rosina's mother stands with her as though she is presenting a prize. She blushes when she recognizes the yearning in Ferdinando's eyes; desire, lust, all there layering the air, yet even though her cheeks are flushed, she is confident her mother doesn't notice.

They get off at the last trolley stop in South Boston. They walk through the crowded sidewalks, past construction sites with scaffolds. The clunking rotation of a cement truck at a storefront forces pedestrians into the street. The atmosphere fills Rosina with a thrilling sensation. The smell of roasted chestnuts from a peddler on the corner, dust of broken concrete flying through the air, along with the bustling herd of people focusing on their own needs, brings an excitement that gives voice to Rosina's thought: *anything is possible.* At the corner of Washington Street, Ferdinando points out a new department store. Taking up an entire city block, it is the most prominent building Rosina has ever seen.

"They call it Filene's. After the Italian name, Fellini."

She laughs out loud, appreciating Ferdinando's desire to find all things Italian in America. Including his own small fabrications, which by now she feels on some level, he needs to believe. Her head buzzes with excitement.

"Maybe I could go inside one day."

Rosina never really enjoyed shopping but is curious about what they could possibly sell in such a tremendous building. Outside of the famous Biltmore Hotel, an organ grinder on wheels cranks out a hollow, tinny song. Rosina always wanted to hear the music from the organ but is disappointed by the tone and the delivery. Ferdinando searches his pocket and then drops a few coins in the rattling cup on top of the organ, making the sound even less desirable. They continue through the revolving doors into the hotel lobby. Ferdinando knows precisely where they are going. He holds her hand as they approach the reception desk.

"I'd like to see the bridal suite, please." He gives the room clerk the date of their wedding. The clerk turns pages of a giant ledger, checking for availability.

The elevator is rich in shiny mahogany with panels of beveled edge mirrors. Rosina whispers to Ferdinando, "It's too expensive. We don't need to do this."

The two rooms are exquisitely decorated with a white brocade material pasted on the walls, and gold painted arches of wooden molding on the ceiling. Ferdinando insists she tries sitting on the bed. When she sits, the down rises around her thighs. Above the bed, the chandelier glitters, reflecting the walls' golden hues. The room clerk stands by the opened door of the room, swinging his key chain.

"We'll reserve it," Ferdinando says. The room clerk bows his head and says, "Yes, sir."

The gesture of a man almost three times Ferdinando's age bowing to him, calling him "sir," makes Rosina uncomfortable. Does Ferdinando feel the same?

As they walk back down the hallway of black and white marble squares, towards the elevator, Rosina says, "It's too much money. We don't have to do this. I'd be happy...."

Ferdinando cuts her short, "My family sent me money. I want to do this. We must begin our marriage on a high note." He tightens the grip on her hand. "Superstition." He laughs.

The specialness of the moment makes Rosina wonder, *is this what Sister Cristina meant when she said, one day, you'll grow into yourself?*

She takes a deep breath. For the first time, she knows a sense of freedom. But is she really *free* attached to a husband, enchanted by his looks, his smile, and the way his amorous gaze sets her on fire? The way he winds her up until the excitement is unbearable. "Superstition?" she asks. "Are you really? Do you also believe in witchcraft?" she smiles.

"Witchcraft? Of course," he says, "There are times I feel possessed. Like now," he says and makes a ridiculous, laughable expression that is supposed to scare her. His silliness makes her lighter, and she decides the foolishness of throwing money away this one time would be okay.

They stop at the concierge desk to pick up the telegram. The older man with snow-white hair directs them to a tiny booth at the end of the lobby where they can read and write messages in private. He takes Rosina by the hand and winks at her and whispers,

"See, *bella mia*, this is how the rich live."

Ferdinando holds the folding door of the cubicle open. *"Entra,* come in. I want you to write something to Matteo, and Nicola, in your own words. I need to show you off. Make my brothers jealous."

The booth is meant for one person. A small built-in ledge acts as a writing desk with caramel-colored telegraph paper and an inkwell and pen. It's so narrow they must stand sideways, facing each other. Rosina worries it will be difficult to get out since the door folds to the inside. She struggles to ignore the claustrophobia which creeps over her. Suddenly she feels the hardness of Ferdinando against her pelvis. He presses his lips against hers and lingers there. A deeper, more lustful kiss than ever before. Greedily, he drives against her until Rosina pulls away to catch some air and notices a woman staring at them through the glass pane of the booth.

"Oh, *bambina*," Ferdinando says breathlessly, still clutching her at the waist. "At night, when I try to sleep, I see you there in my bed...I can't wait." In those few seconds, Rosina knows they have crossed a barrier. She wonders if they'll wait until they're married.

Another woman passes, slowly turning her head, staring at them. Suddenly playful, Rosina wants to stick her tongue out at her but notices a man standing close by and is worried he's waiting to enter the cubicle. She waves the unopened telegram at Ferdinando.

Ferdinando beams as he tears open the envelope expecting to read how happy the family is about their upcoming marriage, but seconds pass and his expression changes from one of joy to a look of shock.

"No. No," he says. He cries and keeps shaking his head no. Rosina touches his shoulder, grasps his hand. He can no longer speak and the telegram slips onto the floor. They stand swollen in the booth. Rosina holds him in her arms. Ferdinando cries into her hair, and her hat slips off her head. A couple passes and pauses to gawk at them. "He's dead, my brother is gone," he manages. "*Mio fratello*, Nicola...*é stato-assassinato.*"

Rosina tries comforting him, yet in a flash of panic, she worries about being stuck in the booth. Trapped. Ferdinando trembles so with tears that she sees him shrinking, diminishing in strength. The air inside turns thick. In her fleeting, bewildered mind, they had formed their own Altar right there in this small cubicle. She will suffocate if she doesn't get out quickly. She pulls the handle on the folding door with such a force that it takes weeks before the bruise on her hip bone disappears.

There are a few more telegrams to and from *Torremaggiore. The* details of Nicola's death are few and unsettling. The bullet at his temple killed him instantly. He was cremated, and his ashes were spread in the Adriatic Sea, as he had wished. Apparently, Nicola had been threatened by an opposing political party several times. He had just returned from Roma, where a hotel building collapsed, killing nine workers. He was organizing a protest for safe and better working conditions and had met with the disagreeable owner of the construction company. Matteo says it could've been any one of them, "*La forza del nemico.*"

Rosina doesn't expect Ferdinando to attend English class on Thursday, but when the weekend comes, and she doesn't hear from him, she begins to worry. She telephones his boarding house a few times, and it rings for a long time. Just as she's about to hang up, the landlady in her gruff masculine voice answers. Rosina says, "I'd like to speak with Mr. Ferdinando Sacco." The woman doesn't acknowledge her, says nothing, and leaves the phone hanging from its cord. It swings back and forth, hitting the wall. She hears the woman yell, "Sacco, get the telephone," then, "Wops. Why do I put up with them?"

Although it is already noon, Ferdinando's voice is gravelly, sounds like he has just woken. He says he can't go to work and has no appetite—he just wants to stay locked up in his room. She tries to bribe him with a home-cooked meal, not really knowing how she'll work in her mother's kitchen, nonetheless, she offers. He repeats he's not hungry. "I just want to sleep," he says and hangs up.

Rosina knows no women are allowed to visit the boarding house but recalls when Ferdinando snuck her in on a Sunday. Apparently, the landlady goes out on errands each day at the same time, so that weekend, on a Sunday, knowing the landlady will be in church, Rosina decides she will visit him.

Ferdinando's room is at the top of a creaking staircase in an old funereal-like Victorian house. The hallway is barely lit, one small bulb flickers in the vestibule. Dark cherry-wood walls. A frayed rug lies at the foot of the stair landing. At the top of the stairway, there are four heavy-grain oak doors, all with octagon-shaped glass doorknobs. She recognizes Ferdinando's door because running down the center, a panel was replaced and never painted. She taps quietly at his door. Ferdinando calls out, "Who is it?"

"It's me," she says practically whispering. Ferdinando doesn't respond, so she knocks once more. Behind the door, she can hear him, obviously disturbed, mumbling incoherent words. When he opens the door, his expression is one of surprise, and fearing the landlady, he quickly grabs her by her forearm, pulls her inside, and closes the door.

"What are you doing here?" he says.

His tiny space is stifling, without air, and when he embraces her, he has the same musty odor about him. "Oh...you feel so good." His lips brush her ear. "I didn't want you to see me like this." The room is a mess of newspapers. Boxes torn open halfway, shoes, shirts, slacks strewed on the floor and on the back of his chair. "I've been going through some of the stuff Nicola left behind and writing about him. I'm sorry if I made you worry."

A black and white marbleized notebook, like the ones children use in school, lay open on his bed. Words written in the blackest ink. She is surprised by the anger and chaos that shows itself, but not by the apparent gloom. The room is permeated with sepia lighting, and a dark brown painted plywood dresser and headboard draped with age-tinted doilies-unevenly placed. He gives her a generous, tight hug, and unexpectedly, she gets a sense of arousal from his touch, and in the space around them.

"I wanted to be sure you were okay," she says.

He has dark circles under his eyes, and his beard, heavier than usual, makes his jawbone stronger, more squared. Rosina finds herself staring at him.

"I know, I know," he says, running his hand through his hair, "I ran out of pomade, and I need a haircut."

It wasn't his beard or his unkempt hair that now fell over his right eye; empathy had been growing in her since his brother's death, and now it was peaking, with all the gruffness, his face was softer, more vulnerable than ever. She wants him to make love to her. She wants to soften his pain, to be a part of his intense grief. Dressed only in a tight sleeveless undershirt and his belt-less slacks, she is more aware of the stocky strength of his body. Still in his arms, she touches the flesh of his back and shoulders. His outstretched hand on her face and neck, she kisses his mouth. A faint taste of strong black coffee is on his lips.

"I've come to take you to eat something. Let's go before the warden returns," she says, knowing these are just words spewing nervously out of her.

Ferdinando guides her to the small bed where he sleeps. "Aren't you hungry?" she asks foolishly as he starts to unbutton her dress. His mouth on her neck moving down to her breast, he gazes at her greedily. She reads him; his eyes damp possesses a look that burns through her. *I want it all,* his voice sweet and sexy. In a matter of seconds, they are both undressed. He presses his body against hers, kissing her ear, her neck, moving her hair off her forehead with his wide hand; *Ti amo, ti amo*, he repeats. She is delirious, caught in a wave of euphoria, threads of tenderness braid them together, she begins to moan.

Afterward, they are like two children, lying under a thin sheet, laughing, kissing, making fun of the landlady who they hear below in the hallway talking to herself, complaining. Keeping their voices low, they joke of ways to get Rosina out of the building without being caught:

"How are you at roof hopping?" Ferdinando whispers, "The buildings are all close together, you'll only have a problem when you get to the end of the street."

"I can jump from the window," she offers jokingly.

"Never, never," he says, kissing her, "I'd rather take the warden out for dinner while you escape. Speaking of dinner. Let's go eat something."

Ferdinando throws on a worn plaid bathrobe, "Give me a moment," he says and goes out into the hallway to the shared bathroom.

She puts on her bra and panties, rolls up her stockings, and secures them with her garter belt. His smell is on her! She'll never wash him off. She is buoyant. So alive. *Is this what being in love feels like?*

She is on her knees, looking under his bed for one of her shoes when Ferdinando enters the room. "Where are you?" he whispers.

"Here," she murmurs, "looking for my shoe."

In the dim light, she reaches for what she thought was her shoe and comes away with something hard and angular wrapped in a soft purple cloth. Sitting on the floor with it in her lap, Ferdinando looks down at her. "It belonged to Nicola. I was holding it for him."

Only the barrel is revealed through the cloth. Ferdinando lifts it from her lap. "I keep wondering. Maybe if he had this with him, things would have turned out different."

"I've never seen a gun before," she says, "not close."

He undoes the cloth and offers to show her.

"No. No. I don't want to handle it."

He slips the cover back on the gun and places it on the desk. "Here's your shoe, *amore*," and he hands it to her.

"What are you going to do with it?" Rosina asks.

"Keep it," he says.

"For what?"

"To protect you." He smiles.

"Seriously?"

"I'm holding on to it. I'm not breaking any law. Besides, you never know when you must protect yourself and your family." He kisses her on the forehead.

"Take off your shoes, let me carry them, we don't want the warden to hear a woman's steps."

At the corner café, they each have a slice of pizza.

"I didn't realize how hungry I was," he says, and then he orders a plate of sausage and peppers.

"Thank you for coming," he says, his mouth almost full. He eats eagerly like a young boy who is just relieved of punishment. He possesses innocence more primal than she has ever witnessed in a grown man.

She thinks of the risk of a gun. She thrills at the excitement she feels. She made love with this man. Ferdinando. Ferdinando Sacco.

"Now I know what Nietzsche meant when he said, '*Bisogna avere un caos dentro di se, per partorire una stella danzante.*'

"Who said that?" she asks.

"The German philosopher, Friedrich Nietzsche. You must have chaos within, before you can see a dancing star. Or dark must come before the light."

7

Ferdinando meets Rosina after work the next day. They will be married. He leans against the metal fence which surrounds the building, reading a newspaper. Something is distant in his manner.

"Can you believe all the money they're putting into this Fenway Park to build a baseball field?" Rosina knows it really isn't a question. "Grown men running around after a ball and pocketing all that dough! It's sickening when this money could help so many people."

"I'm surprised to see you here," she says.

"I want to walk you home. I have a half-hour before I go back."

"You're working tonight?"

"Just for a couple of hours because the boss is away. I have something I want to talk to you about."

Rosina catches her breath. Does he want to talk about delaying the wedding or calling it off? She knows by now that Ferdinando is a romantic. A man with a yen for drama, who perhaps is enriched by romantic tragedy. He has shown deep reverence and respect and passion and love for her. So why is she now suddenly stricken with uncertainty. Is this her mother's voice telling her this is what you get when you open your legs for a man before you marry him? Still, unlike her mother, the piece of paper that bonds a man and woman in marriage means nothing to her. To be governed by a license—censored, is to give in to being controlled. *Little by little stripping your right to be free.*

On the stoop of her parent's apartment house, he says, "Let's sit here for a moment."

Rosina reaches in her pocket for a tissue but finds nothing except lint and an old chewing gum wrapper. Looking into his eyes, sadness still lurks. The initial shock of his brother's death is not yet done.

"I've been writing a story about Nicola to publish in *Cronaca Sovversiva.*"

Rosina has heard of Luigi Galleani's paper and of its support for the people. She knew it to be the leading Italian anarchist journal in the world.

"It will help me. Because I'll be doing something for him." His eyes watered. "He was my hero, but you already know this."

"What a beautiful idea. It'll be a great honor to him," Rosina says, relieved and at the same time angry with herself for allowing in old insecurities.

"I'm also going to make an official announcement at the end of the article, but I wanted to tell you first."

"What kind of announcement?"

It is the time of day when the city buildings darken, drained of natural light, hints of artificial lamps begin to glow through apartment windows. Across the street, a man pushes his way into the tenement doorway, dropping a bag of groceries on the stoop. They watch him in his struggle to re-bag the items.

"I'm going to take my brother's name." Ferdinando sighs heavily, obviously relieved he has spoken the words. "I want to be called Nicola. It's the only way I can honor him and do good work in his name."

Rosina hesitates. "You want to change your name?"

"Yes," he says, "My name will now be Nicola."

It is a simple act, she thinks, one of love. But it puzzles her. A name has so many implications. Perhaps it is way beyond her understanding. Or maybe, maybe she might be jealous he could love someone else with such fierceness. The strength of such love moves between them, bringing tears. Nicola. She imagines saying it. It is foreign; outside of her. But here is her love. Her man. Nicola?

Moving her hands to his chin, she kisses him on the mouth. "You are such a beautiful man," she says. "*Ti amo.*"

He takes a deep breath. "What would I do without you? So that's final," he says, "*Ti amo,* what?"

"*Ti amo.*" She hesitates again.

"Nicola Sacco," he says.

He smiles at her, and his lavish heart melts her.

Although it feels strange, she whispers the name Nicola a few times, endearingly through her lips. It is uncanny, awkward. But it's a plan. His brother's death will eventually move into a place of acceptance. A place that will allow him to function, to return their lives to some kind of normalcy.

"*Amore mio,*" she says. "Nicola Sacco."

8

1917

Occasionally, especially while sewing, Rosina tries to identify the moment she identified the need to return to Italy. Dante, almost four-years-old now, she wants to show him the hills where she was born. Rosina envisions them in the field, near the pond—a chorus of frogs mating so loudly, that she and Nicola would be unable to hear each other speak. She recalls a scent of lavender working its way around the massive pines and the once magnificent cottonwood tree; the aroma fills her pores. She dreamily visualizes them at Nicola's village, meeting his entire family of brothers, and he possibly meeting her parents. Maybe it was having a child that spurred it on, or did this yearning begin when they moved here to Mr. Kelley's small farm? Here in Stoughton, closer to Nick's work, and more than two hundred feet from the Kelleys' home, they have open fields, chickens, goats, and a donkey to care for, and Nicola is finally able to grow vegetables. There is even a small greenish pond where the insects gather. All reminiscent of home on a much smaller scale.

Sewing the last stitch on Dante's blue dress shirt, a commotion at the front door pulls Rosina from her dreaming. The screen door bangs and squeaks open, slams shut. From her sewing room, she is unable to see into the living room. "Dante? Is that you? *Di dové a sei?*" she snips the thread and places the shirt and scissor down on the cutting board. "Hello?" she hears a giggle coming from the living room and finds Nicola and Dante standing in front of what appeared to be a sewing machine.

"*Che cosa è questo?*" she asks.

Nicola looks at Dante. "Tell Mama."

Dante's face is beaming. "This is for you, Mama," and he moves to the side to reveal his surprise.

Rosina approaches the maple cabinet and runs her hand along the metal threader and body. "Where did you get this?" she asks.

"We bought it for you. Right, Dante?"

Her child is filled with pride. "*Si.*"

Rosina is stunned, not by the continued generosity of her husband, but by the temptation before her. "This is too much. I'm fine with using my hands."

"But we have the money now," Nicola says.

Since Nicola worked long hours at Mr. Kelley's Shoe Company, learning the trade of edger-finisher, besides being night manager, they were doing well and banked away some earnings. Besides, she and Nicola were caretakers of the property they lived on, which saved them rent money, and the only thing they had to pay for was coal for the furnace in the winter months to heat their cottage.

Dante begins to open and close the drawers in the cabinet. He runs inside Rosina's sewing closet and comes back with a spool of red thread and puts in inside the drawer. "See, Mama, it fits."

"Yes, *amore. Grazie.*" she kneels to hug him. "Mama likes to use her own hands like you like to use yours when you draw, so we won't keep it." At first, Dante looks puzzled, then he nods his head in agreement. "You can go and play with Pinocchio now. Be careful, do not stand behind him." Dante's deep brown eyes grow large with excitement as he scurries off to the donkey.

"Just give him some water to drink. It's warm today," Nicola calls to him. Nicola sits down for a moment at the edge of the armchair. "Why are you so stubborn?"

Through the opened, screened window, she watches Dante run across the field to the black fence where the donkey is tied. A breeze skips over the flat green land, stretches its way to Mr. Kelley's house and flutters across her face.

In a pull of self-reproach, she says defensively, "It's not stubbornness. My conscience doesn't allow it."

"Rosina, no one is more aware of the hardship of others than me, we've worked hard for our money so we can have the things that will make us happier."

"I know Nick, but it doesn't seem right, having something so luxurious. And besides, what will we do with it when we go back to Italy?"

"We could sell it or give it to someone less fortunate." Nicola was always ready to give. It didn't matter what or how much. For Rosina, the sewing machine standing in the middle of the room is like some sort of impostor: the luxurious maple cabinet and the black cylinder shape of the machine with the name "SINGER" written across in gold lettering might as well read: You too will fall on the face of capitalism. If she believed in the devil and in the evil money brings, she would've believed the devil placed it in her living room. "No. If we start here, it won't end. Perhaps, later we can find one back in Italy. A used one."

She places her foot on the pedal and moves it back and forth. "It's beautiful, Nicola. We can't keep it."

Nicola gasps with resolution and takes her hands in his and kisses the inside of her palms. "How did I marry someone so genuine? Too many convictions." His expression, wide open, amazed. "You are my hero."

Rosina enjoys the fact that her husband understands, but she knows his gifts to be far greater than hers. Since the war, they've both been more aware of prosecution and false espionage charges. The deportation of *Greaseballs, Guineas*," were at a height. At times, she lacks Nicola's sensitivity and passion, his unbridled fury toward injustice.

What passes through her mind is Carlos, Nicola's friend, being dragged from the picket line, beaten with police clubs, and left to die on the curb. Nicola fell into a deep depression. Unreachable. All she could do was wait for his return.

"Now please, bring me a chicken. Susan is coming for dinner."

From the back porch, Rosina watches Nicola lift the chicken from the coop and hold it in his arms. He carries the chicken close to his body, hugging it, the same way he used to hold Dante when he was a baby. Placing the chicken in the holding crib, "Ah. We are truly savages," he sighs. "But my Rosetta, one of the best cooks this side of Boston is calling you. Consider this a privilege, my friend."

The chicken begins to cackle and squawk, running in a state of frenzy from one end of the crib to the other. In the distance, she sees Dante pulling on the donkey's cord. "It looks like Dante wants to ride Pinocchio."

Rosina waits until Nicola approaches Dante before she grabs the chicken and locates the ropey thickness of the neck, reaching the spot she has become familiar with. She snaps it.

Hours later, the house smells of sautéed garlic and onions. Nicola had brought in a basket of zucchini from the garden, and Rosina stuffs them with breadcrumbs and Fontina cheese, then bakes them in tomato sauce.

When Susan enters the screen door, Dante runs to her. "Zia Susie," he yells and jumps into her arms. Susan has put on some pounds over the years but is still attractive. She gives Dante a bear hug, and then, inhaling a whiff of the odor coming from the kitchen, says, "Um—what is Mama cooking?"

Dante, in her arms, looks directly into her eyes. "Sunday dinner."

Susan laughs out loud and smothers him with more hugs and kisses.

Rosina notices the painful grimace on Susan's face as she lowers him to the ground.

"You shouldn't lift him."

Susan waves her off. "It's always going to be there. It will be worth it, my badge of courage, when we get to vote," she sneers.

After meeting Susan that first time, months had lapsed. Rosina never imagined Susan was one of the hundreds of women who were beaten at the Suffrage March. She thought she was like others who always said they'd stop by and then didn't. She and Nicola had read in the newspaper that insults were hurled at the women who marched. Lit cigars were thrown at them. They were spat on, slapped, and beaten with sticks. Susan was in jail with a broken shoulder for two days before they brought her to the hospital. At the time, Rosina never thought Susan was one of the women who were hurt, especially since they claimed over 10,000 women were marching. Susan eventually did stop by for a cup of coffee, and it was then she joked about the guards and how they couldn't take her screams anymore, so they finally brought her to the hospital.

Now stirring the sauce, Rosina again regrets she was unable to attend the rally. Eight months pregnant, she could hardly walk.

"Should I open another bottle?" Nicola asks as he pours the little wine that was left in Susan's glass.

"I wouldn't mind," Susan says. "What about you, Rosina?"

"I've had enough," she says, and catches Nicola's eye to signal Susan had had enough too, not that it made a difference because Nicola was already removing the cork from the Chianti. The wine didn't affect Nicola as much as it did Susan. Once she started drinking, she didn't know when to stop. On her last visit, after Susan left, she had asked Nicola not to keep pouring the wine, and it turned into an argument. "Susan's a grown woman, she can make her own decisions." he said dismissively.

"I don't like what happens to her. She repeats things, doesn't make sense, and with the two of you drinking so much, I begin to feel totally alone."

"She's just having fun—stop making so much of it. Maybe _you_ should drink a little more," he says, as he lies on his side of the bed and falls into a deep befuddled sleep.

That night, Rosina, angry and hurt, tries to make a point by sleeping on the couch. When Nicola rises at four in the morning to tend to his garden and then go to work, he wakes her by moving the hair from her face. "Go to bed. Why are you sleeping here?" He kisses her forehead. "I'm sorry if I said anything to hurt you."

In the end, Nicola didn't understand what she wanted from him. He remained headstrong, and she had decided not to fight over it anymore. She'd have to figure out another way to avoid Susan's drinking.

"We haven't made a dent in this country," Susan says.

"No, no, we have. We just can't see it yet. History will show," Nicola says, taking a sip of wine.

"Papa, what is a country?" Dante asks as he sits on the floor, pulling on loose threads from the top of his sock.

Knowing the conversation will turn to the war, Rosina stands and says, "Dante, you can go in your room and play now." Then she begins to clear away the dishes.

"It's a very jittery time. Strikes everywhere." Susan says, "More and more dirty bombs are being deployed, but nothing seems to be getting done. On top of it, masses of people are afraid of getting the flu. It is now beyond epidemic portions."

"It's the war," Nicola says.

He sits back in his chair and crosses his legs, revealing his Sunday black dress socks. "War, tension, much of our group is in hiding. So, it's difficult to get anything done right now."

"I'm so afraid the military will come after Nicola," Rosina says as she brings the coffee cups to the table.

Susan clicks glasses with Nicola. "*Salute*," she says, "I won't let them take him."

Rosina is annoyed by her flippancy. "Seriously. He's probably going to have to go to Mexico. We've been talking about it."

There are so many implications, some of which she reads on the frown of Nicola's face. He is far away. Finally, shaking loose of his thoughts, he says, "If they draft me, they'll end up deporting me because I won't go to war to fight for the politicians or kill anyone. Maybe they'll throw me in prison. There's a group of men getting together next week, planning their way to Mexico. I'm going to the meeting tonight. *Gruppo Autonomo*, over in East Boston. Will see what they're doing. As much as I'll miss my Rosina and Dante, I can't take the chance of staying behind." He sips his wine, looks down at his shoes, and pulls up his black socks. "They'll get us one way or another."

"I agree," Rosina says, pouring coffee into the cups. "We have no choice. Rich men. War. Politics. I'm sick of it. And we, the small people, have to pay?" There is a bitterness in her mouth before she even tastes the strong coffee.

"Yup, it's a very jittery time, all right," Susan repeats. "This horrendous government led us into war. This pandemic, tension is everywhere." Susan pulls the *New York Times* from her briefcase that is always on the floor, next to her chair. "Look here, darling," she says to Rosina, searching for an article she had read. "With each bombing, they found a pink flier."

Pink fliers. Rosina knows they are documents signed and written by the Anarchist Fighters. Most of the fliers she thought came from their chapter, but when Susan reads the statement on the flier, she doesn't recognize it.

YOU HAVE JAILED US,
YOU HAVE BEATEN US,
YOU HAVE ROBBED US.
NOW YOU MUST KNOW VENGEANCE IS COMING.

Susan becomes teary. "You never got to meet Andrea Salsedo. Talk about justice? He had a printing shop. He printed out the newsletters for us. The FBI held him on the fourteenth floor in New York City at the Federal Plaza Building, right next to the Department of Justice." He was a good man. Look at this article, it's so small, they could hardly waste the fucking ink. They said he jumped from the window after being questioned by federal agents. They held him for eight weeks. Eight whole weeks of torture. Without any legal rights. Not a fucking one." Susan gulps. Breathing heavily, she tosses the newspaper across the table, and Nicola reaches for it.

The version Rosina read in the *Boston Globe* was: "After several weeks of being held captive, questioned and beaten, and some say tortured, Mr. Salsedo was pushed from his fourteenth-floor office building, leaving a family of four children and a wife behind."

Rosina feels cornered. She rejects the fear that twirls in the pit of her stomach and slams her fist on the table. "Okay, we've had enough." she stands, corks the wine bottle, brings it into the kitchen, and slides it under the cabinet.

She hears Nicola; "You see, I already have my own army sergeant here." But he wasn't smiling. Closing her eyes, she stands with both hands on the edge of the sink and is consumed with fright. That same fear she felt when she was thirteen years old and realized her parents were going to leave her at the convent. Her father fighting back the tears, and her mother, tall, rigid by the open door.

"We'll send for you when we're settled in America."

For years, in her sleep, she heard the whoosh of the carved doors in the convent closing, over and over. Even then, she knew that moment would never be erased. They had gifted her with the condition of anxiety; one she had been fighting ever since. *Maybe I should drink*, she thinks. *Perhaps this is how Susan copes.*

* * *

Early spring electrical storms move into the Stoughton area and last for two days. Rosina, afraid of thunder and lightning, tries hard not to show her fear to Dante, but he senses it and hovers close to her in the kitchen. As the bread pudding bakes, Rosina struggles to ignore the thunder and keeps busy playing with Dante and the puppets. The largest puppet, Luciano, covers her hand in his dashing eighteenth-century costume. Rosina's voice, disguised as a man's, pronounces English consonants and vowels in a disorderly fashion. When Rosina sneaks an occasional vowel into the group of consonants, Dante becomes hysterical with laughter and is thrilled to correct the puppet. "Not 'a,'" he screams at the puppet. She uses the smaller puppet, Lucia, to teach Dante to read. This one wears an elaborate blue velvet low-cut dress, revealing a full bosom. Sometimes Dante moves her red tendrils from her shoulders and tries to push her breast down. He giggles and says she is fat. The puppets are from Nicola's family. He and his brother, the first Nicola, brought them over from Italy. They made a promise to each other: whoever had the first child would have the puppets. Even then, her Nicola was confident the puppets would be his, knowing his brother's love of women would keep him from settling down.

When the rain lets up, Rosina puts on her rubber boots and ties on Dante's, and they walk down the muddy path to the mailbox. At the bottom of the road, the branches of the huge maple trees sway frantically. The wind attacks them in a circular pattern, rumbling in her ears. Dante pulls on the hem of her dress. The thunder close by, she knows lightning will come next, so she grabs the letters in one hand, and Dante's fingers in the other. In trying to move faster, she slips on the mud and falls to the ground. There is mud on her dress and knees. It begins to rain hard once more, and Dante starts to cry. "*Non piangere*, Dante. It's okay. *Bambino mio.*" Rosina quickly gets up and presses the wet mail to her chest. Inside, Dante, once again secure on the living room floor is playing with his truck. "See, *amore*, it's nothing—it's fun to get wet."

"But you fell down, Mama," he says with a pout. "I don't like thunder."

In the kitchen, she wipes the two letters with a dishtowel and waits for them to dry before opening them. With the tip of the wet towel, she tries to remove the mud from the envelope and reads: Selective Service—Armed Forces.

9

Susan has Luigi Galleani's information in her worn leather address book. Random notes fall onto her lap as she releases the rubber band holding it closed. She gathers the papers and slips them in the back of her book.

"He lives on the outskirts of Stoughton. I'll arrange for you to visit," she tells Rosina. One of Susan's notes is under her chair, and as Rosina reaches for it, she fades into calm acceptance.

"I don't know what else to do."

"You have nothing to lose," Susan says. "Consider it an adventure."

"An adventure. Now, why would I want to do that?"

"It's the way we move forward. Get things done. Who knows what can happen? And if he can't help, then we'll find another way."

Rosina admires this about Susan, always positive, seemingly fearless. She would have to meditate on this. Yet, just a few days later, as the men gather in her parlor, she realizes it is becoming more dangerous for Nicola to stay in the country. Rumors abound of authorities knocking on doors, jailing, and deporting any Italian they deem suspicious. *There is nothing further to think about*, she says to herself as she brushes out her hair. She has to ask Galleani for help.

It is Sunday, and Nicola is working overtime again. "We need additional money. I'll need some for Mexico, plus I must leave some for you and the boy."

She hates when he says, "The boy." As though Dante is some strange kid, yet she knows it's also the fault of English not being his native language. She reminds herself of Nicola's long working hours. The way his sleep pattern has been broken, and the dark circles which mask his eyes. All is forgiven.

The train ride from Stoughton to Brockton is short. Pea-green buds on the tops of trees flicker by quickly. Spring has truly arrived: Only this morning, a pair of mallard ducks take refuge in the small pond, and she has her hands full trying to keep Dante from throwing stones at them. The hyacinth and Jacob's ladder Nicola planted along the path to the house are beginning to bloom. When Nicola kissed her goodbye that morning, she caught the irritating, close smell of mothballs she had stuffed into the pockets of his light rain jacket last winter, an acrid smell, another indication that spring was here.

The train grinds along, jerks sideways at track intervals. Rosina questions, *Am I doing the right thing?* The next group of men are scheduled to leave for Mexico in a week. There is no room for Nicola, maybe in the next van, two more weeks. *He can't wait for another month. The* induction letter from the Army is in her handbag, where it's been since it arrived. She never showed the letter to Nicola because she didn't think she needed to. He doesn't need the stress of knowing the government caught up with him. Nicola isn't a fighter, or a killer. He's a man who doesn't believe in war. *I'm on my own private crusade*, she thinks. *I'll go to any extent to protect my husband.*

From the train station, it is six short blocks to his house. When she approaches Galleani's slanted porch, she stands there for a moment, reluctant to knock on the door. Overgrown shrubs tangled with large rhododendrons hug the sides of the old Victorian. Masculine laughter reverberates from deep within the house. Music, the opening chords of *Cavalleria Rusticana*, waft through an open window. A pair of muddy shoes sit near the door, a small brownish puddle under them. Fresh. Someone removed them moments before. The longer she stands on his whitewashed clapboard porch, the more unease she feels. She hears the men's voices and is suddenly aware of the thickly stemmed lilacs entangled with the rhododendrons. Their overpowering scent makes her heady in the spring air. She feels entirely alone, in an orphaned way, out of her element. Their voices are louder now behind the door. She turns to leave, but the door opens.

Luigi Galleani stands there shirtless, barefoot with deep green wide-corduroy slacks rolled carelessly up to his shins. Another man, leaving, tips his hat and passes between them. "Mrs. Sacco." Luigi's long, thin mustache lifts to a smile. "Time and I are never aligned. Come in, please."

Rosina flushes, flustered as she follows Luigi's bare back, remarkably broad and smooth for a man his age. *"Prego, si accomodi,"* he says, gesturing to his parlor chairs. *"Mi perdono."* He thumps his chest with an open hand. She notices a few grayish-black hairs between his breastbone. "I'm afraid I'm indecent in front of a beautiful young woman. *Miscusi*," and he walks out of the room.

Consumed with awkwardness and embarrassment, she can't stop her knees from trembling. Being in such a powerful man's home with him half-undressed is indeed forbidden territory. She recalls another time of forbidden territory: before the convent, she was at a house party, and a few girls were gathered in the family's modern bathroom learning how to arrange different hairstyles. Piero, a boy, one whom all the girls liked, wanted to pee. The girls all giggled at the idea of staying to watch him pee. He calmly said, "It's okay, stay if you want." Curious, only she and another girl stayed. When she saw his penis spring from his pants, she found it queer, so peculiar and freakish, to have such an appendage outside the body. "You want to touch it," he said, as it grew straighter, more erect. The band from his twisted shorts pressed against what she now saw as chubby thighs, bringing attention to the darker, wrinkled skin of his balls, in total contrast to the tight, glossy, skin of his penis. Seized by the moment, she was frozen in place. A while later, when the other girls cornered her and asked to describe what she'd seen, she was sorry she hadn't the courage to touch him lightly, and at the same time was perplexed by the excitement she felt. Lying in bed that night, she thought, *what harm would it have done to place my hand there?*

At her feet is a green braided rug with pieces of yellow wool woven in. On the wall, under a glass frame, hangs a collection of three Polyphemus moths, their wings pinned, spread, revealing the four eyes on their wings. A heavily carved sideboard stands across the room. On top are several framed newspaper articles with photographs of Luigi Galleani. Hanging on the wall above, an oil portrait caught his likeness as a younger man. Galleani appears and turns down the music. His slacks are now rolled down, and he's wearing a pair of worn slippers, and a long-sleeved starched white shirt, only partially buttoned.

"Can I get you something to drink, Mrs. Sacco?

Before she can answer, he says, "You'll have tea with me. Come with me into the *cucina*."

She follows him through a narrow hallway wallpapered with bluish-purple peonies. The smell of cooking fills the air, lentils with lots of garlic. Apparently, he used the kitchen as a reading room. Towers of books lay on the floor. An open book with a notepad next to it is on the table. In the corner, piles of old newspapers look as though they're about to topple to the floor. He gestures for her to sit.

"So, tell me. Why didn't Nicola come here himself?"

"He doesn't know I'm here." The seat legs wobble. Assailed by the frailness of the moment, she doesn't want to embarrass him by changing her chair. Now that she is here, she has to go forward.

As he turns to put the kettle on the burner, she notices a rough scar running along his jawline down the side of his neck.

"I remember your husband. The article he printed in my paper—about his brother." He pauses to look at her for a moment, "Your husband is a man with heroes."

Rosina detects a smirk beneath his words. Was he belittling Nicola?

"Yes, Nicola tries to find good in everyone."

Galleani opens the cupboard and brings two delicate, thin, porcelain cups covered with bluebonnet poppies to the table. These aren't cups a man would choose. She wonders about his woman. The thought comes to her that to be involved with this man would be a one-sided relationship. A woman could get buried under a man like this. A man with so many scars, so much history.

Glancing at the ruled pad on the table, she notices his penmanship, unexpectedly tiny, precise sharp lettering. It seems he is preparing a speech or writing an article. He hums along with the music as he pours the water from the kettle into a teapot.

"Susan is a good friend. How long do you know her?" he says, now stirring the beans in the pot.

"We met at one of your study circles. About five years ago."

His back still towards her, he shakes his head. "She has the courage of twenty women."

Rosina knows this courage. Audacious Susan, a dauntless spirit who often makes Rosina question her own bravery. Susan is a free woman. There is no child, or for that matter, no husband who depends on her.

"And you?" He brings the teapot to the table and places it on a square of tapestry with frayed edges. "Are you as courageous?" He is smirking.

"I like to think I am." For a moment, she senses the rush of a door opening, one she had glimpsed years before the rules were set in place by the nuns, ones which regulated her; now before the door slams shut, she decides to slip through, and playfully says, "I'm here, am I not?"

He chuckles and goes to sit down. Although there are three other chairs around the table, he chooses the one closest to her. "Let me see your face," he says. "Take off your hat, please."

"I won't be staying long." She nervously touches the brim.

"Please, I must see your hair."

It was a plea, overbearing and dictatorial—a command. Rosina hesitates then removes her hatpin and hat.

"Such beautiful hair," he beams, "*Lei è una bellissima donna.*"

His eyes on her, he unbraids her little by little. She forces herself to move from this moment towards her purpose. "I've come here to ask if you can place my husband in the next group that goes to Mexico. Susan says you have connections."

He takes a sip of his tea. "Oh yes, connections." He raises both eyebrows. "Why is he in such a rush? I still don't know why he didn't come here himself."

Rosina takes the draft notice from her purse. "This letter came from the government three weeks ago. Nicola was supposed to answer a few days ago. I haven't shown it to him. I'm afraid they will come to take him."

"Mrs. Sacco. What is your first name again?"

"Rosina."

"Rosina," he repeats. "Why did you not give him the letter?"

How could she explain without making Nicola seem like he could be so easily damaged? "Nicola is a kind man. A man who wouldn't even kill an insect. They cannot expect him to go to war and kill." Anger stirs. "We have no enemies. The government makes enemies, and we have to fight for them? It won't happen. Nicola will refuse and then perhaps spend his life in jail or be deported, taken from his family. I can't take that chance."

"So, I see, after all. You are a woman who takes control. Very much like your friend, Susan. Perhaps too much control of another life. Have you asked yourself if this is fair?"

She is slightly wounded by his remark. Who was he to question her ways in their marriage?

"Fair? I'm trying to protect my husband. You don't know, Nicola," she says now trembling inside.

"Such passionate loyalty." He sips his hot tea. "What region of Italy do you come from?"

Rosina is unnerved. She wants to lash out at him. Yet, she knows that coming here has allowed this man into their lives. His pompous, intimidating attitude is one she is not used to dealing with.

"For years, I've been studying people from different provinces of *Italia*. It's amazing what similarities in character strengths and weaknesses have emerged by region. Perhaps one day you'll consider becoming part of my study?" He gives her a catchall smile. Tilting his head to the side to look at her more fully, "I find you most interesting."

She is right, he is capable of swallowing women, *but is she capable of being swallowed by such an overtly narcissistic man?* Still trembling, she tries to direct the conversation back to Nicola. "Can you do it? Can you get Nicola on the next vehicle to Mexico? If you want money, I promise I will get it to you."

"Money? Money is for the capitalist. We—I believe we exist for all. We are here to help one another. Are we not, Rosina?"

As his voice turns inward, a saucy expression begins to grow in his eyes. "To give whatever the other needs."

He possesses a calmness, principles, ideas that allow him to live as he pleases without concern for others. Rosina had sensed this on some level when she first heard him speak, and now he demonstrates it.

"Life is hard," he says, "and sometimes we must do difficult things, things we never knew we were capable of to get past the trouble."

Had she known all along it would go this way? The desire in his eyes, in his movements towards her. She is suffocating. Suddenly aware of how tightly she has been kneading her hands together, as he places his long, thin, fingers on hers in an effort to calm her. Hands so clean, they seem unreal.

"*Si calmi, cara.* Let me get you a muscatel. I promise I will not hurt you." He has the facade of a much younger man as he walks to his liquor cabinet, the look of a man who has just found his virile strength.

She gathers her hair and fastens her comb. Her pulse is racing as she takes a sip of the muscatel. It burns her throat and at the same time, seems to open it. "Will you get Nicola on the next bus to Mexico?"

"*Si.* I'm a man of my word, *mia cara.* A man of my word."

Galleani moves the back of his hand along her chin, over her cheekbone to her hair, where he again removes the tortoise-shell comb Nicola had bought her on her last birthday. He releases her hair with unexpected tenderness, spreading it along her shoulders, and then draws her closer. Her hand flat on his chest to resist, she feels his heart beating furiously. He holds her chin in his hand and leans in to kiss her. His kiss is wet, and she wants to wipe her mouth. She tells herself it will be over quickly.

<h1 style="text-align:center">10</h1>

Dante opens and closes Nicola's suitcase as Rosina tries to pack it. Nicola sits on the bed next to her. "*Vieni qui*, Dante, Come here." Dante jumps up on the mattress and throws his body against his father's, trying to tickle Nicola in that way they always play, wrestling him.

Nicola, never ticklish, pretends, and begins to yowl, proceeding to tickle Dante back. Dante's giggle is comforting, a sign of health and joy: *If I had a relationship with God*, Rosina thinks, *I would thank him for the extraordinary happiness I know in these moments.* Yet she still says *thank you, thank you*, under her breath, throwing it out there in the face of superstition.

Pretending to be a frog, Nicola starts to ribbit, ribbit, and Dante, sitting on his father's belly, puts up his hand to stop, "Papa, wait," he shouts, "Are you a poison frog?" he asks.

Nicola eyes Rosina, "There are no poisonous frogs," he says.

"Oh, yes. Zia Susan says so."

Dante whines, in his "wanting-his-own-way tone."

Rosina laughs.

"Well, if Zia Susan says it, then it's probably true," Nicola shrugs his shoulders. "Right, Mama!" he smiles and rolls his eyes to Rosina. "Go, go and see if you can find a poison frog."

Dante runs off to his room to find a picture of a poisonous frog in one of his books.

"Do you want to take the suede vest or the woolen one?" Rosina asks.

"You decide," Nicola says. "It will be warm there." With his foot, Nicola pushes the suitcase toward the bottom of the bed. "Come, *bella mia*. Forget about it. Lie here," he says patting the spot next to him.

The soft mattress yields to her body. With her back towards him, she rests her head on his extended arm. He inhales her, and she is aware of his desire. "Can we get Dante to take a nap?" he says. They both chuckle at the impossibility and hear him in his room, making frog noises.

They lay silently for a few moments. "At least by going to Mexico, I'll have the opportunity to keep 'The Idea' alive." Nicola's breath, heavy with sighs, he whispers, "I pray we can be safe. Between the Mexican and Russian revolution, and all the bombings going on in this country, maybe we are finally in the winds of change." Pressing closer to Rosina, he asks, "Why are you so quiet, *amore mia?*"

Having discovered her own vein of guilt these last days, avoiding his gaze, managing to jostle time so they'd not be alone. She was utterly paranoid, and afraid Nicola would notice her reluctance to make love with him. It is a week since her visit to Luigi Galleani. Since then, she hasn't allowed Nicola near her, pretending it was that time of the month. But tomorrow, she now believes, he will be leaving. Rosina tries to hide her tears. With his arm around her waist, he draws her in closer. "No, no. Please, no tears. I promise to return as soon as I can," she wants to shout at him. His innocence, coupled with his oppressive naivety, left her feeling so alone. *Don't you see. Don't you see?*

The prospect of Nicola leaving is indeed sad. She had been with Galleani; she'd been unfaithful to her husband. And now she is telling herself it wasn't a totally adulterous act. She'd sneered and allowed him his egoistical remark: *I won't hurt you.* Galleani had prodded and asked questions, yet she saw to it that he knew nothing of her inner life. No clues of who she really is.

She turns and kisses Nicola fully on his mouth. Somehow, it was very much like the first time they kissed. Just as Nicola unbuttons and slides his hand under her dress, Dante enters the room.

Evening, with the spring rain drumming against their bedroom windows, first a slight tapping, then a pulsing and a letting up again, Rosina wants more than ever to be with her husband. She now looks at

Nicola's body with a renewed sense of awe, young and firm, broader, huskier than the older, slighter, intellectual man she allowed to extort her. She didn't want to think of Galleani, but couldn't help it. She had refused to remove her dress for him, just her garters, undies, and stockings, while he, shamelessly shirtless and with no underpants, dropped his slacks to his ankles. With her eyes closed, she felt the thinness of him, his virile substance dissipating around them. A deep-seated disgust for both him and for herself, she can't help it, flushes her blood. Now, fully aware of her husband's glowing strength, she wraps her legs around him. Nicola lets out a tiny wince as her cold feet touch the small of his back. Nicola, always the talker, the tease: "I love us when we're like this," he says, moving inside her, then just about pulling away, prompting her to tighten her muscles, not letting him go. He moves and moans, "I want to be a mythical God."

Rosina laughs softly.

He goes on, "So I can fly back night after night. To penetrate you, only as a God can." He pins her arms above her head, "You'd have to beg me to stop." His words ignite them and she feels him rising. "How much more could I want you?" he says.

Afterward, in the bathroom, Rosina hears Nicola's soft snores as she makes a mixture of vinegar, iodine, and water, and hangs the rubber douche bag on the nail behind the door. They've talked about having another baby but now isn't the time. She inserts the nozzle and grimaces at the sting as the liquid trickles down into the toilet.

* * *

The van is scheduled to arrive at 6 AM. They peer through the frosted glass pane of the kitchen door. "Remember," Nicola says, trying to keep the moment light, "don't allow any governmental officials here, they'll steal the cross right off the donkey." Rosina, momentarily puzzled, remembers the markings on Pinocchio's back, the way the dark, short, stiff hair stood up, splayed along his back, crossing in a tee shape, or as Nicola called it, a cross.

"I will write to you every day unless work gets in the way." He presses his lips to her forehead.

Rosina hates long goodbyes. Goodbyes make her anxious. She waits impatiently for the car to arrive. "Don't worry about us, we'll be fine."

She sees headlights coming, then watches them brighten along the driveway. Nicola hugs her tightly. *"Ti amo,* I'll return as soon as I can."

The sun is beginning to rise, backlighting the outline of his fedora and his broad shoulders as he walks towards the van. *"Ti amo anche io,"* she calls after him. She also sees the shadow of another man beside the driver inside the van. As she watches him step onto the running board, she is surprised that she is relieved. Harboring a secret, one she would have to learn to live with will be easier with him gone; she knows that now. Now she will conjure up his dark *cioccolato* eyes, plant kisses on them. Hold him in her dreams. There is something tender and endearing about loving from afar, something almost pure. All she has to do is close her eyes.

11

Two weeks pass when Rosina receives her first letter from Nicola. She is grateful to read his words. At home, they always try hard to speak English, she has forgotten how beautiful his Italian was:

Mia cara moglie,

> *It took us two days to come to this small town, which we'll call home for the next few months. The roads were wretched, filled with so many holes that a few of the men got sick. But the bougainvillea, the overgrown purple sage, and the wildflowers were beyond expectation.*
>
> *Cara mia, if I were a flower this is where I'd want to live. We stopped to eat along the road. Antonio, the man in charge, had sandwiches made of salami and peppers. We sat under the trees, and each shared a keg of water. Rosabella, a hummingbird came to my sandwich, was inches from my fingers and wasn't afraid. I allowed him to peck on the bread.*
>
> *I've found a friend, a man who is a poet, a philosopher. His name is Bartolomeo Vanzetti. He also lives in Massachusetts. We are staying in a one-*

story building that used to be a coffee mill or a packinghouse.

There are many rooms that contain only bunks for sleeping. The toilet is outside the building, only one for twenty men. This is no place for women. Each day I think, if only I didn't feel this unsettling devotion to "The Cause," And with the threat of being drafted how could we have a normal live? I ask myself each night, why must we possess this burden?

Three days later, another letter arrives.

Carissma,

We have found work picking coffee beans and we begin tomorrow. We took a drive to the seashore, and Bart and I were amazed that no one lives near the ocean. Such a beautiful sea, it doesn't seem possible.

We wanted to spend the night at the beach, but there was no way for us to return. It was many hours away. At night the temperature here goes down to 14 or 15, so it's not too cold, but during the day the temperature reaches almost 45. We are excited to work.

The driver, Antonio, has somehow set up an incredible mail system for all the fifty or so men here. He also brings a newspaper each morning. I read that here the revolution is escalating. Zapata is gaining strength.

I saw you and Dante in my dreams again last night. You came to me like in a fresco painting; of all the Madonna's, you were the most brilliant. A masterpiece. Your eyes intensely warm, a look so penetrating, I carry it with me all this day.

Vi Manco cosi tanto. I think only of you, Baci e Dante.

Nicola keeps his promise. The letters, although dated consecutively, arrive sporadically. Sometimes, two a day and then none for a week.

Carissima bella donna,

I got your first letter today. My hands trembled with joy as I opened it. I cannot believe that Dante read his first book. I'm so proud of both of you. You for teaching him and him for learning so well. I am happy to hear that you and Susan are getting involved with a new play. Send her my love. We must hold our fellow human beings close to our hearts and not allow the institutions to oppress us further.

We were informed of a group of men who were falsely arrested for burglary while going out on strike in New York. Part of our earnings here will be going into a fund to pay for their lawyers to get them out of jail. Each of us deserves to experience a life of equality.

I miss you and my Dante so much, I'm having difficulty sleeping at night, but love the outdoor work. I have to close this letter quickly; my fingers are sore from picking. They'll need a few days to heal.

I read in the paper that Zapata says, "It is better to die on your feet than to live on your knees." Are we socialists not great philosophers?

You have my heart forever.
Nicola

12

Rosina waits for the streetcar on the north side of town. Susan will be waiting for her at the old playhouse on the south side. The autumn air is an early surprise, brisk against her forehead and cheeks. Across the street, the empty lot is filled with debris. Blackened clumps of unraked leaves from last fall twirl about in the spiraling wind.

She hadn't slept well the night before, so she's glad to find a a seat on the streetcar. As she journeys downtown, she finds herself dozing, but the occasional high screech of metal-on-metal of the streetcar is vexing. Nicola's voice comes to her, or what she believes is his voice. Was she forgetting the calm vibrato of his speech? No longer able to envision the intensity of his eyes, the curve of his full lips; she knows his face better than her own, but now struggles to see it. It has been three months since Nicola left. It seems like it's been a lifetime. She longs to hear his footsteps on the craggy porch; the rough and tumble way he throws open the door. Last night, longing for him, she took a shirt from the closet and brought it to bed with her. n an urgent and greedy attempt to be close to him, she washed and pressed all his shirts the first week after he left and was upset with herself for having washed away his scent.

Now only two letters arrive each week. We miss you. Dante misses you. Come home. She wants to tell him but doesn't for fear of putting him in danger. Instead, she writes: *the war is becoming unpopular; vigilante justice is ongoing in Boston and New York. People are being sent to jail for speaking out against war. We must whisper our thoughts, amore. American flags are everywhere—Nationalism is at its prime.*

Yesterday, she sat at their kitchen table, the gauzy curtains she had just finished sewing and hung, cast a soft opaque light as she opened Nicola's letter. His response to her news was, *"These are good signs. Political change, class struggles, we know they take time."* She finds it so absurd; how can he still possess such a positive attitude?

The window on the streetcar is clouded over, like someone attempted to wash or coat it with oil or tar, leaving heavy streaks. Still, she can see the remnants of another eviction when they pass Garrett Street. Tossed out onto the curb on the sidewalk are mattresses, dressers, a couch, boxes of toys and books, and a rocking horse with its head at its feet. Commonplace these days, it doesn't matter if the breadwinner is dreadfully ill, unemployed, or dead. The blessed truth is the landlords have the law on their side. Thoughts of cruelty towards oppressed families nibble away at her. Rosina shrugs miserably, tries to rid herself of such notions, then notices her stop approaching and pulls on the cord.

Stepping off the streetcar she sees Susan a few doors down, sitting on the stoop of the old playhouse. She wears a cloche hat. A raccoon boa she'd acquired from the Salvation Army is wrapped around on her shoulders. Rosina admires the daring way Susan has taken to dress lately: slacks with pleats and pockets, French lace blouses you can see through, scarves with feathers. Her own hips were set too wide to wear slacks: *You have the body of a childbearing woman. Nicola's words run through her head.* She sees his face flush with desire, a memory that still arouses her. Speaking of Susan, Nicola had voiced that it was strange a woman would want to dress like a man. Rosina knew her husband found her attractive when she wore dresses, bared her calves.

"You're going to love this one," Susan announces, puffing away on her cigarette.

"What?"

"This play is going to be a farce," she says sarcastically.

"I suppose that's good," Rosina says, "We could use some laughs."

"We probably won't be able to laugh about this one. It's about the accidental death of an anarchist. Sounds too much like the story of Andrea Salsedo." She holds up the script. "Another 'freedom fighter.'"

Susan had been throwing the term "freedom fighter" around lately, especially when she heard someone accuse the groups of being terrorists.

"It's like the writer copied the life of Salsedo. You remember, my friend, thrown from the New York skyscraper?"

How could she not. Susan cried about it for days and swore to somehow get even.

Susan tamps her cigarette into the ground. "Let's go in and see what this guy has to say."

The "guy" Susan refers to is a playwright new to the area. His name is Romeo Scaglioni. Susan had heard of his success in New York at a small theater in Greenwich Village. One night the theater had broken out in flames and the authorities blamed him, closing him down. They ordered him to leave New York City, or the police would make his life wretchedly unhappy.

* * * *

The small theater is four steps down, in the sub-level of the building. The walls are laden with a marine blue paint, thick and bumpy from too many coats. There are probably seventy or seventy-five seats. With the house lights up the once plush wine velvet seating looks worn and shiny.

Romeo is sitting on the edge of the stage, his legs dangling. His eyes are a light, opaque gray. "*Benevenuto, Signore*," he speaks clearly, softly. "Come sit with me." Rosina heard he originally came from Trieste. His Italian is so pure; he makes Rosina realizes how much she misses the language. She could listen to him speak all day. Most immigrates she met in Massachusetts were from the southern part of Italy and owned the habit of chopping off the ending sound of words. Romeo is the first northerner she's met in the States. High Italians, that's how they were quickly coming to be known among the southerners, and Romeo wore this title flawlessly.

He crosses his legs, revealing the soles of his shoes worn in thinning circles. He hands her a script. "I've given one to Susanna, and this is for you. Please study it. We don't have much time. We open in three weeks. Your name again?"

"Rosina," she says, nervously.

Her eyes avert towards Susan, who looks like she has just swallowed the script whole.

Romeo excuses himself and walks behind stage.

Susan grins and whispers, "He's never going to learn our names."

Romeo returns with a burlap sack filled with papers and cardboard, something you might find in a room for kindergarteners.

"Stupendous," he says, shuffling through his bag. "I want you, my radiant ladies, to study this and think about this throughout the entire play. This is our theme." He holds up a poster with large lettering. "All Anarchist are philosophers," he says. "If you ever question this, remember what Anatolia France wrote." And he turns the poster over so they can read it:

THE LAW, IN ITS MAJESTIC EQUALITY,
FORBIDS THE RICH AS WELL AS THE POOR
TO SLEEP UNDER BRIDGES,
TO BEG IN THE STREETS,
AND TO STEAL BREAD.

He recites the message in Italian from memory: *La Legge, Nella Sua Maestosa Uguaglianza Proibisce Ai Ricchi Come Ai Paver Di Dormire Sotto I Ponti, Mendicare Per Strada E Rubare Pane.*

"This sort of irony is all around us, we are immersed in it, and this attitude is what we'll pursue in our play. Sit here, *Signore*." He points to two of the seats in the front row. One could almost see him thinking. The frown on his brow, the long white fingers searching for intangibles. The occasional closing of his eyes; it is all there, the creativeness, struggling, grasping at whatever worthwhile thing will come to the front of his mind.

Looking over the script Rosina is glad to see it was only a one-act play, with two characters. One female and one male character. She nudges Susan, points to the script and shrugs.

"I want to hear your speaking voices. Read the first couple of lines in the script. No, wait. Just tell me about yourself. In your most natural speaking voice."

Rosina's mouth goes dry. The words will never come. "My name is …."

"No, stand please."

As she stands, she shakes slightly. "I don't know why I do this!" she announces with that nervous laugh of hers she has grown to hate.

"Oh, well, that we can philosophize about later," he says, waving off her remark, making her feel even more unfit for the stage.

She thinks of her nickname when in the convent, *Timida,* and wonders if by labeling one eventually they became that. She wishes she was more daring, had some "moxie," a word she recently learned from the Russian pharmacist. Calming herself, she takes a deep breath and tries to imagine all the money the play will raise and how many hopeless families it can help.

"My name is Rosina Sacco, I'm the wife of Nicola Sacco and the mother of four-year-old Dante. Originally born in the province of Brescia, I arrived in the United States and went to work as a seamstress in a factory at the age of sixteen."

"You mean a sweatshop?" he says. "Okay, enough. Now, I'd like you—eh—Sophia, to do the same thing."

Susan stood, "My name is Susan. Susan Morrissey." Susan's all moxie.

"*Mi scusi,* I'm very bad with names. When you reach my age, you find them unimportant. Please continue."

"I was born in Maine and moved to Massachusetts with my parents at the age of eleven. At the age fifteen I became aware of the issue of class, thanks to an uncle, my mother's brother, who made a lot of money—padded his pockets with the blood and sweat of the poor workers."

"Enough, Susan. You have a strong presence. I'd like you to play the part of the male journalist. And Rosalia, you'll be the wife of Arturo Fagotti, the man who was unfairly persecuted, thrown from a window on the sixteenth floor." He coughed. "I'll have other actors, who will be policemen, moving about the stage." He looks around the theater. "If they show up. Now, are you both familiar with the death of Arturo Fagotti?"

Rosina and Susan look at each other. Romeo lets go a sigh of frustration and hands them each a folder of newspaper articles about Arturo Fagotti and his inescapable death.

Rosina is relieved, the wife's part is much more suited to her. She'll handle it better than the male part. Yet she still feels stage fright; nervousness hitting her at the back of her neck, tightening in her chest. Her mouth so parched she swears over and over the words won't come, but somehow, they always do.

After the first few lines she is able to transform herself into character and become detached from the small audience. In another life, she thought, she might've been a star of the stage. Oh, the wonderful warm rush of satisfaction that raced through her when it was over; the hug of applause around her. Still, she'd struggle with the frivolousness of such behavior, impersonating, playacting. Thinking of a family dispossessed, destroyed; of Arturo Fagotti, editor of a newspaper, or Andrea Salsedo splattered on the pavement in front of the Justice Department in New York City. Is this all pointless? How can putting on a stage play really help? The cure seems too wide a gap. At what point, finally, would humanity be served? *I can only try*, she mumbles to herself. Mumbling, something she started doing right after Nicola left.

13

That evening Susan reads Dante a story before going to bed, while Rosina cleans the supper dishes. Susan's appetite makes her smile—so like Nicola's. After devouring her third sausage without any hesitancy, she tells Rosina, "I only eat like this when you cook." But Rosina knows better. Still, her voracious appetite is part of this pressing passion that surrounds her being. There is never any guessing at what Susan loves or hates. Yes, "love" or "hate"; never anything in the middle. Rosina understands this. Her own heart is very much the same. Rosina's ideals are clear-cut, never any doubt to her opinions, yet she doesn't speak up as loudly as Susan does. Rosina feels it unnecessary. *It's a kind of vanity*, she thinks, *after all, who would really care.*

The sound of Susan's footsteps crosses the hallway into the kitchen, where Rosina is just hanging up her soiled, damp apron on the slanted cup hook. "He made me read the book three times. That kid is exhausting! Oh, but such fun." she sits at the table and reaches for her cigarettes. "Sometimes, I really wonder how you mothers do it. Never having time for yourself." Susan presses her cigarette into her new cigarette holder and lights it. "I guess I'm too selfish to have kids. Not that I ever had the opportunity to find out."

Susan had many lovers in the past, but none of any importance since Rosina met her. The last man, George, fifteen years her senior, broke her heart. Susan told her, "After seven years of living together, he decided to go back to his wife, he said he needed a more nurturing woman in his final years."

"What did you do with the vino?" Susan asks.

Searching in the cupboard for her covered dish to store the leftover broccoli rapini, Rosina asks, "Are you sure you don't want to finish this?"

"I've had plenty." Susan spreads the *Boston Globe* out on the long wooden table. "But I wouldn't mind another glass of wine."

Rosina's loneliness has pervaded the day, ever since she woke in the morning. Perhaps it is the start of the new play and not having Nicola to share it with. Dante's reading and writing is blossoming along with his fertile personality, and Nicola is missing it all. Everything. Whatever it is, she feels further away from her man, and has been teary for days, in the same way she is more emotional a day or two before her menstrual cycle; something she and Susan had once discussed, deducing they would never admit this to the opposite sex.

Susan is now rummaging through the kitchen cabinets, looking for the bottle of wine. "What did you do with it?"

The kitchen is very big. Large in a way that in the evenings the light fixture which hangs over the long wooden table provides only a soft cone of light, leaving the corners of the room darkened, full of shadows. Rosina sees Susan in those shadows, muted, reminding her of the benign Sister Cristina, opening and closing the low cupboard doors searching for the water-color paints she had hidden so well—inadvertently misplacing them for her little "Rosa."

Rosina closes the icebox door and turns to Susan. "Promise me, you won't have more than two glasses, and I'll take it out."

Susan's eyes widen, stunned, as though Rosina has pushed her against the opened cabinet door. "Jesus, Mary, and Joseph. What do I look like, some kind of child? You're going to count my drinks?" the look on her face is one of hurt. "I can't believe you're actually telling me this."

"No. I don't mean it like that." Rosina's tears come quickly. "It's just I need you to be here with me tonight. I've been feeling so lonely. And when you drink too much, I feel all alone. You are just not there." Fearing the timing of her tears might be manipulation to get Susan to do what she wants she wonders how much of the nuns' behaviors she really adopted!

Susan retrieves a napkin from the holder on the table and places it in Rosina's hand. "Why didn't you just tell me this before?"

"I'm trying. I don't want to hurt you. I simply need to talk."

"Okay. I'm here." Susan is at her side, nuzzling her to her bosom. "Now, I'm going to get you a drink."

Rosina begins to laugh and cry at the same time, and points to the cupboard where the liquor is. Knowing Rosina likes an occasional aperitif, Susan places a bottle of Campari on the table, along with two glasses.

"I don't want wine anyway," Susan says, "It always makes me too tired. Have this." She hands Rosina a small glass filled with the garnet red liquid. "Do you want some ice?"

Rosina takes a sip and nods. Susan puts the glass to her lips, "Ugh," Susan says, her lips pursed together, frowning. "I need some ice, or something."

Rosina laughs and takes Susan's glass to the icebox where she lifts the French blue bottle and siphons seltzer water into her drink. "Try this," she says.

"Better. But not great!"

Wiping away the last of her tears, Rosina catches a whiff of the lavender scented talc on Susan's shoulder. Susan douses herself with powder each day after her bath. Rosina reaches for the pick in the drawer and chips a few pieces of ice from the block in the icebox. "This should make it better."

"Um," Susan tastes the bitters, "It's a little better. So." She takes a deep breath and settles into the chair across from her. "Darling, I don't like seeing you so upset."

Rosina is grateful for Susan on so many levels. She's the closest thing she ever had to a sister. *Better than a sister*, she thinks, *because there is no competitive spirit*. She could tell her anything, be herself without being judged or ridiculed. "I'm sorry. I didn't mean to hurt you."

"I guess we all do it from time to time." Trying to make light of it, she hums a tune and sings lyrics from a song Rosina isn't familiar with; something about hurting the one you love.

"I want my life back, with Nicola," Rosina says, moving Susan's legs aside on the settee to make room for herself. Susan adjusts her position and tries sitting with her legs crossed under.

"This used to be easy," she says, untangling herself.

Rosina gets up, "I'll sit in the chair," she says.

"No, stay." Susan continues. "It won't be much longer. I'm almost ready for sleep." She takes a sip of Campari. "The war is winding down and...."

There is a knock on the door. "At this hour?" Rosina says as she goes to see who it is. At the parlor window, she moves the newly embroidered curtain to the side and sees Mr. Kelley, the landlord.

"I hope it's not too late, but I saw your light on."

Mr. Kelley was also Nicola's boss; he owned one of the shoe factories in the area. "I was just wondering if you knew when Nicola was returning." Dressed as a gentleman, his tie loosened being the late hour, he held his fedora in both hands at his chest.

"Please come in." Rosina gestures for him to enter.

"No, no. It's much too late. The missus is waiting. I just wanted to know if you heard."

Apparently, he had walked from his house, and not driven his car. Rosina sees the reflection of light on his front porch. Always lit, it brings her comfort during the dark hours, especially since Nicola's absence.

"I'm sorry, I really don't know yet. We were just talking about it. Nicola says he'd let me know soon. Are you sure I can't get you anything? My friend Susan and I are just having a, what do you call it? 'Cap of the night'?"

Mr. Kelley laughs, "You and your friend enjoy your nightcap. I was just checking. Tell Nicola I'm anxious for his return, but please, tell him to be careful."

"I can't thank you enough, Mr. Kelley. Please, if there is anything I can do for you."

"Don't worry, Mrs. Sacco. You've got enough to handle with him being away."

Once they had Mr. Kelley and his wife to dinner and Nicola and he became friends. It was obvious he respected Nicola's enthusiasm for the shoe industry: His artistic eye, and the care he took in tooling the leather, but mostly it was the interest he took in Mr. Kelley's business. That night during dinner, he said, "Other than myself, I never met another man who had such a passion for the shoemaking business."

Sympathetic to their cause, Mr. Kelley had encouraged Nicola to leave, to avoid the draft at all costs, guaranteeing his job on his return. However, Mrs. Kelley always remained indifferent and rather distant.

Rosina says goodnight, closes the door, and enforces the slide lock, knowing Susan's plan to sleep over once again.

"I can't believe how lucky we are to have Mr. Kelley. He is a man of great *vitalita,* great principles. You can see how much he loves Nicola."

"Ah, well, Nicola is easy to love." Susan unties her boots and slides them off her feet.

Rosina sips the Campari. "The Sisters would say, *'Dio benedica sempre.'* And I, the atheist, say the same."

She doesn't know if it was the little Campari; the earlier release of tears, or the sight of Mr. Kelley reminding her of how safe he makes her feel, but things seemed better. She was less alone.

"Okay, now tell me what's on your mind."

"Maybe we should practice the play."

"The play?" Susan looks bewildered. "No, no. You're not getting off so easily. I've put the newspapers and my article aside so we can talk."

"Okay, but first tell me how your article is going?"

Susan is writing an article. She says, "It's about the immigrants of America."

Susan retrieves her notebook from her satchel lying on the floor and reads. "The Irish lay claim to the "whiteness of America," she looks up at Rosina. "I'm trying to draw a parallel with the Germans, who claim to be the superior race. It's not easy," she laughs, "especially since I'm supposed to have both bloodlines."

"How far along are you? I'd like to read it."

"Believe me you will. I'll need your opinion."

She loves this. Susan's trust and confidence make Rosina feel like she somehow really belongs in the United States. For so long, she and Nicola had trouble with many words, but one Christmas Susan brought them the very thick Webster's International Dictionary which is splayed open on the small oak table in her sewing room. Both she and Nicola fell into the habit of having it near when they read in English.

Rosina finishes her drink and decides to make another for herself. She isn't going to offer Susan one. If she wants, she'll get one herself. It has been a long time since she felt the pull of relaxation surround her.

"As I said earlier, I'm really missing Nicola," she says.

"Of course, you are," Susan says, tucking her notebook back in her bag that has toppled on its side.

She doesn't know why, but Susan's quick affirmation annoys her.

"Being without Nicola was bearable until about a week ago, then suddenly it's become too, too long."

Susan attempts to tuck her bare feet under her once again but fails and resorts to crossing her legs. "Maybe if your parents were still here in this country you'd feel differently. Me? I'm used to not having family around." Susan's mother died when she was sixteen years old, and her father married the lady who had cared for her dying mother. Susan never got along with the woman who reminds her of the worst time of her life.

"My parents?" Susan had never met Rosina's mother and father. "What, and have my mother teach my son to throw stones at me?" she says jeeringly.

"They're better off in Italy. My mother never wanted to learn English, which was a problem, and my father, well, he tried, but it was too difficult."

She remembers her mother dragging her or her father along to do the shopping because of her refusal to learn English. When Rosina lived in the convent, she spent a lot of time reflecting on her mother. The anger she felt towards her. In those early years she was too young to know what caused her mother to be so close-fisted, so contemptible. Her only memories of her grandmother were cool—neutral ones, and if that was any indication, then her mother followed suit.

She recalls one late winter afternoon at the convent, helping Sister Cristina build a fire in the dining room fireplace. Handing her small twigs cupped in the apron she was required to wear each day. She had told Sister how angry she felt towards her mother. Sister Cristina never looked up, just continued to poke at the smoldering twigs, the two of them flinching, trying to avoid the dancing sparks and inevitable grey puffs of smoke.

"Your mother wasn't born that way, something made her that way," Sister Cristina told her. "Did you ever think, little Rosa, that your mother is trying to shield you from the hard life she had?"

Her words resonated for Rosina in small moments. Months and eventually years later, it helped to soften her anger. This much she thanks the nuns for. And now, at twenty-two she gave up trying to analyze her mother's past. For years, she was afraid she'd be that same impassive woman, but the moment Dante opened his eyes and caught hers, she was free of that thought. There was no doubt. She would love him with all she had inside of her, without criticism, without judgement.

Seeing Susan's raccoon boa draped over the rocker, Rosina places her empty glass on the coffee table and wraps the boa around her shoulders. "This is very glamorous," she says, "deluxe." She brings it closer to her neck, and the light hairs tickle her chin.

"I wonder how many raccoons it takes to make such a thing."

"Oh, please," Susan scoffs, and then yawns, "don't even worry about it. If I do, I won't be able to wear it. I manage by telling myself I wasn't the one to kill them."

Rosina takes another sip from her Campari.

"Besides," Susan continues, "they probably all died of old age."

Rosina had seen this before; the way Susan rationalizes her actions. She had formed so many principles—her soapbox declaration was the unfair distribution of wealth—the need for all humans to be equal. However, she was easily tempted by an elite lifestyle. Hard for her to resist temptation, she would say, "I need an outlet."

Rosina settles on the sofa, next to Susan. "Let me have a puff of your *sigaretta*," she says, playfully, and reaches out for Susan's holder then take a long, deep inhalation, and begins to choke.

"Take it easy," Susan laughs. "You have to inhale slowly, like this," demonstrating, but Rosina is done, and gives her back the cigarette holder and goes to get a drink of water.

It is a warm evening, and she has left the windows on the front porch open. Moths swerve around the lightbulb of the small lamp on the side table.

Moths, she wonders, how long do they live? How long does any insect–animal live? "I still don't know how you can wear a dead animal around your shoulders."

Susan's head rests against the sofa pillow, her eyes closed.

Remembering Galleani's mounted moths, she says, "I slept with him. I slept with Galleani." Somehow unable to bring herself to say his first name out loud.

Susan opens her eyes and stares at her closely, as if to be certain this was the woman she knew. Suddenly alert. "You didn't."

During the silent moment that follows, Rosina worries Susan might not understand so she begins to blurt it out. "You remember, I never showed the draft letter to Nicola. Well, when I went to his house that day, he manipulated me. If I didn't allow him, Nicola would've never been in the van that morning. I didn't have a choice."

Susan sits upright on the sofa and takes a deep breath. "Wow. Holy shit. I never thought."

Suddenly Rosina has the urge to close her eyes, to bury herself in sleep, but she needs to wait for Susan to digest what she just told her.

"Now that's what you call a real sacrifice for social justice," she chuckles. "I would've never expected this from you." She moves from the sofa to touch Rosina's shoulder. "I don't mean it the way it sounds, really, it's okay. You did what you had to do. Once when we had to have some literature printed for the Suffrage March, we had no money, so I ended up sleeping with the printer. It was the only way we could get the pamphlets out." She smiles. "Besides he was kind of a handsome fellow. And I did see him for a few months afterwards."

Rosina realizes Susan is missing the point. "But you weren't married."

"Yes, Rosina darling, but isn't it all about the end result?"

She couldn't argue this point. The end result. It was the way the world worked. It didn't matter how you got there, as long as you succeeded at what you set out to achieve. As Galleani said, "we do what we must."

"I douched so many times that day and the next, it felt like I burnt my insides." And she had avoided Nicola that week. Pretending to have a stomachache, allowing Dante to stay up later than usual. Rosina inhales deeply. Relief. "Nicola must never find out. Never. It would destroy him."

"Of course not," Susan says, wholeheartedly. "Of course not."

"What's done is done. I just needed to tell someone. And who else could I tell?"

"You can tell me anything," Susan says. And then she yawns. "Excuse me. I admit, I'm exhausted."

"Me too," Rosina says.

Faces washed, teeth brushed, and in their nightgowns, they kiss each other good night. But Rosina wants to hold her. She feels an even deeper connection to Susan, one she had never experienced, a sisterhood of trust. "Thank you," she says and hugs her hard and long, releasing her in time to hold back the tears about to flow.

14

There are no letters from Nicola for almost three weeks. For a moment, Rosina stops clearing the supper dishes to ask the question once again: *Why is he not back. Maybe he is hurt. In a hospital. No. I can't be doing this.* She continues to pick up Dante's uneaten flat green beans and resolves to make them with eggs and Parmesan cheese for lunch the next day. A week of dense humidity, and with no window screens, the houseflies have moved in. Chasing them from the leftover chicken legs, she swats the air with the flyswatter. "Shit," she cries as she misses. The heat and humidity presses upon her, making her cranky and tired. She is having terrible dreams lately. Always, the loud swoosh of the convent doors closing. Heavy carved doors sucking in unseeable things that leave her feeling edgy when she wakes. She hasn't thought of the convent, about the founding nun who is buried under the rectory, for so many years, so why now is she dreaming, forced to think of disembodied ghosts during her waking hours. *You will not haunt me; she* says out loud. *I was never yours to haunt. She* pours herself another glass of vino.

The Adventures of Paddy the Beaver, a book she is reading to Dante, is spread across the table at Nicola's place. Three-and-a-half months have passed since Nicola left. She wills herself to see him seated there. Well-groomed. Tidy. Knife in his left hand, and fork in his right, resting them only when he is finished eating. She sees him swabbing the sauce from his bowl with a chunk of Italian bread. His innocent look, his spirited eyes. *I've been alone too long. Thinking too much. Absurd dreams.* She presses on, turning pages to the back of the library book for the return date. September sixth. Schools are opening soon.

She is glad she doesn't have to decide about Dante attending school yet. *Public schools* with *their propaganda, and their heavy dictatorial hand, designed to break a child's spirit.* She always dreamed of schools being more like community centers, always open, where any student can wander in and out of the libraries and workshops. Each student choosing what they wish to learn. Hands on with nature—acquiring knowledge, to live in *this* world on their own terms. Not a teaching imposed through a whitewashed sanitized history, built on untruths.

She recently heard from one of the comrade's wives about *Casa dei Bambini* in Roma. A modern school opened by *la dottoressa* Maria Montessori, a woman from Ancona. The unstructured program, or lack of one, seemed idealistic to Rosina. She had read Montessori schools were starting to come to America. *Wouldn't that be wonderful,* she dreams, *here in Massachusetts.* She wants her son's heart to stay pure. Not be corrupted by boundaries and rules she and Nicola have tried to avoid for so long now.

Closing the book, she sighs heavily, and remembers Dante's rollicking laughter when the young Beaver's logs began to float chaotically in a difficult stream. That sticky spider web he put his hand through to see what it felt like; the way he cried when he saw he destroyed it. She had to convince him the spider no longer needed her web, she moved on to another location. Thinking of her son's care and concern for all living things, she becomes teary eyed. Maybe she's had enough wine.

Peeking into Dante's room, she lifts his pillow from the floor. His top sheet hangs by the foot of the bed. She rearranges the cover over his tiny body. Pillow on her lap, she sits by the side of his bed. The small lamp on his nightstand reflects on her clunky black shoes, laces securely tightened. The plain cut of her housedress spins dreams of another life.

Susan, who was fashionably dressed, was off in New York, "adventuring," as she liked to call it. She was taking risks, owning her splintered shoulder, which they now referred to as her badge of courage. Rosina wonders, almost jealously, *where is my badge of courage?* She sees herself there alongside Susan. *Free like a man,* she says out loud.

The vino envelopes her in a fog, and somehow she hears the squeaky hinges of the shutter outside her window of the convent. *Parents, convent, husband, child.* Never really "free."

When you're young, who thinks about freedom? The Italian brainwashing: *You must marry young before you're too old, or no man will want you.*

She chuckles out loud at the absurdity of this statement, inducing Dante to turn in his sleep.

Dante's skin glows ivory, an angelic look. His face is serene; even when asleep he appears to be smiling. Raphael's cherubs. *A perfect angel.* The pillow on her lap, she wonders what it might be like to hold it gently over his face. To watch him struggle, gasping for air. Terror strikes her, reverberates deep within her body. Fear tethers to her being. She is paralyzed for a moment. *What's wrong with you?* And she throws the pillow to the other side of the room. In trying to recover from her vision, she kneels at the head of Dante's bed, and kisses him on the cheeks, the forehead, then lays her head near his; she smells the sweetness of his breath, and sighs in gratitude.

In the bathroom, she stumbles as she slips her nightgown over her head. Hearing a mosquito buzz, she stands perfectly still, waits for it to land, and slams her forearm. Blood spurts from the insect. The ugly olive-green walls make her skin look sallow in the mirror. When will they have time to paint? As she washes away the blood, the thought descends on her it's not only Nicola that she misses but also the meetings. She needs the fellowship of like-minded people. To be involved, to have a purpose more than a housewife and mother.

Her bedroom begins to spin. She falls into bed. Just as she begins to doze off, she hears the sound of an automobile coming, or going. Why would Mr. Kelley be stopping by so late? in her thin summer gown, she searches for a cover up and quickly grabs the cotton throw at the foot of her bed and wraps it around herself.

She hears scraping on the porch. "Who's there?" her voice should be bolder. Her judgment is off, and she tries desperately to be more aware. She cannot remember if she locked the door. Her bare feet on the wooden floor move towards the kitchen, to the knife drawer. She hears the squeak of the front doorknob turn, and then opens. There in the dark shadows stands a man wearing a flannel shirt and baggy slacks. For a moment, the scene doesn't seem real. She is outside her body. Gripping the knife tightly, she lifts it above her head, ready to strike, and then hears a familiar call. "*Mia cara, Rosina.*"

Her husband's voice floats in the darkness. Stunned, she's unable to move. "*Dio mio!* she drops the knife on the floor and explodes in joy.

They fill their arms with each other. "*Ti adora. Ti adora.*" Over and over again. Nicola holds her at an arms-length distance, "*Come stai.* Let me look at you."

He smells awful. A mix of sewage and rotted potatoes. She laughs and weeps and the same time, "You smell like a dead horse."

"I feel like a dead horse," he laughs, and taps his small protruding belly. "Lots of beans and cheese."

His eyes are puffy, and his face is tanned. He is exhilarated and exhausted. "I've missed you and Dante so much," he murmurs in her ear. "I'm willing to take a chance. Should they come looking for me, we'll worry about it then," he says. "Anyway, there is rumor that a family man would be the last to be drafted."

It was true. Rosina remembers Mr. Kelley saying that he read it in the *Globe*. But she didn't trust, didn't want to think about it; maybe she wouldn't have felt she'd had to go to Galleani had she not been so consumed with fear.

Rosina notices the broad-stripped cloth satchel on the floor. "Where is your suitcase? Where did you get these awful clothes?"

"Someone robbed it. The first day I arrived in Santa Ana. No one knew where it was, and no one saw it. An old Mafioso tale," he says quickly, smiling without concern.

A pounding headache wakes Rosina in the morning. She hears Nicola in Dante's room. Despite her heaviness, she feels the familiar warmth of her home come full circle. The sound of his voice, *how* she reflects, *how can one person bring so much light into someone else's life?* Even the olive-green walls in the bathroom look brighter. When she walks into Dante's room, Nicola is showing Dante some tools he got while in Mexico. "This is called a pincer; I can use this for pressing the leather together." He looks up. "Ah! My sunshine is finally awake."

Moments later, over coffee, he asks, "Did you leave the door unlocked last night?"

Remembering her crazy thoughts about Dante, she's ashamed. "I was just about to lock it, when I heard the car approaching," she says.

15

It is a few days before the American day of Thanksgiving. Rosina decides to go to Via del Marceto, in celebration of Nicola's return. This is the street where shop windows hang salami and provolone, and bakeries display *sfogliatelle* and *cassata* cakes. Here, in the north end of Boston, she will find that perfect ricotta, and black Sicilian olives, sharp and wrinkled. At the butcher shop, she purchases sausage to stuff the turkey. Because of their steep prices, she has only shopped here once before during the summer. At the Italian delicatessen, she chooses a bulbous provolone hanging from a hook, the wax on it so tight and shiny she can almost see her reflection.

Rosina remembers the way the older women, once proprietors, dressed in black, sat on their crates in front of the shops, fanning themselves with a handkerchief or dishtowel while keeping a sharp eye for problems. Now, with a clear sense of snow arriving, doors are closed, and the smell of the pasticceria's freshly baked cannoli crust is only for those who enter. She is smiling, practically giddy, throughout her shopping trip, excited to celebrate and have Nicola back home. Yes, grateful—this one American celebration seems like a perfect fit for her.

Rosina is curious to meet Nicola's new friend, Bartolomeo, who will be coming for dinner. Nicola is excited. They haven't seen each other since they departed from Mexico together. Nicola rarely brought friends home. She wondered if it was because most of his friends were more subversive, more rebellious than she would've liked.

Waiting for the trolley, the winds begin to pick up. Rosina lowers the packages to the ground in order to button her coat, and then notices the Italian newspaper headline at the tobacconist shop. *SPLOSION UCCIDE NOVE POLIZIOTTI E UNA PASSANTE.* She rushes to buy the paper before the trolley comes. Fighting against the wind, the paper flutters chaotically as she reads:

> The worst incident of terrorist violence in the United States. The bomb was found in the basement of a Catholic church in Milwaukee. Aimed at a right-wing curate. After having been discovered by the police, it was then transported to the station where the bomb accidently erupted, killing nine policemen and one female civilian.

It was a large black powder bomb with an acid "delay" detonator. A heavy investigation is underway. They attribute it to the anarchist group—*Galleanisti*, followers of Galleani.

The heat rises in her face, and she immediately folds and shoves the newspaper into her bag. The man who is also waiting for the trolley is now seated across from her, staring. She hears Nicola's warning: Never read a foreign, especially Italian, newspaper in public. So, with the turkey on the floor between her feet, she presses her ankles tightly against the bag, then grips her purse along with the remaining bags on her lap, closes her eyes, and pretends to nap.

Thursday morning, while Nicola and Dante are still asleep, Rosina gets up early to prepare the turkey. At the last-minute, Mr. Kelley told Nicola he and his wife would be coming for dinner, so she is even more eager to have everything perfect. The bombing had been the main topic of conversation the day before, but now Rosina wants to make this a family day. A safe, warm setting.

Knowing Susan is coming and Nicola's friend and Nicola's need to share his thoughts, it may not be possible. There will be little or no talk on radical groups in the presence of the Kelleys. She will try to keep them longer. In her own dreamy intentions, she is imagining trying to arrange some sort of union between Bartolomeo and Susan. She had asked Nicola what he thought, but he said flatly, "It would never work. Susan will eat him alive." He snickered in that confident, masculine tone he used when he was with his comrades. Yet knowing men know little about what they really want in a woman, not until they actually see her before them, she dismisses his opinion.

When Dante wakes and comes into the kitchen, he insists on having a *cannoli* for breakfast. Rosina tries to reason with him. His tears summons Nicola to the kitchen. "Oh, let him have it. It's a special day today. We have much to be thankful for." Still in his pajamas, Nicola tousles Dante's hair as if to have it match his own messy mane.

Dante stops crying and sits at the table with wet eyes and cheeks, a pathetic look upon his face. He waits for the outcome of his father's remark. Nicola has been trying to make up for time lost—afraid the bond he shared with his son has to be solidified, made strong once again. Rosina sighs. She knows she's going to have to give in a little bit. So that Dante doesn't understand, she speaks in Italian, telling Nicola that giving Dante his way is not an act of love. "*Concedergli tutto non e un atto d'amore.*" Moments such as these come tumbling down on her. Is she too stern, like her mother? This thread of doubt is the weakest part of her mothering, and yet she knows she will never learn the truth until Dante is a grown man.

When Bartolomeo arrives, Susan is already helping Rosina get ready. Placing the platters on the dining room table, Susan is able to see him enter the parlor. "He's got books in his hands."

Rosina catches Susan's eye as she removes the hot lasagna pan from the oven. She can't tell by Susan's expression if it is a good or bad sign. Turning off the stove, Rosina wipes her hands on her apron and goes into the parlor to meet him.

He is at least a head taller than Nicola, with a striking mustache which hangs dolefully. His style is what she would expect to find in a "*borgo antico*" somewhere in the hills of Italy. He shakes her hand robustly. His skin is coarse as if he mixed cement for a living and never washed. Yet in a most soft-spoken voice, he says, "*Felice di incontrarvi.*"

"I'm happy to meet you also," Rosina says, surprised at his appearance. His shirt is tucked carelessly and a frayed rope around his waist holds up his wrinkled pants. He appears old, or was it old-fashioned? Any thoughts of matching him with Susan are quickly erased.

Grasping Susan's hand, he says in English, with a thick accent, "Nice to see you. My name is Bartolomeo Vanzetti."

Back in the kitchen, Susan whispers to Rosina, "Wow, when he says his name, it sounds like music...the beginnings of an aria." She smiles pleasantly. "How do you say his name?"

"Just call him Bartolo or Bart. I'm sure people here call him that already. He's in America now."

Susan nods in agreement.

Dante takes to Bartolomeo immediately, as he does with most visitors. He shows him the wooden truck his father made for him and pulls him by his shirt sleeve to go outside to meet Pinocchio. Later on, when Nicola is able to get Bartolomeo away from Dante, before the Kelley's arrive, Rosina hears them over a glass of wine talking about one of the men who was in Santa Ana with them.

"Remember him, his hand-painted shirt? on the back he wrote, 'As Long as There is Government—There Will be no Freedom.'"

"*Si*, he had signs all over his shirt. I don't remember his name, but I remember, 'Die with dignity. Say No to War.' Right on his sleeve. He was always laughing," Bartolomeo says.

"*Allora*, well now he has nothing to laugh about. He was arrested for carrying explosives, and they're deporting him."

When the Kelleys arrive, Rosina arranges the seating around at the table. Nicola reveres the idea of giving thanks. Setting a day aside to honor gratitude. All of them now seated, the lasagna cut into generous portions and the bird waiting to be carved on the sideboard, they wait for Nicola to say blessings.

"Bartolomeo, my dear Rosetta, and me, we come to America to find work, to make our lives better, instead we find many problems, much unfairness. Some of us, like my dear friend here, lived homeless for two years." Bartolomeo purses his lips together and nods his head..

Nicola continues, "They call us Birds of Passage, but we here at this table, are not. We are here permanently. To make better our lives, to help the poor and the needy. But today, I speak of what we have, not what we don't have."

Rosina is relieved. Glad she doesn't have to interrupt him. "We are grateful for all of this: Our guests at this table, the food my beautiful Rosetta has prepared, and for my job, for Mr. Kelley."

Dante jumps in his chair and shouts, "And what about me?"

During the quick round of laughter, Rosina whispers to Susan. "Dante is the true blessing."

Nicola's so-called blessing could've been tainted by a long political lecture. Rosina is grateful. She urges, *"Mangia,* everything is getting cold, Nicola."

Nicola gazes around the table, and nods. "Today I hope for fairness of wealth and health for all. Freedom from laws that chain us down."

Rosina clears her throat in an obvious way. Coughs.

Nicola looks at her. "Okay, let's eat. *Mangiamo.*"

There is laughter, clacking of forks and knives, and an occasional toast. Even Mr. Kelley, his glass filled with a special beer Nicola bought for him, toast's Nicola's return and in a surprise announcement, he says he is promoting Nicola to foreman. Bartolomeo understands enough English to participate in most of the conversation. And Susan, as always, is there in all her naturalness, part of everyone's conversation, especially Dante's, whose questions to her are ceaseless.

Rosina sits back and takes in a deep satisfying breath. The house is filled with her guests. The dishes, the embroidered tablecloth, the serving plates brimming with food, the short water glasses they used for wine and the decanter filled with the ruby vino on the sideboard with its glued legs. All of it, how did they do it? She never really saw it happening. It all grew from nothing. It wasn't material things; it was the wholeness, the completeness of a world that now, like a room of gifts, tumbled around her. She reaches for Dante, *"Ti adoro,"* she says. Although miserly with his hugs, her son allows her a quick embrace before pushing on to do or say something else.

When Rosina passes the stuffing and turkey to Mrs. Kelley, who is sitting on her left, she nods, takes the dish, but never once looks Rosina in the eye. She consumes small bites of food and seems very frail. At first, Rosina guesses she might have some kind of *malattia,* and wants to ask if she is not feeling well, but there is something about the woman. As frail as she seems, Rosina has a suspicion she will tell her to mind her business, *stay away from me.* She offers no conversation at the table, only an occasional whisper to her husband's ear. It's as though she has a burning prejudice towards Italians—forced to be among them because of her husband. Rosina's sympathy is growing for Mr. Kelley—he deserves a happier, more endearing woman sitting at his side.

As expected, the Kelleys leave early and Rosina, exhausted and relieved to be rid of the Mrs., doesn't bother to ask them to stay longer. Dishes are piled in the sink, and a bowl of grapes and walnuts still are on the table. With Dante asleep in his bed, the four remaining adults relax in the parlor. Rosina feels accomplished, sophisticated, alive; warmed by the company, and by the swift alliance she has formed with Bartolomeo. Surprised to hear him articulate so many words in English. His way with language is poetic and his expressions can hold any audience.

"When I earn extra money, I want to buy a violin and learn to play. Music is important to man. I find it most calming" he says, affirming, nodding to his own thoughts. "It makes us feel and think. More sensitivity to the world around us. In our working days, we sometimes forget who we really are."

Susan asks him, "What are you reading?" indicating his books now on the end table.

He hands them to her. One is titled, *What's Wrong with the World?* and the other is a book of poetry. "The poems," he says, "by different Italian poets."

Susan briefly flips through the politically inclined book. "I'm impressed that you can read in English."

"Hardly," he laughs. "I struggle. But it's good practice."

"I really have to do more reading." Susan put the book down. "Lately, all I seem to be interested in is the newspapers."

"Newspapers? When she's here, they're everywhere. She reads at least, what is it? Four newspapers a day?" Rosina says. "From front to back."

"Well, now I'm inspired by your reading," he says to Susan.

Each of them knew what Bart meant.

"Did you read about that young woman who was arrested for transporting dynamite on a train going to Chicago?" Nicola asks.

Bartolomeo crosses his legs revealing frayed cuffs on his slacks and nods.

"Yes," Susan says, finishing what is left in her glass. "She was Italian also. Her name was Gabriella-something-Antonlino. She was only nineteen years old. I don't know if she was part of the Chicago-based group or not."

"The only information she gave was a false name. She refused to talk," Bart says, lighting one of the cigarettes Susan offers him.

"Well, now they know who she is, and she's going to jail for fifteen months and then she'll be deported. So, what good did it do?" Rosina says.

Nicola stretches his neck and moves his head side to side, some pain he brought back from Mexico but no memory of how it happened. "She validates our cause," he says. "Shows we're not giving in to the institution of crooked governments. Not without a fight, anyway."

Rosina wants to say, *yes, I'm sure her parents are very proud of her.* Sometimes she gets so tired of the "fight." Unless she actually sees it happening before her eyes, like she had many years before when she and Nicola went to the Lawrence Textile strike. There she witnessed the beatings by police and the death of a child from the water pressure of the fire hoses. She felt such anger then, it fueled her for years. Since she became a mother, her view of the world and how much she tolerates or accepts has become more fluid in her mind. A struggle that seems more and more layered through the years.

Yet now, after putting on a superb American dinner, Rosina is joyful; grounded in her world. Nicola was now safe at home, and fear of the draft resolved. Maybe their lives really could return to normal; free of chaos. She decides to voice this, if necessary, in the quiet of their bedroom. She excuses herself to the kitchen, where she begins washing the dishes.

16

Several months later, Rosina's wishes come true. The war is winding down, or so it seems. Nicola has been busy with his new position as foreman. Working longer hours there is little time for the "cause." When Bartolomeo visits sometimes late in the evening or on a weekend day for dinner, the exchange of ideas live on. But mostly everyone's life seems to be affected by the "La Grippe." Some even blame war as the cause of the epidemic. Claiming the lean soldier's, who made it home safely, carried the Spanish Flu with them. And now the Government propaganda is blaming the death of so many men found in the trenches saying they were killed by the "vicious" flu and not gunshot wounds.

Bartolomeo, his tone fatalistic says, "The pandemic is spreading across the United States to Europe, Japan, worldwide. Six thousand cases alone in the state of Massachusetts." His long fingers twist at his mustache.

Nicola brings home masks that Mr. Kelley gives out to his employees. When Rosina goes to Market Street, she sees people not only in masks, but with strings of garlic and onions tied around their necks. Fear dominates the news and Rosina is determined to keep Dante near her. She fiercely monitors his whereabouts to keep him out of harm's way. She reads about germs possibly coming from animals, livestock, so when Dante wants to go outside to play with Pinocchio and the other animals, she makes him wear a mask. At first, he likes the idea and pretends to be a bandit. But after a while, he gives her a difficult time and refuses to wear it; until one morning, she has the idea to paint a dog's nose and whiskers on it and names it Bruno.

During this time, one of the wives from their Galleanista group is taken with the flu. Although she survives, she fatally infects two of her children. Everyone at the funeral parlor wears white paper masks except for the parents. Nicola and she are both uncomfortable with masks on in front of the grieving parents, so Nicola removes his and embraces the man and woman. He consoles them with hugs and attention, while Rosina finds herself frozen in place. Why take a chance and bring germs home to Dante? She feels sick. The odor of what seems like a thousand carnations makes her nauseous. Seeing two young boys in their coffins is unimaginable, surreal. At one point, she is convinced she sees their chests move up and down, so she walks to the back of the room where Susan is seated. Their eyes, more prominent now because of the masks, meet, and as she looks into Susan's eyes, an outrageous roar takes hold of her. A strange chortling begins to build inside of her. Susan starts, "Isn't this…" and her voice takes on a cracked, almost elated sound, "awful."

Rosina is unable to respond to her. Perhaps it's the fumes, the gases from the funeral carnations. Laughter begins to roll up, pushes its way up out of her mouth. She presses her hands to her face, over the white paper mask, and rushes out of the room, muffling her laughter enough so that everyone thinks the sound coming from her is a cry of grief. Susan follows right behind her, pretending to be crying, but much less obvious. They hurry through the funeral parlor doors and once outside let it all out. When the uncontrollable frenzy of laughter begins to subside, Rosina draws a hanky from her purse and wipes her eyes. The lacy edge is rough against her lids. "We are terrible. How could we laugh?"

"This is the tenth funeral I've attended. If I don't laugh, I'm going to cry forever, and I don't want to cry forever." Susan blows her nose.

They sit on the stoop. Frost from the night before coats the streets lightly and now snow flurries swirl chaotically. Rosina nods in agreement. Too many funerals, too much sadness. She knows of love and hate. *Italians believe they are the same, just different sides of the face. Can it be that grief and joy, as well as laughter and tears are the same? Perhaps these emotions are on the same plane, toying, testing us—*

making us closer to a kind of madness. All emotions are a form of madness. Oh, the parents who lost their children—such a deeply-seated love, the way it conquers, lifts one's life. The way it can unexpectedly shatter a person into millions of pieces, transforming a once exuberant life to a hollow shell of an existence. She leaps from the stoop.

"I'm going home. I want to see Dante."

17

Sunday arrives and it's the first day Nicola had off in a month. Sundays should be family days. At least this is the way she'd like her family life to exist, but with Nicola working on weekends and no real family around it is hard to instill even this small custom. Lately, she has felt a greater need to anchor all she holds dear.

Part of Rosina's unorthodox family includes Susan who was in Boston for a few days, working as a "weekend reporter." Rosina is unable to keep up with Susan's projects. When Nicola asks that morning if Susan was coming for the day, she tells him Susan is volunteering for the Red Cross, but then moments later realizes her error, which she never bothers to correct. She admires Susan's willingness to constantly volunteer, and Rosina really wants to do more herself, but with Nicola working long hours she finds it difficult. She doesn't want to leave Dante with the nanny who had recently been exposed to a child with flu. She will look for a cleaner, more appealing woman; she considers this as she hears Bartolo's and Nicola's voices in the parlor.

From the kitchen window, she sees the snowman they had made a week ago. The three of them patted and rolled the snow to make the round shapes. Dante had jumped up and down, impatiently holding the carrot. Nicola had set the eyes of coal and placed his old fedora on its head. Looking at it now, Rosina thinks it is still perfection. Later that day as they struggled to remove their wet boots on the porch, she remembers later how safe she felt. The danger of flu still lurked in the back of her mind, "We are so much safer at home."

"The flu is passing, *non `c `e quasi piu*, it is okay now. Stop worrying," Nicola had said.

Bartolo and Nicola enjoy their time together. Bartolo teaches Nicola how to play chess. At first it is difficult for Nicola to catch on to the game, and he teases Bartolomeo. "It's that high forehead of yours that makes you smart, and me, mine is too short."

Now, Rosina hears them yelping when one of them makes an aggressive move or moaning when it's not. After the game, she brings black coffee and biscotti out on a tray and sits with them on the settee in the parlor. Politics already underway.

Nicola is speaking about congress passing the Sedition Act: "The law says any United States citizen that talks against the country, the flag, or the government can be prosecuted."

"That includes any of our notes, or printed materials, anything of this nature," Bartolo says.

"They've already begun to deport aliens who they say spoke against the land." Bartolo shakes his head in disbelief. "The worst part is they don't have to prove any of it."

"Whatever we write for Luigi we must be careful not to keep any papers on us. Even our own scribbled notes. They've been checking people randomly. Everyone is suspicious."

Bartolo nods his head in agreement, as he chews his second biscotti.

"We can't disappoint Galleani. He's counting on us. We must keep information current for the *Bulletin* at least once a month," Nicola adds, sipping his drink.

"He has other writers. People who can contribute also," Rosina says, annoyed that Nicola always puts Galleani on some kind of pedestal, as if he were a God.

That next evening Bartolo and Nicola are scheduled to make the rounds in North Boston to collect money for anarchists' activities. "There must be a constant flow, or the cause could stall, lose its momentum." Nicola repeats this phrase so often heard at Galleani's meetings.

They decide to meet at the Brigham train station.

At night in bed, after contemplating Susan's overwhelming commitments, Rosina tells Nicola she wants to go with him to collect money. "Next time," he says. "It would be nice, like the old days, except now we'll have to get a babysitter. She feels a slight irritation by his remark, *of course they'll need a babysitter.*

As is his habit each evening, Nicola gets up to crack the window. He can't seem to sleep without the fresh night air entering the room. His pajamas are buttoned wrong, but she doesn't say anything. Back in bed, he fixes the blanket over them, another nightly ritual of his.

"Ti amo," he says, and kisses her good night. His head on the pillow, his breath in her ear, already his eyes closing.

Thinking of tomorrow night when he'll meet Bartolo she says, "Please, be careful. Just be careful."

Unable to sleep, she thinks of the eel Bartolo brought them for dinner. She had prepared it in spicy red sauce. Over these last few months, Bartolo had been selling fish, now calling himself a "fishmonger" and smelling like it too. He says it is a better life, not being told what to do all day long by some capitalist. Besides, he enjoys being outdoors, even during the below zero winter temperatures. Her thoughts drift to her mother, pieces of cut lemons always on the sink, washing her hands with them especially after preparing fish. Rosina decides to offer Bartolo some cut lemons.

18

Rosina is excited to tag along with Nicola to deliver his story to the newspaper. The piece he wrote is on the suppression of free speech. Just a few days earlier they had read a commentary where a congressman said, "Italians are inferior beings." This infuriated Rosina, and Nicola felt compelled to answer this in his article, naming all that the Italians had given to the world, and more.

"The only ones who will read this are Italians," Rosina says as she moves the hot iron over his white shirt. "You're wasting your breath." Nicola just looks up at her in silence suddenly struck with a sort of malaise. From the ironing board where she stands, she notices his morose expression and counters her words. "I suppose it does help to put it down in writing though," she says.

Ready to leave the house, Rosina remembers the article Bartolomeo wrote. She looks to the white envelope on top of the dictionary. "Let's not forget Bartolo's paper," she shouts to Nicola, who is finishing shaving in the bathroom. She considers Bartolo's words, 'Immigrants blocked... no freedom for them. Ironic," Bartolo wrote, "Freedom, and free speech is the very reason most migrated to the United States to begin with."

Nicola says, "Let's not rush, it's safer to deliver the stories as late as possible. Late at night there aren't as many policemen on the streets. During day hours, they appear quickly on horseback or by automobile, always when you don't want to meet up with one, it seems."

The key to the newspaper office is in Nicola's pocket, on his keychain. He checks to be certain he has it. The plan is to leave their stories on Galleani's desk.

It has been a while since they were out together without Dante, and they are both energized. Nicola asks, "Would you like to stop for gelato on the way home?" Rosina remembers the last time she had ice cream that she didn't make herself: They sat on the edge of a park bench, the pistachio dripping onto her hands. The vendor had run out of napkins and Nicola had unbuttoned his vest and invited her to wipe her hands on the inside of his vest. Oddly, she feels like they were like children then.

They exit the train a few blocks from where the newspapers are printed. When they arrive at Galleani's office, they find the front door boarded up. Large planks of wood are nailed across the door and police warnings taped on the boards:

ANYONE ENTERING THIS PROPERTY
WILL BE PROSECUTED
TO THE FULLEST EXTENT OF THE LAW

Nicola and Rosina stare at the words longer than they should: A patrol car passes slowly, then stops. The policeman stands and shouts from the opened car door, "What are you doing there?"

Rosina, aware she has a lesser accent then Nicola, quickly says, "We're just reading the sign."

The officer, six feet from them, still standing by his car, says, "Well, get going. No one's allowed to hang out here."

Nicola tips his hat, "Good night officer," he says.

His heavy accent thick in the night air. She wishes he hadn't spoken. And they begin to walk back to the train station.

On the ride home, Nicola is stunned by what they found. "How can they close down a newspaper? Isn't that against their precious Constitution? I wonder if Luigi knows. I must try to contact him."

Rosina's thoughts race, thrash about inside her head like the thump and jolts of the train that is taking them back to the suburb. Gripped by ideas that fills her with fear: "It could've been worse," she says, "what if they came to close him down while we were there?"

Her throat tightens at the thought. "We could've been arrested. *Dio,* what would've happened to Dante?" Lately, she had been overcome by a great ambivalence. Raising a child, being totally responsible for another human being, filled her with contradictory feelings, feelings she wasn't ready to voice for fear Nicola will not understand. The *seduction of idealism—this fight for justice—turning their backs towards capitalism and what and if there will be a price they must pay.*

Galleani having stressed more violence recently, while she'd always felt peaceful solutions were the answer. *Is fear my motivator? Am I a coward? Where is peace in this world, is it only for the wealthy?*

"Lately, many stories that were printed have been very aggressive. Threatening—on so many levels. Maybe that's why they shut the place down," she tells Nicola. But he doesn't pay attention. His brain is working hard, trying to figure out what he should do next. "First thing. I must get hold of Luigi."

All the next day Nicola tries reaching Galleani from the pay telephone at work. He tries early in the morning and then before going home, but it appears his phone lines are down, turned off. They search newspapers for any word on Galleani. When Susan arrives at the house, she retrieves the *Boston Globe* from her briefcase and reads out loud,

> As a result of the Anarchist Exclusion Act which
> was passed with flying colors of red, white, and blue,
> all anarchist or any resident aliens involved in any
> revolutionary political organizations will be seized
> and deported. The editors of an anarchist newspaper,
> *Cronaca Sovversiva,* namely a Luigi Galleani and four
> of his adherents, will be held in prison until such time
> that a decision is made for deportation.

Susan throws the newspaper on the table. "Bastards. So much for freedom of speech."

In the evening, Bartolomeo brings his friend, Aldino Felicani, to meet Nicola. He is in his early twenties and seemingly a very successful editor of another anarchist, libertarian newspaper called *La Notizia.* Now with Galleani out of the picture, Felicani is preparing to put his own group together for a new newspaper called *L'Agitazione.* Aldino moves and speaks with such fire, and such speed and determination, that Rosina finds herself enjoying the entertainment he provides. He spins agitation, along with a candor she has never witnessed. She couldn't possibly dream up a better name for his newspaper. Rosina knows the calmness is amplified by the boot-legged wine Aldino has offered. She is suddenly her true-self, full of hope, and excited to live in a world where Galleani will be far from her.

"Aldino wants to publish our words in his newspaper," Bartolomeo says, "Do you have our stories?"

Nicola is edgy all day, pacing, crossing his legs when he sits, shaking his foot. Silent, until an idea crosses his mind. "Wait. Let's talk about this," he says. "Luigi may get out soon and he can go underground with the paper."

Susan also seems restless, standing, drinking from a glass of water, which surprises Rosina especially since the huge bottle of wine is on the table. "We can't wait for that, Susan says, "If that happens, it may take him months. And what if they deport him? It's important we keep the logs burning."

Rosina sees how difficult it is for Nicola to let go. Galleani had been right, and she hated it. Nicola is indeed a man who needs heroes. Yet she also knows how much Nicola struggles with change. When they returned last evening, she hid the articles in the back of the dictionary, and now she finds herself waiting by the table, the book laid opened, ready to hand the envelopes over to Aldino.

Aldo, as he likes to be called, speaks with excitement as he picks from the olives Rosina has offered, along with the cheese and crackers: "*Ho grande rispetto per voi ed il vostro lavoro. Bartolomeo mi ha detto interamente circa voi. Possiamo lavorore insieme per far del benne per la classe lavoratrice.*"

His praise of Nicola and the work he's done in the past leaves Nicola unchanged. He continues to sit in the mission chair they bought at the Salvation Army. His arms rest on the wide wooden arms, his legs crossed, as he studies this excitable young man. Everyone else is standing, pacing, except him and Aldo. They are like two heads of state coming to a decision. Rosina tries to read Nicola's mind; he's questioning this young man. Perhaps thinking: younger than me, how much can he really know?

Finally, Aldo says, "*Fidati di me questa volta.* Trust me, Nicola."

Bartolomeo puts his arm around Aldo. Nicola hesitates, lets out a deep sigh, then stands in compromise, and he and Aldo grasp each other's hands.

19

Rosina puts Dante to sleep and keeps dinner, lamb with roasted potatoes, for Nicola by covering his plate with a clean dishtowel and placing it into the still warm oven. He was rarely this late. Perhaps Mr. Kelley needed additional time from him?

In her sewing room, she begins to alter the trousers she made for Dante only four months ago. He is growing so fast she must adjust the hem once again. An hour later she presses the pants and one of her dresses, and places them on hangers. It is almost ten o'clock when she lowers herself onto the settee and picks up *The Profits of Religion*, by Upton Sinclair. Susan had purchased the book for her when she was in New York. Sinclair's words validate Rosina's ideas about religion being institutionalized, profit-making. He speaks of the way the true meaning of Jesus is exploited by man.

Once again, she finds her bookmark missing. Dante has gotten hold of the book. He sometimes pretends to be reading. She never liked bending the pages over, it seemed disrespectful to the writer, besides being messy. Now turning the pages of the book, looking for the last chapter she read, she tells herself she's not going to worry about Nicola. There are so many spur-of-the-moment meetings lately. Some of them on the outskirts of Boston or in the city itself. It takes time to get there and back.

Months had already passed since Galleani's arrest, and Nicola, wanting to visit with him was aware of rumors that this was exactly what the authorities were waiting for. At one of the secret underground meetings she had attended, it was the main topic: They were holding Galleani in a local cell longer than necessary in order to see which of his compatriots would visit.

Finding her place, she rests the book on her lap. Rosina can't seem to concentrate on the words before her.

L'Agitazione, has taken off. Aldo said there were now close to 12,000 subscribers. Nicola was free to write his weekly column alternating with Bartolomeo's. What she appreciated about the paper was that it didn't stress violence, only reported it. Mostly it was aimed at justice. Justice in a free society.

She recalls the evening she sat in the parlor with all three men. Although Aldo was twenty-four, only four years younger than Nicola, Nicola nicknamed him "*Ragazzo,*" he said. "He looks like a boy."

In turn, Aldo called Nicola, "*Vecchio mio.*" Nicola liked his nickname, he felt the term, "old man" commanded more respect.

Bartolo, who was out of character, had told a joke and they were all laughing. Aldo was drinking only water, even though he had lugged a huge bottle of boot-legged red into the house once again. "I need to get back to the office and don't want to fall asleep from wine." He took a long gulp from his glass then asked Rosina, "What if we printed an English edition of the newspaper?"

She was sitting on the settee and thinking it was another funny story. "Is this another joke?" she chortled.

"No. No joke. You complain that the only ones who read what we write are Italians, so why not allow the general public to see what we're all about," Aldo said. "It would advance our cause, finally others would be able to connect to the working class."

His words stoked her, and she found herself jumping out of her seat, uncontrollably. "*Un grande momento,*" she shouted.

The men had broken out in laughter. "You knew?' she asked Nicola, then rushed over to hug him. He grabbed her by the waist, in the way he would when they were alone. The memory of Nicola's glowing eyes and grin now brings a smile to her lips as she finds herself drifting into sleep.

The slamming of the front door startles Rosina causing the book to slip off her lap onto the floor. Nicola looks strained. Dark circles are under his eyes. His hair is longer than usual and although generally straight a few pieces curl at the nape of his neck. At this late hour, his heavy beard is beginning to show.

"They've deported Luigi," he says, throwing his coat over the chair.

It takes her a moment to swallow what he is saying. She had been waiting for this for so long now. It isn't really a surprise.

"He's on a boat to *Italia* with the others."

Rosina is secretly thrilled. What intense relief. She has lain awake worried that Galleani might intentionally slip, somehow send a suspicious flare to Nicola. She sighs deeply. *It's over. He's gone.* How foolish she was to worry; there were probably many women. Who knows if he even remembered her, she reassures herself and searches for something to say. "At least he's not in prison any longer," she manages.

"No consolation. They'll probably lock him up the moment they dock in Naples." He bends to kiss her on the forehead and begins to unbutton his shirt. "I need to bathe and get to sleep. I must be up again at 4 AM."

"You don't want something to eat?"

"No. Just pack it up for my lunch tomorrow."

Rosina perches at the edge of the bathtub washing Nicola's hair. She's enchanted with the sight of his body. His stocky strength still excites her; his broad chest; his forearms thick and muscular. His eyes closed, his whole body yielding to the warm water. She knows, sees how tired he is, tired of the messy fight, but now she feels him softening. "So far, they've deported 4,000 men," he says, strangely relaxed now, as though talking about a small incident at work.

She remembers his plate of food in the oven but begins to wash his belly and slowly moves her hand down to his groin, washing lightly with the cloth, then allows it to float away, now only using her hand. Nicola opens his eyes. She loves the look of arousal on his face. She had been thinking for months, even talked with Susan, but now she felt it; she was ready to have another baby. Nicola grows erect, the tip of his penis rises above the tub water like the *la canne* she'd seen at the convent's lake: Virgin reeds reaching up for light. Nicola lets out a soft, familiar moan. He reaches for her. It comes as a shock, the fall, she flounders, water rolls over her, soaking her body quickly. She hears it trickling over the edge of the bathtub onto the floor.

He kisses her fiercely, biting at her lips. "Sit on me," he says. They struggle to undo her wet housedress and underwear. There is something holy about water, the way it lifts the flesh, frees one to move in ways it wouldn't ordinarily. Her legs grip his hips as he guides her, lowers her onto him. They laugh out loud when her muslin drawers get caught around their genitalia. How can he make her feel so loved, so unshakably free? Her role as wife doesn't exist at these times. She feels more like his mistress; wanting to pleasure and to be pleasured.

20

The news of Galleani's deportation surfaces, and outrage hits the streets. A band of bombs, thirty or so, were sent to the homes of leading capitalists: Rockefeller, Morgan, Judges, and Attorney General Palmer's home. The bombs went off at midnight all along the east coast, as well as some in Chicago. The newspapers said an unnamed group of anarchists claimed responsibility.

Nicola says it was Mario Buda's group, but Aldo and Susan say they're convinced it was another band from New York. Later that same day, they learn, Valdinoci, a gentle man and an excellent violinist they knew from their chapter, accidentally blew himself up on the steps of Palmer's residence. Another senseless act Rosina can't put her mind around. This is a man who said very little, never demonstrated any anger, yet he was able to commit a "solo" act of violence.

The next evening Rosina goes along with Susan and Nicola to *Gruppo Autonomo*, where Carlo Valdinoci is praised and is added to their list of "*Grandi Anarchici.*"

Scare tactics are okay, Rosina thinks, *just as long as no one gets hurt*. Some in the group insist on mailing bombs. Their intended victims are politicians who endorsed the anti-sedition act and deportation.

Nicola says, "None of the mailed bombs are meant to kill or harm."

He knew. Nicola knew, and never mentioned it? Yet, one package, sent to a senator in Georgia who sponsored the Anarchist Act, was opened by his Black house servant, and her hands were blown off.

Nicola and Rosina, sick over Valdinoci's death and the innocent maid being deformed, call together a meeting at their home a week later to address the heightened level of violence.

Sitting on Dante's bed, Rosina tucks the blanket around him. "Our friends, the men will be coming by for a meeting tonight, so I want you to go right to sleep." He had gotten up at 5 AM that morning, and as she moves to smooth hair off his forehead, she sees the day has worn him out. "So, if you have to use the bathroom, use it as soon as I finish reading to you. There will be no glass of water, no calling Mama." She had been working towards ending his resistance to sleep. She will have to repeat this again before she kisses him goodnight and closes the door.

"Why can't I stay up, and why do the men have to come here?"

"Do they keep you awake?" Rosina asks.

"I don't know what they talk about."

"One day, you will. When you become a young man."

"How long is that?" asks Dante. Rosina opens *Just So Stories* and begins to read "How the Camel Got His Hump."

A small group of angry men shows up. Galleani had shouted out for vengeance, and it seems to be foremost in the minds of these men in her parlor. One of them keeps biting his nails, his fingertips puffy, red and swollen, another says he has boxes of fireworks in his basement, which he intends to use as an additional scare tactic. Nicola expresses his concern, keeps using the term "*fuori controllo.*" Things are out of hand.

In the kitchen, when Nicola comes in to fill the pitcher of water, Rosina whispers, "The men are on edge, waiting for the next comrade's arrest or the turn of injustice so they can release their anger even more."

Nicola nods in agreement.

"You knew about the bombs being mailed? Didn't you?" Still upset with her own innocence and that he never mentioned it.

"Later," he says, and rushes back to the parlor.

Authorities have a list of subscribers to *Cronaca Sovversiva*, and there had already been a number of arrests. "We're being watched," Nicola warns the men. "Hoover, along with pig Palmer are working hard to end our activities. We mustn't be foolish."

The only men who believe in violence are here in my parlor, sitting on my settee, pacing, leaning against our furniture—drinking our wine, and the ones who aren't are in their warm, comfortable beds. Without saying a word, she makes her way down the narrow hallway to their bedroom and prepares herself for bed. Head to the pillow, she sees Carlo Valdinoci's body spread across Palmer's steps. *The pointlessness of his death. How, just how will he make a difference?* She recalls the quietness of the convent. The bare, narrow marble-walled corridors, a crucifix every twenty feet or so. Silence. Peace.

* * *

The first article published in the *Bulletin*, the English edition of *L'Agitazione*, is about the striking Boston Police Department. Governor Coolidge calls them "deserters and traitors." the police respond with tremendous, wounded pride, saying: "At best, months ago, when we returned from the war we were hailed as 'heroes and saviors' of our country, and today because we are in need of more solid working conditions, and better pay, we are now called 'traitors.'"

The policemen Aldo interviewed went on to say they never desecrated the flag and had the misfortune of leaving some of their friends in the trenches in Europe. Aldo, with his ability to inflame a subject, wrote at the end of the article: *These are the same men who were on the French and German front, and now Mr. Coolidge will you please tell the people of Massachusetts which war you fought in?*

Arrests come day after day, flooding the news. Unfounded apprehensions, claiming that most foreign-born, especially Italians, are radicals intent on destroying society, and are considered dangerous. In early January, snow still covers the ground. There is wild enthusiasm about radio transmission. Wireless waves that can cross the seas. The name, "Marconi" had been popular amongst them, and their comrades, but now he is known to most Americans. Mr. Kelley makes himself a crystal radio and offers to make one for Nicola and Rosina. Nicola is so grateful for Mr. Kelley's gift that he offers to work overtime for free whenever he needs.

Each evening after Dante is asleep, Nicola and Rosina huddle close to the radio, sharing the earphones. They listen to Public Service announcements and classical music, which periodically breaks into harsh static. News of deportations were reported sporadically. Deportations. Red Scare. Palmer Raids. Lists of radical immigrants, all become words they hear on the radio, and see printed in newspapers day after day—words that wouldn't go away. Reports of arrests of foreigners across the country were now at ten thousand.

Aldo and Bartolo visit late one night, and they take turns listening to the radio: Aldo rages, "Five-hundred men-chained together, forced to march through the streets of Boston. Dragged from their homes, without coats, in below zero temperatures."

Aldo says, "I have a friend that works for the *Sun*, and he says that newsmen are being warned not to report brutalities for fear of making heroes of the condemned."

Overwhelmed, Rosina moves from the sound of their voices into the kitchen. The tightness in her throat, as though a pit is lodged there, is with her almost daily. *Tea. Tea with honey.* She puts on the kettle of water and glances out the window and sees snowflakes soar in the wind, melt against the glass pane. In the distance, the Kelley's home holds an unusual glow, their porch lights, amputated by wind and snow, move circuitously. In the parlor, men sit on the edge of their chairs, hunched over, elbows on knees, intent on every word.

"Deer Island?" Aldo shouts, "They're bringing them to Deer Island? Fuck. There's nothing there but an abandoned warehouse; no heat or electricity, no fucking toilets." Aldo is pacing the parlor floor. "Those sons-of-bitches."

The longer the fight, the more hatred of authority builds in her. The *authorities want to keep us down, to kill us, dominate and control us. It's all a mirage,* Rosina whispers to herself as she pours the boiling water into her cup. *Justice is a mirage just like the view from this window is a mirage.*

Evening. Instead of one-hundred times, she can only pull the brush through her hair twenty times. Nicola, already in bed reading, stops reading when she puts the brush down. "Is that all?" he asks.

"We should go home," she says, watching him through the stained mirror.

"We are home," he says, bewildered.

"We are not going to change things. They want to smother us, blot us out." She takes the loose hairs from the brush and twirls them around her finger.

"Come to bed." Nicola holds the heavy woolen blanket up for her to get under. In bed, he fingers the tips of her hair and draws them to his nostrils.

"Ah...I love your hair."

She hates that he's talking about her hair, when in reality they need to take a full *inventario* of their lives and where they're headed.

Rosina hears the wind sweeping the snow drifts up against the window.

"Tomorrow, tomorrow is another day, my Rosetta. You'll see, things will be better," Nicola says.

21

Early March and the promise of spring once again. The Jacobs ladder outside the living room window is showing its dainty blue flower. Rosina, overjoyed that Susan is returning after three months in New York, prepares a *Zuppa Inglese* for her homecoming. Dante hovers at the stove, wanting to help.

"Here, now beat the egg yolks until I tell you no more."

He is all smiles. "When are we making my birthday cake?" he asks.

"We have plenty of time. Your birthday is in two weeks. And besides, it is a surprise cake. You're not supposed to know about it."

She measures out the flour then pauses to kiss the top of his head, *Ti adoro*.

"How old are you, Mama?"

"Oh, me? Your Mama will be twenty-four this year. I'm an old lady," she smiles.

Having just learned from his father how to whistle, Dante proudly whistles away as he beats the eggs with the beater. His growth astonishes her. *Seven years. Gone so fast; he is no longer a baby.*

Babies. She had been dreaming of having another child. She didn't want Dante to be an only child, to have him face this world alone as she was forced to. A baby girl, she thought, someone Dante could look out for, someone Rosina herself could share her small feminine world with. She had told Nicola, "I want to have another child. I want a baby," and he acquiesced with such passion she thought by now the seed had been planted but was disappointed when she found blood on her panties.

When Susan arrives, it's all about Emma Goldman. Rosina can't help but be jealous. Envious, she missed the "Glorious Goldman Marathon." Susan bubbles over with excitement. The legs on her chair keep scraping the floor as she pushes away with enthusiasm—then scoots back in towards the table to take a sip of coffee.

"We took newsreel footage of her lectures, and we had pretty good views of the police dragging her off." Susan takes a deep breath. "Listen to what she said. I wrote it down." She hunts through the pile of papers in her briefcase. "You had to see her...no sign of fear. Listen...this is the kind of stuff that just spews from her lips....*Patriotism assumes that our globe is divided into little spots, each one surrounded by an iron gate. Those who have had the fortune of being born on some particular spot, consider themselves better, nobler, grander, more intelligent than the living beings inhabiting any other spot. Therefore, they believe it is the duty of everyone living on that chosen spot to fight, kill, and die in the attempt to impose his superiority upon all the others.'* No wonder they deported her," Susan continues, and sighs deeply. She folds the paper and stuffs it back into her briefcase. "She has to be the most threatening woman they ever came across," Susan. "Funny thing is since deportation she's become more popular. She has even more followers."

Rosina takes the coffee cups to the sink and throws them in with force. The sound of broken china startles, and when she turns to look at Susan, her eyes are opened wide in alarm.

"What's the matter?"

"Why do you think something is the matter?"

"Come on, Rosa, since when do we throw good china into the sink?"

Rosina blurts out. "Why should you care? You are an American. You don't have to be afraid of being thrown out of the country." She is building her emotional base: memories of these last weeks, men chained, being dragged through the streets, the horror of imprisonment, the brutal deaths they endured, all come flowing back to her, weakening her for a moment, bringing tears.

"Maybe you don't know what has been going on here?" she turns away, trying not to look at Susan, ashamed of her resentfulness.

"How can you say that to me? What do you think I was doing in New York? Going to parties?"

"Well, that's what it sounds like." She isn't being fair and doesn't care. "You never once asked how things were here. You don't know how terrible it's been. How many of our Italian comrades have been deported and even killed."

Dante runs into the kitchen. "Mama, there's a man here. He's coming up the steps."

The young man stands on the porch with a gold-colored envelope. "Is this the home of Ni-nic-Iowa Sack-o? I have a telegram for him. From overseas."

Returning to the kitchen, Dante holds a pencil in one hand, and the brown butcher paper Rosina saves for his drawings, in his other hand. He begs Susan to play tic-tac-toe with him. Frowning, Susan marks her X quickly. Looking up at Rosina, she makes an effort to articulate. "What is it?"

Susan looks fatigued, and Rosina feels a pang in her chest; sorry for having put her through her jealous rage. She puts the telegram on the table and stares down at it.

"It's for Nicola."

"Aren't you going to open it?"

"Come on, *Zia*," Dante demands.

"Don't worry, Rosa. The government or police, none of them send telegrams when they want to interrogate you."

Rosina makes a sound like a laugh. "It's from Europe. Italy, I'm certain."

Susan makes her mark once again, allowing Dante to win. "You won. Go, go play now. Mama and I have to talk."

Hating how she feels, Rosina walks over to the back of the chair where Susan sits and puts her arms around her shoulders. "I'm sorry. I don't know what comes over me sometimes." She wants to be honest, and hates to play psychological games. "I guess I want everything. Your world seems—so—so—charged. So meaningful, that I'm jealous. I wish I were American. Not to worry about deportation all the time. I'm frustrated, Susan."

"Oh, Rosa, look around you," Susan says. Tears rim her eyes. "You have so, so, much. A husband who cherishes you, a child. Something—something I'll probably never have."

"Forgive me, Susan. I'm such an idiot. I guess I can't have it all. Family, free to travel, help to promote our cause. I really haven't been myself these days. I can't even use the excuse that I'm pregnant."

She smooths the dirty-blond hairs off Susan's forehead and rests her cheek there. Picking up a hint of lavender shampoo from Susan's hair, she says, "You always smell so good." Thank goodness she has Susan back. "We baked a *Zuppa Inglese* for you."

Nicola knew of his mother's illness but didn't expect her to die so soon. The telegram his father sent spoke of her sudden death, and also said, *"Torna a casa. Sei stato via per troppo tempo."* Come home. It's been too long.

Over two long weekend days, Nicola sits cemented in his mission chair, newspapers sprawled across his lap, pretending to read whenever Rosina asks if he is okay.

"I loved my mother so much. I left her so young. Why do we do that?" he asks her. She knows it isn't really a question. Not wanting to leave him alone, Rosina irons their clothes in the parlor. "It's not too late for your father. We can go back to Italy and see your family, and perhaps my father, my mother."

He nods in agreement. "But to go back home and not see my mother there..." His forehead rests in his hand. Earlier, she had tried comforting him, but he pushed her away. He wanted to be alone. So, she stuffed a freshly ironed handkerchief into his hand and took Dante for a long walk through the woods behind the house.

* * *

The newspaper was so successful it didn't take much for Aldo to persuade prominent American authors to contribute articles: John Dos Passos, Edna St. Vincent Millay, and others that Rosina was just beginning to know of.

After much pleading from Aldo and Bartolomeo, and her husband, Rosina decides the one thing she can do without leaving her family is to write for the newspaper. In the morning, after Dante is in school, she carries the English dictionary to the kitchen table and stares at the blank pad for a long time. Emma Goldman comes to mind, as she remembers what Susan read to her.

Because... Rosina writes the first word. *Because one man belongs to a different tribe, comes from a different part of the world, makes more money, or doesn't make any, there really is no difference. We are all made from the same pottery.* No, she stops to look up the word. *Clay, we are all made from the same clay. We want to be happy...to be free to live our lives as we choose. I reject Capitalism—it breaks us down into categories, sets human beings up to be labeled...the poor are the steppingstones, the worker ants that allow the rich to grow more prosperous. We become objects the government spies on, regulates, controls, censors, taxes until we are repressed. I reject religion because it wants to dominate us...thou shalt not, or thou shalt. I firmly believe order without government will relieve us of greed.* Errico Malatesta said, *"By definition, an anarchist is one who does not wish to be oppressed nor be the oppressor. He wants the greatest well-being for all human beings. He has respect and love for humanity.*

Malatesta's words have been this anarchist's guide for most of my life.

Further, Rosina writes, *in this world of grossly unfair distribution of wealth, we must hold tight our philosophy and spread the word as moral human beings to live fearlessly and continue our work for all.* Rosina turns the pad over, takes a deep, long breath, and walks to the sink for a glass of water. It's not time to reread what she's written just yet. She will allow it to cool like the biscotti she makes on Sundays, anticipating gratification from having done something well.

When Susan arrives the next day, Rosina asks her to read the article before giving it to Aldo. She feels a tingle inside, as though she is on display. Unable to watch Susan reading, she busies herself in the kitchen and tries lighting the gas burner several times. Nicola had promised to check the gas line but hadn't done so. The stove emits a sulfurous odor, and Rosina is convinced the leaking gas is making her dizzy. So much paranoia, lately. And fear. *Paranoia and fear go hand in hand.*

Susan puts the pages down on the table. "This is terrific, Rosina. I couldn't have said it better myself."

"Really?" Uncertainty itches under her skin.

"Without a doubt. I didn't know this Malatesta. Aldo is going to love this."

Rosina had finally mustered the courage to put what she felt down on paper. And now, all she wanted was for the others to feel the way as Susan does.

"Don't tell Nicola," she says. "I want him to be surprised."

It is almost suppertime, and the light of the day still glares through the windows, upsetting Rosina's schedule. She watches Nicola picking through the Russian sage he had pruned back early spring. The cat mint he had planted, so like lavender, lines the walkway. He pauses to pull weeds. He then stops at the bleeding hearts to feed them water.

"I'm still having a hard time putting Dante to sleep at seven-thirty," Rosina says. "He thinks it's too early when he sees the sun is still out."

"Leave it to the politicians and their corporate buddies to make your life more difficult, anyway they can," Susan says as she files her fingernails. "At least now, the poor businessmen will have time to go home and play golf. Never mind that the workers have to get up in the dark and start their day while it's still night out. How people can be manipulated and brainwashed!" Susan had been on the rant of daylight savings for some time now. "It's absurd." she tosses her nail file back into her opened satchel that is lying on the floor next to her chair.

"Don't you get tired of carrying such a large purse?" Rosina asks.

"Ah, *mia cara*, my whole life is in here," Susan says.

* * *

With the help of funding through an anonymous foundation, Aldo is able to print the *Bulletin* twice a month. The Justice Department and the Palmer Raids continue. All scheduled anarchist meetings are held underground, literally underground, in various empty warehouse basements. Many comrades continue to believe—convinced that a revolution is coming.

Mid-April, the *Bulletin* prints Rosina's article. On the same day, the essay is published, Nicola takes off work to go into Boston to obtain their passports at the Italian Consulate. That night, Nicola, just in the house, hangs his coat on the tree rack, unbuttons his vest, and says, "I wasted a day. The photograph is too large. We have to take a smaller one and bring it back to the consulate. That means taking another day off work."

Rosina can hardly concentrate on what he is saying. She is anxious to show him her article but decides to wait until after supper when she knows he'll ask for the newspaper. Finally, after dinner, she hands him the paper, but can no longer wait, and says, "Read page two." He frowns, looks so serious when he has to read in English. She can't take her eyes off him, and soon she sees a change in his expression; a slight grin, wrinkling of the brow, and then a smile. He slaps the newspaper on his thigh.

"Rosina Sacco, *Che bella sorpresa! Brava la mia scittrice! Brava, brava.*"

The moment is worth all the trepidation she felt while writing the article. The strength of her convictions now validated; she could dance. As if Nicola can read her mind, he hurries to the phonograph, and the tinny sound of mandolins erupts. He takes both her hands in his and starts to twirl her around. He playfully plants kisses on her forehead, cheeks, and mouth until Dante comes out of his room-sleepy eyed in his pajamas, wanting to join them.

A few hours later, as was now his habit before bed, Nicola puts on earphones and listens for any news of the day. Rosina, in the bedroom, brushes out her hair as she gets ready for sleep. Removing her feet from her slippers, she notices the worn wool where her big bony toe rests.

"It's probably time I buy new house slippers."

The mattress moves as Nicola gets into bed. "Slater and Morilli were robbed, and some people were killed."

"Slater and Morilli?"

"*Si,* another shoe factory. Mr. Kelley knows the owner."

"Where are they?"

"South Braintree. They robbed the payroll, more than $15,000. Two men, Italians, were shot and killed. I might have met one of the men. His name sounds familiar. Bernardelli. He was the payroll master."

"Why were they delivering payroll so late at night?"

"No. It was early today, in broad daylight. Some witnesses said there were five robbers. Terrible. I'm sure they were family men. Awful. Now the workers will never get paid."

Rosina reflects on bringing children into the world. "*Viviamo in un mondo crudele, perche vogliamo coinvolgere un bambino?* Such a cruel world," she balks.

"*Forse per renderlo migliore,*" Nicola says. "Maybe, we hope the children will make a better world." His voice shows signs of weariness. "I have to get up at four."

With Nicola working overtime and training another workman in preparation for their trip back to Italy, it seems the only time they have to talk is right before they go to sleep. Whenever he mentions the apprentice, he and Rosina end up talking about their return home.

Nicola lies on his stomach. His arm spread across her chest; Rosina tries to remember the names and ages of all his brothers and wives. "Who is Francesco's wife again?"

Nicola half asleep. "I don't know if he has a wife."

"But you told me he was married?"

"Oh then, *possible*."

Through the open window, a fresh, scented breeze passes over the newly formed lilac blossoms in their yard. Eyes closed, Nicola sighs, and instinctively pulls the blanket up over the two of them.

Since their decision to go back to Italy, Rosina has trouble falling asleep. She struggles with the importance of family. It has been so long. Blood, the dictator of all. And then the voice of her long-dead grandmother comes to her, whispering in her soul:

Who but family knows who you really are?

Ah, and she conjures up images of her mother and father, and the mood shifts—she laughs to herself. How ridiculous. Her parents know little of who she really is. They never wanted to. But they are of the same blood, the blood she feels streaming through her veins. She will always belong to them. She can never escape.

22

Rosina becomes accustomed to having strange men coming in and out of her home. Unexpected meetings, boxes of printed materials dropped in her hallway. The coffee pot and tea kettle are continually going. Occasional bottles of boot-legged wine. White boxes of left-over pastries and biscotti brought in by the visitors sit on top of their cabinet in the kitchen. Cigarette butts clipped in the ashtrays. But it's the cigar-smoking she can't handle. The men are arriving in an hour, so she hurries to get Dante in bed. He is exhausted from helping his father plant the tomatoes and the basil. Nicola bought him a small shovel, and they both spent the afternoon putting in the vegetable garden. "I made all the zucchini holes today," he murmurs, almost dreamily. She cherishes these moments—a day uncontaminated by the outside world, as she sits on his bed, tucking the blanket around him. In the Parlor, Nicola wipes out the ashtrays and places them on the coffee table.

"Please, Nick, ask them not to smoke cigars."

Mario Buda will be one of the men coming, and he always smoked Cuban cigars. She remembers the first time he was on their sofa, the ashtray in front of him with the cigar smoke fogging over the room. The stench of it lasted for days.

"I can't do that!" Nicola says.

"I don't know why. He doesn't smoke it anyway. He just lets it sit in the ashtray. The smell makes me nauseous."

She was slightly queasy. Maybe she picked up the stomach flu. Or maybe the gas pipe on the stove is leaking again.

"Listen, we don't know this guy well enough. Don't want to upset him. He has a car we need to transport the materials."

"I don't ask you for much," she says. "This small thing you can't do?"

"I will, but not tonight. Rosina, we have more important things to deal with!" His tone impatient, emphasizing her name at a level she isn't used to hearing. She walks away, displaying enough anger for Nicola to notice. He calls out to her, "Rosa, my Rosetta, don't be angry, one day you'll understand."

I'll never understand you, she thinks, *not defending your wife*. A bold stubbornness invades her. She decides to ask Susan to say something to Buda.

Susan arrives early. She stands next to Rosina at the sink while she cuts the stems of the hyacinths and crocuses Nicola picked in the early morning. Rosina, still thinking of cigars, says to Susan, "Just tell him you have emphysema, or that you can't breathe. If I say something, I'll embarrass my poor husband's manhood. And we know we can't do that. After all, he is a man."

Through the kitchen window, they see Nicola turning over the earth with a pitchfork, getting ready to put in the annual flowers.

"It looks like Nicola is making use of the daylight savings time," Susan sighs, "Well, it's what we do. We can't fight everything."

Mario Buda is a good-looking man with an enormously kind face. He's lived in the States for a long time. He knows his way around. But too many gold rings on his fingers and a thick gold cross hanging from his neck confuses Rosina. His attention to material things. She immediately disliked him when she first met him. What was his purpose? His philosophy? Was he really interested in the working-class man?

Several of the men huddle together, all of them referring to "radical literature" that had to be hidden. A man she had never met before says,

"Authorities are clamping down, busting into homes, dragging off what they call "suspicious characters." His voice is gravelly from smoking too much.

Bartolomeo isn't present this evening. He and another member went to New York with a lawyer to investigate why the authorities are holding two of their comrades for weeks without legal representation.

One of the men ventures into Rosina's kitchen as she's filling the sugar bowl. Nervous, wound tightly and cautious, he looks down at his shoes when he speaks, "*Per cortesia, potrei avere un bicchiere d'acqua?*" Rosina retrieves a glass from the cupboard. Nicola, walking in behind him, pats his back, and introduces him as Gino, the pharmacist. "Gino is going to water the plants, take care of our vegetable garden until we return. He'll also distribute the crops to the families in need. I've already given him a list of names."

When Rosina hands him the glass of water, she sees a scar, spread out like a starburst on his half-opened eyelid, and realizes he is the man that was burned with acid, the one who lost his eye when a bomb exploded near the State House. The soft timbre of his voice and his faint appearance sear through her. She turns from him and her eyes well up with tears. How vulnerable she is lately, how tender.

"Did you see the gold cross around his neck?" Susan says, bringing her glass to the sink, noticing Rosina's expression. "What's wrong?"

"I don't know. Just feeling sensitive. Forget it." She wipes her cheeks with the sleeve of her dress. "Do you mean Buda? *È un ipocrita*. He's so much a hypocrite."

Susan nods. "Well, at least he hasn't lit any cigars. Yet."

23

When Bartolomeo returns from New York, he is morose, visibly upset by the news that they must hide, or dispose of, any literature in their possession. The New York chapter validated fears of the authorities breaking into suspicious homes. Bartolo, in his nervous habit, pulls and twists his mustache. "If no evidence is found, it doesn't matter. If you're one of the chosen, they'll manage to plant incriminating proof to use against you."

A few days later, the front page of the *Globe* reports that one of the men who was being held in New York turned informer—giving out names of so-called Galleani destructionists, had thrown himself out of an office building window.

"We'll never know the truth. Whether there is a list of names or not," Nicola says, lowering the paper to his lap. Newspapers sprout on the braided rug next to his chair. Dante is kneeling at the coffee table, eye-level with his finger-sized metal cowboys and Indians making war noises.

Nicola reads the headline out loud:

"RED'S DEATH— PLUNGES 18 STORIES."

"Anyone who doesn't agree with their politics is a Communist," he says.

Rosina calls to Dante, "Take your toys in your room, *caro. Andiamo.*"

Preparing for an early start to meet Bartolomeo the next morning, Nicola shaves his beard over the bathroom sink. Rosina already under the thinning cotton blanket in bed, hears him say, "We have to pick up Mario Buda's car in Bridgewater at the repair shop, and then we're going to gather as many materials as we can and bring it over to the warehouse so they can be destroyed."

"We must start to be more careful about what we say in front of Dante," her voice louder than usual. "He's getting older now. He's still young enough to understand or, rather, misunderstand a lot of what we're saying."

Nicola sits on the edge of the bed and acknowledges her with a grunt. She'll have to talk about this further when she has his full attention.

"Do you have to go with Bartolomeo tomorrow?" Rosina asks as he performs his nightly ritual of adjusting the blanket over them. "I really need you here to help me with the packing."

"I must do this *one* last thing before we leave. Bartolomeo doesn't know all the stops, all the places as well as I do. Once we get the car, it won't be long. We're only going to a few locations to pick up literature and dispose of it. Aldo already has a few teams out."

There's no sleep for her now. She's fired up. Her body tingles, her legs restless. Maybe it is the excitement of their trip. Ah, but now she realizes this familiar sensation; this uneasy lavish, warm feeling that courses through her body. This is the same way she felt when she was pregnant with Dante. An inner glow, lit with a kind of happiness. Smiling to herself, something she'd also been doing a lot of these days. She makes the decision to wait until they arrive in Italy to break the news to Nicola and Dante. A celebration with the whole family.

* * *

Rosina decides to take another suitcase for the small gifts she made and purchased for Nicola's family. She wishes Nicola were home to help her make some decisions on what clothes of his to pack. All morning she's felt a sneaking foreboding—a premonition that something was about to happen. She blames it on her fear of change, even the good kind. Leaving the security of home. Packing. *Such a long passage to Italy. So much could occur.* Since her marriage to Nicola, she relishes the idea of life built around a sense of permanence: Before going to bed each night, as she places her metal wedding band in the tea-rose porcelain cup Nicola found in the Salvation Army, and then slips her misshapen big toe out of her molded slippers, comforted by knowing they'd still be at her bedside each morning. Small rituals—a meditation of their lives, not taken for granted, anchors her to the illusion of a secure existence.

She settles her thoughts by reminding herself she was this way when she carried Dante; this was merely an overall sensitivity to things that didn't seem to matter at any other time. Like the way she broke down and cried when she'd found she overwatered the ivy plant, killing it, then telling Nicola, "I can't even take care of a plant, how can I take care of a baby?" Moments later, the two of them laughed at the absurdity of her words.

She remembers to pack some of Dante's baby clothes for one of Nicola's sisters, but now removes one item from the suitcase. The sailor suit, a romper with a marine-blue trimmed collar, was the first piece of clothing she made for Dante. She was so proud of it. A boy or girl could wear it easily. Fingering the cloth, she again changes her mind. *I can always make another.* She wraps it in brown paper and puts it back in the suitcase, on top of her magenta cardigan.

Rosina falls asleep in Nicola's chair in the parlor. Hours later she wakes from Dante's call. "Mama...Mama." Dante had been having bad dreams at night and, dazed from her own unexpected deep sleep, she hurries to his bedside.

"It's okay, Mama is here." She holds him; wipes the perspiration from his hairline. "You know it's just a dream. Dreams don't come true."

Having heard this before Dante acknowledges by shaking his head pitifully. Rosina is disoriented. Why wasn't Nicola home yet? *He never stayed out this late.*

The ritual of getting Dante back to sleep takes only a few minutes, and once he is sleeping, she tiptoes from his room only to find herself pacing from the kitchen to the parlor.

Maybe they were in an accident. Perhaps the garage didn't repair the car properly, and the vehicle broke down again. They probably got lost, or it's just taken them longer than Nicola thought. She sees no light coming from Mr. Kelley's house. Still, she wants to ask to use his telephone to call Bartolo at his boarding house. Three in the morning. How could she wake everyone up at this unreasonable hour?

Sitting in Nicola's chair once again, she lifts the newspaper from the top of the pile:

PALMER WARNS NATION: NEW TERRORIST PLOT
TO OVERTHROW GOVERNMENT
WILL ERUPT ON MAY DAY

Sick of seeing the name Palmer, she tosses the paper aside. May Day was well over, and nothing happened. Hopefully, people were catching on to his "fear tactics."

On the dining table, she sees Nicola's keys. Under the keychain are their tickets for passage to Genoa. The name of the ship is printed on the envelope: *Vi da il benevento a bordo Il Dante Alighieri,* and beneath in English, *Dante Alighieri welcomes you.*

Nicola had told her, "Let's not tell our boy the name of the ship. I want to surprise him." Rosina had just finished pressing the pleats in his slacks, put the iron back on its plate. "It won't matter to him, he's too young. It will just be a name to him."

Overwhelmed by the preparations for their trip, she had tossed off the remark, "What's in a name anyway?" And just at that moment, she remembered Ferdinando. She stole a glance at Nicola, reading the *Globe*—and was glad he hadn't been paying attention.

Rosina's neck is sore from the wooden armrest of the settee, uncertain if this is what wakes her, or the heavy banging on the screen door. Alarmed, she suddenly remembers why she is on the sofa. Nicola's keys on the table come to mind, and she rushes to let him in. Through the small glass panel in the door, she sees the frame of a taller man with a long, thin neck. As she gets closer, she recognizes Aldo's pale, narrow face. Fear rises in her chest as she opens the door. Aldo's growing goatee makes him look grubby.

"It was a trap." Aldo touches her elbow, "Come sit down," as he guides her to the settee. "They were arrested. We've already got a group together." Aldo talking at the speed he usually does. "We'll have them out in no time."

Alarmed and confused, Rosina asks, "Who was arrested?" Fear prickles through her. "What happened?"

"Nicola and Bartolomeo were on the streetcar...."

"Arrested? Streetcar? What happened to the car?"

"I don't know for sure, but I think it wasn't ready, or it was part of the trap."

"A trap?"

"They were pulled off the car and arrested as "suspicious characters.""

"Suspicious characters?"

She only seems capable of repeating Aldo's words.

"They'll probably be home this afternoon. Our compatriots, *nostri Fratelli* are working on it right now."

She hadn't noticed how really tall and thin Aldo is, but now he seems spare. How can he stand so straight without hunching over?

He rattles off slogans, "defense committee, political arrest, unlawful," words that reach into her like one stitch at a time. Rosina's insides being pulled with each word—darning her tighter and tighter, layer by layer until Aldo's parting statement: "Courage...*Coraggio*, Rosina."

Alone in the parlor, her gut goes taut as if one small, tiny sound from her will rip her open. She puts her clenched fists to her lips, and then, so not to wake Dante, she pushes the needlepoint pillow from the settee over her mouth—to smother her sobs.

Hours later, she moves methodically through Dante's breakfast. Prepares only toast—dresses him and herself to take him to the new nanny, Mrs. Hayes, a friend of Aldo's mother. Aldo had said, "She's sympathetic to our cause, and has agreed to be available whenever needed."

Rosina immediately liked her appearance, a plump, motherly woman, who had her own little boy that Dante could play with. On the walk back from the nanny's, the day holds brilliant sunshine, so bright she notices sharp shadows everywhere. Too much light for such a dreaded day ahead. Last night was only a small nightmare she tells herself. Today it will be over, and tomorrow we will leave for *Italia*. She decides to make pasta with ragu sauce for Nicola for dinner, and tries desperately not to imagine him being jailed overnight.

When she returns to the house, she sees a police car and two mounted police horses tied to the porch column, and her front door wide open. As she steps onto the porch, an officer asks, "Are you Rose Sacco?"

Stunned by his presence, she nods her head.

"Don't move," he says. A halting hand in her face. "Stay there until I tell you it's okay to come in."

From where she stands, she hears drawers or closet doors banging. In the kitchen, the silverware drawer sounds like it's being emptied into the sink. Rosina turns away from the door and sees a grouping of black butterflies on the lilac bush. They rest on a gnarled stem pumping their wings as though unable to fly, yet seconds later, lift off. She remembers the pamphlets under the porch. Nicola's gun in the shoebox on the shelf in their bedroom closet. Her nausea rises.

She doesn't know how much time has passed before the oversized officer allows her to enter the house. At first, she sees her cushions on the settee thrown to the floor—books spread opened, scattered everywhere. The philodendron plant that Nicola had trained to climb is turned over, ripped in half, pulled from the curtain rod. Broken pieces of the clay pot and soil are on the windowsill and floor. An officer comes from the bedroom, swinging an opened suitcase, "You wops planning to go somewhere? Guess you'll have to cancel your trip." When he flings the open luggage, she feels something drop inside her. "Come on, boys, we're done here." Two other cops appear from the back rooms, and as they walk towards the door, she hears them laughing, and one of them says, "Did you see those tits? These I-talian women aren't so bad looking. She could make me happy." More laughter.

Rosina rushes to lock the door after them. She walks through the rooms like a stunned deer she had seen in the field weeks ago. In Dante's bedroom, she sees busted toys, his bed turned over, then unexpectedly, her legs crumble under her, and she plummets to the ground. "*Bastardi*, fucking bastards," she cries out.

Remembering Nicola's pistol, she climbs over the sheets and blankets that are thrown onto the floor in their bedroom. Now at the foot of their bed, she sees the top shelf of the closet, and the box appears to be untouched. Suddenly she knows she will be sick and rushes into the bathroom, where personal items from the medicine chest are strewn about. The heavy oak door of the chest hangs from the loose hinge. Cold sweat tingles through her, stomach clenching, she kneels over the toilet bowl and releases its contents right on top of the bottle of aspirin bobbing in the water. Her washed menstrual cloths also thrown about. She picks one off the floor and wipes her mouth with it.

She can't seem to move. *Susan where are you?* She hears her father's voice: *I knew no good would come from such a man whose ideas are so dangerous to himself and his family.* She covers her ears with the palms of her hands as if to block out his voice. *How? How do you prepare for such a thing?* "Get up," she screams out loud, "you're no good to anyone sitting here. Do something."

In the bedroom, she lifts the sheets, blanket, and pillows and tosses them onto the bed. She takes up what's left of Sinclair's *The Profits of Religion* and places the loose pages back on the night table, then suddenly remembers the boxes of literature under the front porch, and adrenaline in full gear, she races to see if they're still there.

Outside, it already feels like the heat of summer. The earth is warm on her bare knees. The boxes appear untouched. She had never bothered to see them before. It looks like three of four boxes of pamphlets. Nicola's wheelbarrow leans against the side of the house, and when she sees it, she decides to wait until dark to remove them.

Back in the bathroom, she salvages what she can and prepares a hot tub for herself. Aldo will pick her up soon to go to the courthouse. She must try to fix herself to look like the wife of a gentleman. She will spend extra time on her hair. She wants to make a good impression on the judge. He will see that Nicola is not a bad person, just a man with ideals—like the rest of us. If she must, she will stand straight and tall and tell him that Nicola is an ordinary man, just one more sensitive to the human condition, a person who wants to better the lives of the working people, nothing more. She will tell the judge when a mouse comes into their home, she is the one who must find it and kill it. When she prepares the cacciatore, she is the one who must twist the neck of the chicken. The judge will see. *He will understand,* she says out loud, as she presses the light rouge powder Susan had given her onto her cheeks.

24

On the drive to Dedham, Aldo shakes his head in anger. "They had no right to come into your home like that without a search warrant."

Rosina is suited in a tweed outfit with a brown velvet collar, with her hair pinned back loosely. Aldo turns quickly to look at her, and she wonders if her appearance is sophisticated enough, but more important—will it matter?

"Don't worry," Aldo continues, "We'll get this all straightened out."

The landscape around the Dedham County Courthouse seems picture perfect. Huge oak and elm trees surround the gleaming white, domed building. May flowers bursting open, line either side of the stairway leading up to the heavy double doors.

Inside, the mahogany-paneled walls, glowing chandeliers on high ceilings, and wooden doors with filigree gold-plated doorknobs only validate her feelings of constitutional greed, of sovereign wealth.

Pointing to a highly polished mahogany bench with claw feet, in the long narrow hallway, Aldo says, "Stay here a moment, let me find out where to go."

She sees no one. Hears only the sounds behind closed doors. A woman walking in heeled shoes, typewriter keys rapidly moving.

Aldo hurries over, "I have to make a phone call. Are you all right?"

She nods, but now she's hoping, even praying to whoever wants to listen, that Nicola is deported. She is ready. They will go home and live a quiet life. She decides to tell her husband about the baby as soon as he gets back that evening. It will make him happy, and will help put this incident behind him.

A long half-hour or so later, Aldino Felicani walks slowly over to the bench where Rosina sits. He looks tired and worn. Surprised by the appearance of his bloodless complexion, fear embraces Rosina. Watching him shuffle through the papers in his briefcase, knowing Aldo loves Bartolo like a *fratello,* she must take care to include him in her concerns. She manages, "Where are they?"

"Incredible," he says. "They're at a photographer. Having their pictures taken!"

Rosina is puzzled. "Why? Why should they take their picture?"

"Nothing to worry about." Aldo stops fishing through his papers but leaves his searching fingers limp between the files. "Whenever someone is arrested, they take photos as a way to identify them."

"A mug shot!" her voice, louder than usual, echoes down the corridor.

Aldo stands, and paces back and forth. His thumbs pulling on the slanted pockets of his black vest. "They haven't been charged with anything, so they'll probably let them go."

Aldo's uncertainty surrounds them. He seems fuzzy. He runs his hand through his hair.

"Don't worry, Rosa. They just want to scare them."

She has the sensation that Aldo is treating her like a child.

"We've jumped the gun by coming so soon. Let me take you home. This could take hours. We both know the court system takes their time. No sense staying here."

"What? What does this mean, jump the gun?"

"Mi'scusi, Rosina it means we are here too soon. That's all."

On the trip home, there is little to say. A void seems to have swallowed up the interior of Aldo's automobile. They stop at Mrs. Hayes to pick up Dante. Mrs. Hayes's little boy, Jimmy, along with Dante begs to have a "sleepover."

Aldo will drop off his small sack of clothing and toothbrush.

Alone in the house, Rosina is relieved, knowing she can dispose of the so-called incriminating literature without Dante witnessing it.

The sun almost spent, yet enough light left to retrieve the cartons. Kneeling in the dirt, Rosina reaches for the box nearest her. Although heavy, she manages to slide it out. Crouching further on her knees, the third and last box is buried deep under the slatted, sagging porch. She will have to come back for it. She questions why she didn't ask Aldo to help. Perhaps, his neat attire, she reasons, then says out loud, *How stupid! What do his clothes have to do with it?* She was so surprised by Aldo's sensitivity towards her needs. He's already done more than she could ask for. More than enough, she says to herself.

Donning Nicola's work jacket, she rolls up the sleeves and begins to push the wheelbarrow over the uneven ground. Struggling to keep it balanced, she presses on into the woods behind the house. Not far from the house, the trees are dense. The barrow is heavy, and she must be careful, keep it steady, or she will lose the pamphlets. Moving along the path, through a thick of trees, the front wheel gets caught in a cavity of earth, and it takes all her strength to pull it out without tipping over. She advances slowly to a clearing she had come to before when on walks with Nicola and Dante. There she releases the handles. Overheated, she removes Nicola's jacket. The white ash and walnut trees circle around her, out of harm's way. She begins to throw the papers on the ground, then decides it will be safer to burn them in the wheelbarrow. Opening the box of wooden matchsticks, she walks around, lighting all sides, then watches as the flames slowly rise. When she bends to pick up the pamphlets off the ground, she carelessly leans on the cart, and her dress sleeve ignites quickly. Grabbing hold of Nicola's jacket, at a furious speed, she quickly tamps out the flames on her forearm. She begins to cry, not from the pain, but from the frustration of having to do this. Of not knowing what is happening. Consequences. *Always consequences even when trying to do good—these are not the results I expected.*

When the flames turn to ash, she finds it easier to turn the wheelbarrow onto its side, then lifting a curved limb she finds under a tree, she scoops the ashes onto the ground. Now she will go back for the last box. Tendrils of gray light appear through the branches of the trees— steering her back to the house. She must be positive. Her father used to say: *Cade anche un cavallo che ha quattro gambe.* Even a horse with four legs can stumble. Yes, she tells herself, this is merely a stumble.

Back behind the house, she finds a flashlight in Nicola's wooden toolbox. The last carton is far under the porch. Flashlight in hand, she crawls her way to it. The ground is damp and chilly. Wet. She should've put on a pair of Nicola's trousers. On her belly, her arm burning, she elbows her way towards the corrugated box, places the flashlight on the ground, and begins to pull with both hands. The corrugated box, much heavier than the others, makes her feel crazed. Angry to find herself here among the worms and mice droppings and cobwebs, she continues to tug and push, her anger strengthening her until the cardboard gives. A corner seam has expanded, splitting open. Something passes over her hand. Rosina jumps in surprise: a mouse? Taking up the flashlight, she sees, bulging from the seam of the box, dozens of cardboard cylinders, tubes with a single string or wire, sticking out of the center of each one. Dynamite!

* * *

Nighttime, like a thick fog, reaches in, drawing to the surface fear and uncertainty from Rosina's sleepless mind. When she dozes off, the pain from her burnt arm wakes her. Looking at her forearm smeared with olive oil, she sees the shape of a dynamite stick. And then, a dream that her arm explodes, waking her to the sound of her own scream. Finally, purplish light peers through the windows, once again preparing for sunrise. She paces the room. She must see Nicola. They need each other. Aldo, she tells herself, Aldo will be driving him home soon.

Still, in her brown terry bathrobe, she hears knocking on the front door. Susan's forehead is visible through the frosted glass pane.

Susan enters in a fury, slamming the door. "What the hell is going on?"

She has on a new flapper style cloche hat with a large rose flower on her ear. Rosina wants to comment on its attractiveness but can only stand there soaking up her friend's warm hug, allowing her tears to surface.

"We still don't know why they were arrested," Rosina manages.

"I know. Aldo telephoned me."

Rosina shakes her head, and like a child needing attention, she rolls up the sleeve of her robe to show Susan her burn.

"What happened to your arm?" Susan removes her light jacket and hangs it on the coat tree waiting by the door. "We better bandage this."

Walking towards the bathroom, she says, "And look at this place!"

Rosina looks around, as though surprised by what she sees. The settee cushion is still on the floor, and the pastoral farm scene Nicola prizes is hanging crookedly from a wire. Her crocheted coverlet is strewn in the middle of the room, along with papers and the maps that Nicola likes to study.

At the table, Susan rolls out a line of gauze and cuts it with a scissor. She begins to apply burn salve to Rosina's arm. "Look at the shape of this burn, Susan. What does it look like?"

Susan backs up to get a clear focus of her forearm....

"Probably a third-degree burn! How did you manage this?"

"No, the shape. Don't you see it's the shape of dynamite? It looks like the sticks of dynamite I found under the porch last night."

"What? Dynamite did this? Impossible."

Rosina tells her about the wheelbarrow, and the fire in the woods, and then of the box of dynamite which is still under the porch. "How could Nick put us in danger like that. What if it exploded?"

Gauze hanging from both hands, Susan says, "You weren't aware of the use of dynamite?"

"Of course, I am" she says, indignantly, "but I never thought Nicola would use it! Or store it under our porch."

"It doesn't mean Nicola used the sticks. He was probably just keeping it safe. You know a lot of our comrades live in apartments with families. It would be impossible to store in a small apartment. Where else could we store it?" She begins to wrap the gauze around her arm. "Don't be angry with Nick, he's just doing his part. You and he always felt the same. Right, Rosa?

"Yes, but why did he have to keep it a secret from me. This is what I don't understand."

Susan let out a small giggle. "Why? Look how you're reacting now that you know."

There is the sound of footsteps coming up the front stoop.

"That must be Aldo, let him in. I have to get dressed."

From her bedroom, Rosina hears the voices. Aldo, always distinct in his sharp, quick pitch, but the other voice, quieter, steady, unfamiliar. Lifting her breasts into her bra, she feels the sore, hot glands are already preparing. A deep sadness washes over her. Couldn't she just stay in bed and weep? Just for a while.

Susan already has started a pot of coffee. Rosina meets her at the stove and squares on her, takes her in. She had removed her hat revealing a new shorter bob. Susan probably knew about the dynamite, *everyone did*. Susan's face is serious, solemn. And there is Aldo and another man in her kitchen. A grim mood hovers in the air, sobering her.

Instinctively, Rosina takes a deep breath. "What's happened?"

"Come and sit down." Susan's pinkish complexion washed away.

"Don't tell me to take a seat. What's wrong? What's happened?"

Newspapers are spread on the kitchen table. Photographs of two men on the front page. The headline reads:

MIKE SACCO AND BERT VANZETTI,
TWO SUSPECTS HELD IN CUSTODY
FOR BRAINTREE MURDER AND ROBBERY

For as moment she's confused by the names Mike and Bert, but then recognizes her husband. The photographs are ghastly. Nicola's heavy beard makes him look like an unkempt man. His mouth tense, his shirt collar unbuttoned and his tie crooked. Bartolomeo's mustache hangs mournfully, and his cap low on his broad brow creates an evil expression, one that would never belong to him.

Aldo is talking behind her, "We're on this already, Rosa. They have nothing. They say Mario Buda's car was the getaway car and because they were the ones to pick it up. It was some sort of frame job."

Over Aldo's voice, she hears Susan whispering to the other man, "You'd think they'd bother to get the names right."

Rosina's legs are wobbly. She takes a seat and begins to read the caption under their photographs. Aldo paces around her and the table and chairs, his words like little sharp knives flying through the air. "Sit down!" she screams at him. "All of you sit."

"When can we see him?" Rosina asks, her voice tiny and cracking.

"I'm working on that today. Luca and I are going down to the courthouse as soon as we leave here," Aldo answers.

"Luca?" she looks at the man standing next to Aldo.

"*Scusa,* Rosina. This is Lucciano Bianchini, an old friend who will be helping us put together a defense fund. In case we are in need of one."

Glancing back at the newspaper, her eyes catch the word guns. "No, no. Nicola didn't have a gun. His gun is here."

She rushes into their bedroom. "Aldo, come, take it down. Take it down." When Aldo hands Rosina the empty shoebox, she cannot believe her naivety. "I thought...." Nausea begins to build. The baby hormones mix with fear and twirl inside her. She moves quickly to get to the toilet, but the room begins to whirl, and she drifts towards the floor.

A strange, baritone voice floats over her, "Are you okay, *Signora*?" the man that Aldo had just introduced her to is kneeling on the floor next to her. Susan removes a wet washcloth from her forehead. "Let me help you up." He has a calm, distinct way of speaking. A deep scar, shaped like the letter "C" is carved near the corner of his eye. She thinks of the branch that scratched her neck as she hurried through the forest and wonders if he too was once in the woods.

"*Posso aiutarti ad alzarti*?" He wants to lift her off the floor.

"No," she says, and he helps her into a sitting position.

Susan brings a glass of hot water with a piece of lemon floating in it. "Here, drink," she says.

Rosina chuckles, looks intently into Susan's eyes. "This is no time to be having a baby." her voice weakening, she's about to weep again. She moves to stand with Luca's assistance.

"How long was I out?" she asks, not waiting for an answer.

"Oh Jesus," Susan touches her arm. "You're pregnant?"

"Baby or not. I have to be strong. Maybe twice as strong." She gives Susan a half-smile. At this moment, she wants to sink into the chair. But instead, legs wobbly, she forces herself to stand tall. Taking a deep breath, she says, "Someone, please take that dynamite from out under the porch. I don't want it here. Now... what are the steps we must take to get them home?" The tone of her voice is strange, not at all like hers, but one of unpracticed authority.

25

The building housing the jail looms large on a grassy incline. A glossy magazine picture, a typical American scene: A tall church steeple adjacent to the courthouse peers over its roof. Red brick with mortar and welcoming tall white pillars at its entrance. Ivy clings along one side of the building, neatly trimmed from the arched windows. A row of white weeping cherry trees lines the walkup, and Rosina wonders if Nicola can see them from his cell window. Her insides shake as she enters the building. She must be strong...for Nicola and the children. *Children.* It is the first time she uses this word. She prays the news will help Nicola in some way.

A guard ushers her into a door that has a sign: HOLDING ROOM. Inside, a small square of space. They take her light jacket and her handbag. A person in a blue uniform comes through another door, and she's uncertain if it's a man or a woman. A belly and chest round and formless encompass the entire body up to a double chin. A hint of rouge on the lips reveals her gender, and the woman begins to pat Rosina down.

"Arms out," she demands. "Turn around and take that hat off."

Rosina begins to feel light-headed; then realizes she has been holding her breath. When the woman finally removes her hands, she says, "Follow me."

When she reaches to take her jacket and purse off the hook, the guard roughly gropes her hand.

"Nope. No outer clothing allowed, and no bags or hats."

"I...I've brought some biscotti for my husband. I made them this morning. Can I take them to him?"

"What is that? Let me see." She peels the dishcloth from the tin tray.

"Cookies," Rosina says.

"Hand 'em over. I'll have 'em checked out."

Looking down at the burn on her arm, she is sorry she didn't wear a long-sleeved dress. Not knowing Nicola's emotional condition, she didn't want to bring up the dynamite. Not yet anyway.

She follows the woman into the reception room where the sun tumbles down from three high windows, painting a broad strip of light across the long oak table. A low divider made of mesh stretches across the length of each table. She's reminded of the article she had read about a game with a silly name, Ping Pong. The room smells sickening of overheated Minestrone soup.

"Sit on this side. Here." The guard taps the bench with something that looks like a larger version of Dante's toy bat and then leaves through the door behind her. In the silence, she quivers with anticipation; soon, she'll see him.

At the far end of the room, a door opens and out walks Nicola with two men also in dark-blue uniforms. His wrists and ankles are cuffed, and he wears a tan jumpsuit. His eyes glow at the sight of her. She begins to rush towards him, but the guards stop her. "No touching. Sit." He points to two separate benches. They sit across from each other. Rosina uneasy, this place—guns on the guard's hips. Her stomach turns in disgust, the belittling of chains, to see her husband as a prisoner. The humiliation sits like a stucco wall between them. Yet, Nicola's face still radiates his love.

"*Cara mia, va tutto bene,*" he says.

The guard shouts, "Hey, only English. We're in America. No wop language."

Rosina has no respect for this man in uniform. She wants to spit at his feet. But she's smart enough to fear the authority he possesses. She doesn't want to do or say anything to make it worse for Nicola.

"Don't let him bother you," Nicola says, "They want to cut us down to size. It's always the first step."

She calms herself by looking into her husband's eyes. His complexion is pasty, and the cleft in his chin is more pronounced from poor shaving. Worn and drained, yet he still possesses that light.

He looks up to the two large arched windows high up almost at the ceiling.

"Ah, you and the sun, all at the same time." Then in a whisper, "*Guarda il sole*," he chuckles. "You know, I haven't seen the sun in months."

Should she ask? "You don't have a window in your cell?"

"A window? No," he huffs. "Nothing but a wooden door with a small slot at the bottom."

How can this be happening to them? They're in a trance, one from which they'll soon wake.

"How are you, *amore mia*? he whispers. I want to tell you so much about what has happened to me in this awful place, but we don't have time. Tell me good things. I want to hear something to make me happy. My boy, how is he?"

"Dante is fine. He adores the new nanny, Aldo's mother's friend, Mrs. Hayes. He now has a best friend, her little boy, Jimmy."

Nicola is chewing, biting the inside of his cheek. His eyes now glaze with tears, yet she knows the tears are misplaced.

"This makes me so happy to hear," he says.

Their hands barely touch under the net on the table. Nicola's fingertips against her own cultivate even more sadness. Tears begin to form. Her voice cracks as she speaks, "Aldo has been the best friend. He told you about the team he's put together. The Committee for Sacco and Vanzetti."

"Yes, such an official name. You know what, I think something good might come of this. It will probably be just a few more days before I'm out of this place. They're getting in touch with the man in the passport office, to prove I was there when this murder—robbery was committed."

"I've made you some biscotti. They'll bring it to you later. They want to be sure I didn't put an escape map inside them."

They make an effort to chuckle to one another, as though they're sitting in the parlor of their home.

"You must get out of here, *amore*." She needs to tell him; she can no longer wait. "We're going to have a baby. I was planning to tell you when we got to *Italia*, but now..."

It takes him a moment to grasp the news. It happens so quickly, him jumping up, shouting excitedly, "We're going to have a baby. Oh, my Rosetta *mia*." Rushing towards her in small, chained steps to embrace his wife, his handcuffed wrists over her head for a hug. The momentary warmth of his body against hers. And then, the thud of a police stick at his back.

"You guineas don't know about regulations, do you?"

The guard pulls Nicola's arms from around her, forcing her to crouch over, his cuffs caught in her comb, pull at the roots of her hair.

"*Ti voglio tanto bene...ti adoro*, Rosetta *mia*," Nicola shouts, as the guards drag him away.

Fear consumes her. The comb Nicola had given her for her birthday hangs from threads of her hair. Strands of hair mark her neck. Her heart is being ripped away. The large white-faced clock situated on the wall above the door ticks loudly as she waits for the guard to open the door. It flashes through her mind-that he never noticed her burned arm. She sobs, knowing there is no luxury of God's grace, she screams out, "Why? Why! Damn you. Damn you."

<h1 style="text-align:center">26</h1>

Although it's been raining for five days and the puddles along the path to the house are muddy, Aldo and comrades keep coming to her door. All in the effort to bring Nicola and Bartolo home. Rosina is grateful for the passion she witnesses within Aldo, and the others, but is exhausted from the clamor. There are moments when she doesn't want to talk.

At night, finally alone in bed, she wonders if she can cope much longer. Her mind swivels to a place that is hell, then back to taking care of Dante, and then to the demands of the growing baby inside her. Hoping her weakness is only a temporary condition. She cannot let go of the shame. Shame so deep and mortifying, a wearing-down kind of emotion she cannot verbalize or unravel.

Three months since the arrest, and still, there is no indictment. Each visit drains Rosina more and more. When the men go to see him and Bartolo, who is now in another prison, twenty miles or so away, they tell her what good spirits he and Bartolo are in. But what about the last time she saw Nicola: sitting across from him, strangely watching his body shrink. Uncertain if it was because of the slump of his shoulders or the way he hung his head when he spoke.

"I've been dreaming of home," Nicola had said, "asking myself why I come to America. We had vineyards. Plenty to eat. My papa had horse-drawn carts. We lacked nothing. So much land. Here I come to a place of tenements and factories. There we shouted out about socialism, anarchism, fascism, we complained a lot, but we did our work in peace."

Always a neat, close-shaven man, she saw the short dark hairs in the clef of his chin, the shadows, and darkness under his eyes deeper.

"Here… I come here, and workers are expected to be quiet, not complain. There is more government here." He'd looked at her, the same way Dante would, questioning, childlike. "More rules, Rosina."

She kept nodding her head in agreement. It was all she could do.

"Now, now I live with a tin cup to drink from and an enameled pot to shit in, and the worse of it is I can't even see the stars at night."

She longed to hold him.

He continued, "I need to work, Rosa. They won't allow me the privilege. Better they should kill me right now."

She felt his need to labor, to exhaust his body til spent. His yearning to be one with Mother Nature. She wanted so badly to hold him, to be in his embrace, to tell him everything will be okay, like it used to be, but all she could do was search for his fingertips, which were not there. Everything. Everything they had worked for was moving further away.

* * *

Luca Bianchini sits at Rosina's table, along with Aldo and Susan. "We are gathering more and more supporters," Luca says, "philosophical anarchists, without a doubt." He casts a broad smile towards Rosina. "Artists, writers, intellectuals, and even some conservative members of high society. Can you imagine that!" he says with more joy and excitement that she can relate to.

Watching Luca light his pipe, she muses at his calm, level-head. A man who seems capable of avoiding outrage in all forms to accomplish whatever is on the agenda. The woodsy smell of his tobacco brings a kind of inner peace to Rosina. She recalls when her parents first brought her to the convent; abandoned, she cried herself to sleep each night. Eventually, it was time that befriended her. She learned that time was the great healer, and now, in pain she wishes for time to pass quickly to mend this pain that is tearing her family apart.

The friendly voices around her table are wrapped in a murky wadded cotton, allowing her thoughts to dash through her mind: Reading stories to Dante at bedtime—holding him in her arms—even when he pushes her away—these moments give her purpose. But without Nicola by her side, she's aware of a sense of defeat that claws at her. Even Dante's new habit of biting his nails seems to be too large a problem for her to handle. The looming question was, how would she live, get on with two children—an infant? How would she live without money?

She says out loud, "I should've kept the sewing machine." Her words draw silence at the table. "Years ago, Nicola bought me a sewing machine. I said no, take it away, it was too much of a luxury."

Susan asks, "Why do you want a sewing machine?"

"I have to start working. I'll need money," Rosina says sternly. She's irritated that Susan has to ask. Why doesn't she know this? Once again, she is reminded that their worlds depart when it comes to privilege and entitlement.

Without pause, Aldo chimes in, "Rosina, we've created a fund for you and the children. Try not to worry about money right now."

This only makes her feel more inadequate. "I can't take charity from strangers!"

They all speak at once. "Nonsense. All these years, you and Nicola have done so much for our comrades, now it's your turn to be on the receiver's end."

Susan manages, "Yes, it would be foolish not to."

"It's not charity. We look out for our brothers, don't we?" Aldo adds.

She knows this is the way their inner system works. She's grateful, however uneasy. She nods "yes."

Luca says, "Another thing you could do. I don't know if you're willing, but you might consider renting out a bedroom. Perhaps that could work for you."

Rosina contemplates for a moment. This might work.

After much discussion it is agreed, word will be sent out; there is a room for rent. She would move her belongings into Dante's room. Maybe it will be good to have a boarder; some adult company until Nicola returns.

"We wouldn't be able to have any meetings here," she says.

27

Each visit to Nicola is more unbearable. The other men continue to speak of how well he is doing, a collective performance for her benefit. On her last visit, she had made one of Nicola's favorite dishes, pasta fagioli, and by the time they finished inspecting the soup, it was brought to him cold—late in the evening, and he refused to eat it, saying they had no respect for the work his wife endured.

September, and still, he and Bartolo have not been charged with any crime. When Rosina awkwardly lowers the bulk of herself into the chair across from Nicola, his face reveals sinking hope, fueling his words: "Please, Rosa, don't bother to come to see me anymore. I don't want you to hurt yourself or the baby." His blank expression is now one of indifference.

His words hurt, but she too can hurt. She wants to say, *yes, no more. I can't take it any longer. Seeing you here tears my heart out.* During his months in jail, Nicola had hardened. That bright, innocent look he held whenever he first greeted her, had now turned into an overbearingly deep depression. He had developed a tic, shrugging his right shoulder quickly, and blinking his left eye simultaneously as if a shock of electricity was passing through him. He was reading Victor Hugo's *Les Misérables* and felt plowed down and persecuted like Jean Valjean.

"I'm a caged man! Pacing my cell for hours! My hands idle for months on end. Why won't they allow me to work? They're stripping me of dignity. Human dignity!"

She senses his need to get up and pace but knows in this hollow shell of a visitors' room, even this he is not allowed. She wants to tell him the day is a perfect Indian summer day, the kind of day he would so enjoy working in his garden, but uncertain how it will affect him.

"I miss talking with comrades. Bartolo...if only I could speak with him. I wonder how he is doing?"

Bartolomeo had been indicted for another hold-up and was sent to the Charlestown State Prison, twelve miles away. Everyone thought it best that Nicola didn't know about the indictment. He'd become more depressed.

"The men say Bartolo is doing okay. I would like to visit him, but it's too far away," she tells Nicola.

"No, Rosa. Not in your condition. Ask Susan to go. She came to visit me with Luca Bianchini, he seems like a smart, nice fellow. Susan seems to like him a lot. He wants to help, but I told him there is nothing he or anyone can do." He clears his throat.

"Don't say that *caro*, they can. And *are* all helping. You know we're trying to locate the man at the Italian Consulate—the person you saw when you went for our passports. They'll find out where he lives, and he'll say he saw you there that day."

"What are the chances? He must have seen thousands of Italians that day. He probably won't remember me."

"Everyone remembers meeting you. No one forgets your politeness and your handsome face," Rosina says, offering up empty words—trying to encourage his mood.

When they part, she wants to embrace him, even for a moment. The cruelness of no human contact thickens around their hearts—growing more severe with each visit. He never even asks if she found a midwife. *Are you getting ready for birthing?* Oh, how he held her body when she gave birth to their son. His firm grip of her arms and shoulders as she labored through a contraction. The midwife, sitting on the cushion, between her legs on the floor, and Nicola's soothing voice, his breath in her ear. *Not this time. Not this time.* Her heart clenches.

* * *

Ten days later, after five endless months, Nicola and Bartolo are indicted for first-degree murder and robbery. Unable to attend court because Dante has come down with the measles, Rosina learns about the expected indictment from a note Susan slips under the front door, the next morning. In quarantine with her son and her unborn child, she keeps Dante's room darkened with heavy drapes tightly drawn day and night. The white lotion Rosina applies to his skin to stop the itching dries into a powder. She worries the powder is infected with the disease and will take him longer to heal, so she changes the sheets nightly. Dante's fever had been a solid one hundred and one for two days, and now washing the thermometer in tepid water, it falls hard into the deep porcelain sink and cracks along the tip. She watches the odd, silver-blue mercury circle around the porcelain sink and disappear down the drain.

Later, under a dim lamp, she sits on Dante's bed reading *Just So Stories* by Rudyard Kipling. She shields his eyes with a folded handkerchief. School has just begun, and Rosina is glad to have the schoolwork dropped off by a classmate. Besides reading, Dante has to make a drawing of his family. Dante, scant in his undershirt, his thin limbs, and undeveloped muscles make him appear even weaker. He sleeps a lot during the day, but Rosina selfishly wishes he had the energy to stay awake. At night, when she hears Dante's even breaths, she closes his bedroom door and quietly tiptoes to the settee. She's closed off from a world she is accustomed to. She wraps her arms around herself—rocks back and forth. She too is a prisoner, *like Nicola*. For the third time this day, she takes Susan's note in her hand and reads:

Dear Rosa, it's just as well you didn't attend court this day. It was only a matter of five minutes when Nick and Bart stood before the judge. Neither one of them reacted to the indictment, and they were immediately taken away. There was no time to talk with them or even say a hello. But it looked like they were at least able to talk to each other when they were brought into the courtroom. Aldo says our fight has only begun. Remember, they have no proof of any kind. If N and B did it, who and where are the other three men? And where is the $15,000.00? The gun is even a different caliber. Try to remember these things. Many hugs to you and Dante, who I hope is doing better today. If you want to write to me, leave the note in your mailbox. I'll try to stop by tomorrow.

She presses the note to her chest, and sees for the first time, writing on the other side: *PS: We've found a woman who is interested in renting your room.*

Picturing Nicola's jail cell, she imagines the slit at the bottom of the wooden door. Sees him positioning himself on the cell floor to try and see the stars through the arched window down the corridor. Now she reconsiders her own feeling of imprisonment and detests herself for making such a selfish comparison.

Before retiring to bed, Rosina writes a note to Susan, reminding her to give her maiden name, Zambelli, to the woman who is interested in boarding. Also, she asks her to please purchase a thermometer at the pharmacy, and she leaves a couple of dimes in the envelope.

When she walks out into the chilled night air to place the note in the mailbox, she cannot help but notice the stars twinkling brightly. This nudge from heaven ushers unexpected tears. The wooden post holding the mailbox had weakened over the winter months. Nicola had meant to repair it, and each day she finds it more and more tilted to one side. Rosina kicks it slightly to see if she can straighten it, then kicks it again, and then once more, harder, until she cannot stop kicking it.

A newspaper left at Rosina's door, just a few days later, headlines:

TERRORISM STRIKES WALL STREET. 38 DEAD. 300 INJURED. DEADLY WAGONLOAD OF DYNAMITE. SHATTERED WINDOW GLASS RAINS DOWN FROM THIRTY FLOORS IN FINANCIAL DISTRICT, SCREAMS OF BLOODIED VICTIMS. AN ANARCHIST ACT OF VENGEANCE

Palmer proclaims: all civil liberties suspended. Announces his Secret trials and mass raids will be continued. The terrorist left a note: "FREE POLITICAL PRISONERS OR IT WILL BE SURE DEATH FOR ALL." The Italian anarchist, Mario Buda, and his gang are the main suspects.

* * *

There is no choice. Against Rosina's wishes, Dante must go to the public school. She can see it now, trying to remove the propaganda from his teachings. Yet, needing more time to visit with Nicola, and to help work for his release, she cannot worry about this now.

At the jailhouse, Nicola speaks softly, determined: "All along, I thought we were arrested because of 'the idea,' not for a gunman's murderous job." Besides his newly acquired tic, his movements are strange, tense in his shoulders and neck. He glances down at his shackled wrists in gloomy acceptance. "That man Katzmann, the District Attorney, asked us only about our political beliefs. Never mentioned anything about a crime. Naturally, I thought we were arrested for being against government. Bartolo and I denied we were anarchist, but he kept pressing us, asking why we went to Mexico."

Each time she sees him, all the energy and spirit he possessed is dissipating more and more. "Don't come. I don't want you to see me like this."

Don't come. Devoured by his own pain, he's unable to see her suffering. She must get past the rejection. Nicola isn't himself, she knows this, yet it is still hurtful. Perhaps, she resolves, once the baby is born, I won't be as sensitive.

In preparation to interview the boarder, Rosina combs the house for signs of her husband's presence. She gazes at the photograph of him with Dante and herself, the one he had taken to the passport office, now leaning up against the ruby-glass fruit bowl. She had meant to put it back into its frame. For a moment, she holds it against her bosom, remembering that infamous day when he was arrested. Emitting a long, far-reaching sigh—she slips it into a nearby drawer.

Wanting to be especially hospitable, she takes biscotti from the storage tin, and tastes a piece to be sure they aren't stale, then places some on a blue and white plate, and keeps the water simmering on low for tea or coffee.

When Rosina opens her front door, a tall maternal-looking woman appears, leaning on an embossed silver-tipped walking stick. She is big boned. Industrial looking, as if this is at all possible. "Rosa Zambelli?"

Rosina reaches for the palm of her outstretched hand and finds it in a tight grip. "Letty Wheeler."

Letty Wheeler has a short bob, sort of mannish, coarse black and white wavy hair. She wears a tailored snow-flaked tweed suit with tuxedo lapels to which a large, enameled songbird, perched on a pewter swing, is pinned. Although larger in frame than most women, she appears clean and neat, which pleases Rosina.

"Please, come in."

She moves like a woman who doesn't need a cane. Long strides. Steady on her feet.

"Oh dear," the woman states, "you look like you're ready to pop!"

At first, Rosina doesn't know what she means but then sees her looking at her protruding belly.

"Yes," she smiles, probably another month."

"Oh, I remember those days," Letty says, as she sits on the settee.

"How many children do you have?" Rosina asks, not really interested, but knows she must be friendly. The woman has a strange odor about her: the convent comes to mind, crushed cardamom or fennel seeds, pulverized, added to the bread yeast.

Letty takes tea with milk, a foreign notion to Rosina.

The small wooden wagon Nicola had made for Dante, along with some of his other toys are in the far corner of the parlor. She watches Letty as she inspects her surroundings, now focused on the toys.

"Oh, you have more children?" she asks.

"Yes, one son. Dante, he is in school now."

"Dante," she chuckles, such a *grand* name! "And your husband?"

"My husband is in Italy. He went there to work, several months now...that's why I'm renting the room."

"Oh, my, Italy? So very far away. What does he do?"

Rosina does not hesitate. She's already worked it out. "He's a builder. He and his brothers run a construction company. They needed him for a big project."

"Oh, that's a long way to commute!" she laughs effusively. "Seriously, does he always go to Italy for work?"

"No. Only sometimes," Rosina repeats, "his brothers called for his help." Rosina cannot believe how easily she finds lying to a person she doesn't know.

"Oh, so what are they called, the Zambelli Brothers?"

Letty Wheeler begins a lot of her sentences with the word, oh.

"Exactly, Mrs. Wheeler. Good guess." Although she smiles, she has the sense that this woman is patronizing her, so she quickly changes the subject.

"Would you like to see the room, Mrs. Wheeler?"

"Oh, Letty will do."

Rosina's bedroom now stripped of their small personal items, the porcelain cup that holds her ring at night. The photo of Nicola and his brother, the first Nicola, taken around the same time she met him. The small sewing basket with needles and buttons, and the books she has now taken to read at night to help her relax since Nicola's incarceration. She had also removed their special blanket from the bed and covered the bed with the woolen blanket her mother had made for them.

After looking around, walking the length of the room, Letty says, "Okay, I'll get my things and will move in tomorrow morning."

She opens her tapestry handbag and removes a green-velvet pouch and hands Rosina two dollars. They agree one dollar and a half would be fair.

As Rosina takes the money, she wonders why does a woman of middle age needs to live alone in a small furnished room? As though Letty Wheeler has read her mind, she says, "It will only be for a few months while the contractors finish renovating my home."

28

There is no cohesion in Rosina's world. Everything seems disjointed. She's unable to even enjoy Dante's continuous chatter and playfulness. In her mind, she replays over and over Nicola's words on her last visit: "If I have to stay in jail another six months, I'll figure out how to hang myself." She had walked up to the young guard and whispered, begged him to allow her to stay longer, she couldn't leave him so depressed. The officer was *simpatico,* young like Nicola, and a simple nod of his head was all she needed.

A few days since she last saw him, and still, she lives with the dread of his words and her emotional response. "How can you say this? With a wife and a child, and another on the way—it's so irresponsible of you." she had screamed at him. "Look at me, *caro.*"

"Irresponsible? No. You look at me, Rosina. Am I taking care of you? Am I doing what I can for you and the boy?" His shoulders hunched; his body curled towards his handcuffed hands. "They've taken my manhood from me."

"No...no. It's because you are a brave man, who has the courage to live by his values, his beliefs, that's why you're here. Don't you see?"

He didn't hear her. "I'm no longer a man. *Non più un uomo.*"

Fear rolled over her, she had stood and banged her fists on the table.

"Don't say that! It's up to you. No one can take that from you, Nicola. No one."

Just then the guard with the pear-shaped belly entered the room and shouted, "Sit down, lady."

"Please..." she then whispered, lowering herself in the chair. "Don't you see how hard this is for me. I need you to be strong for the children and me."

Just when she thought she could no longer cry—her eyes burned, ached from dryness, as though they might be bleeding. "I need your strength now, especially now with the baby coming." her voice cracked.

"I'm sorry, Rosina...*mi spiace*. I don't want to upset you. If you were locked up... robbed of your days. No labor. No purpose. A man is nothing without his work." He gaped at the two arched windows above. "Forgive me. I'll try harder for you and the children. I promise. But tell me. When will this end?"

* * *

With Letty Wheeler in the house, Rosina takes comfort in knowing she can drop Dante off at Mrs. Hayes to play with little Jimmy, so she can attend meetings. The meetings have become her very breath. She needs to be with like-minded comrades. Conversations of bringing the men home is the only time she looks forward too.

Letty Wheeler carries a large wooden-framed tapestry bag into the parlor. "May I sit?"

Rosina, just back from dropping off Dante, is in the kitchen washing the breakfast dishes.

Letty exhales deeply as she sits in Nicola's chair. "This quilt is taking me longer than I thought." She places small squares of material on her lap, picks one up, and begins stitching it to the larger square. "This is from my poor husband's shirt. He loved this shirt."

Rosina is compelled to observe. The quilt appears to be a patriotic statement. Stars, stripes, American flags, mostly red, white, and blue.

"How big will it be?" Rosina asks.

"I don't know yet. Maybe I'll hang it on my wall or give it to my daughter."

"How many children do you have?" Rosina hesitates to make conversation.

"Just the one," she says, "And how are you feeling, my dear?"

"I'm fine. Just on my way out to see a friend."

"Can I be frank with you, my dear?" she doesn't wait for Rosina to answer. "Why doesn't your husband come home with you, now that you're in this state. He should've never left you alone at this time." Letty's eyes are on her, scrutinizing.

"We're okay," Rosina says. She hates the fact that she must lie and move quickly to get out of her own house.

After that, whenever she has the opportunity, Letty speaks to Rosina with an unconvincing, concerning motherly tone. Rosina wants to tell her to mind her own damn business, to stop putting her nose where it doesn't belong. Sometimes, she mumbles it in Italian along with a few curse words. As if she's resolved the matter.

Moving her distended body along seems to be getting more and more difficult. She doesn't recall feeling this way when she was in the ninth month with Dante. Mrs. Hayes had given birth to her second child only a year ago and has arranged for her doula to meet with Rosina. She is consoled by knowing she'll have the help she needs when labor begins. Susan had already stated, "I'll be with you. But won't be able to help, not really. I'll probably throw up!"

Seeing Susan fraught with paleness the day Dante fell from the high fence and hit his forehead on a stone, and then running into the house with blood pouring over his face, she knew then she wouldn't be able to count on Susan.

In Aldo's old slated-roof house, with its battleship grey painted, crooked floors, he offers, "Here, Rosina, my most comfortable chair."

Rosina winces as the springs through the worn upholstery pinch her bottom, but says nothing. For the first time, she asks herself why so many of their male comrades are unmarried.

They sit in a circle, around a low table with stacks of papers, notes, and opened books. A growing pile of energy, an exhaustive undertaking. This monumental effort to set the men free makes her muse: she should be more grateful. But she is exhausted, and there isn't much gratitude to muster.

Carlo, a man she recalls from other meetings, says, "Since their arrest, there's been chaos. Lots of threats. Compatriots have set bombs, blew up safes. Warnings, some say more like threats have been sent out to politicians. And pig Palmer and his raids have come down even harder." He lights a cigarette. "I want someone to tell me to where the money is that was taken at the robbery and why the hell aren't they even talking about the other so-called three men who were part of the gang?

Someone shouts, "They're not even looking for them."

"No one cares who they are. They've got what they want." Luca's baritone voice is murky. "A mockery of justice," he says. Something he constantly repeats...words that wake Rosina in the middle of the night...*mockery of justice.*

"We've learned the passport agent who had agreed to identify Nicola has gone back to Italy. We must find him," Aldo says. "He returned to Italy months ago with failed health. Some lung problems." Aldo's long narrow face, his preoccupied frown directed at Rosina. "His name is Giuseppe Andrower."

"*Un altro muro di mattoni.*" Rosina sighs heavily. "Has someone told Nicola?" she asks.

"Rosina, no worry, it's not a brick wall. We will find him." He coughs, "Yes, I saw Nicola for a few minutes this afternoon, he knows. I had to wait until a reporter left to talk with him. I also met Elizabeth Gurley Flynn from New York," Aldo continues. "She's one hell of a ferocious young woman with quite a reputation. They call her the "rebel girl. She can help."

Aldo shuffles through some papers on the table, finding what he's looking for, he appears to be in a really good mood. "A reporter, Mary Heaton Vorse, was there with her. She's interviewing Nicola, and we hope it will be in the newspaper this week. Needless to say, the more exposure, the better our case will be."

"Who is this Elizabeth? Her name is familiar," Rosina remarks.

"She's the young woman who's known for the demands she made at the textile workers strike in Lawrence. She gave some stirring speeches there and has been very active in helping the worker ever since. She is also very well connected. Her family comes from money. Part of the Boston Brahmin clan."

"I met her once," Susan remarks. "Yes, she'll be very valuable to have in our corner. You'll like her, Rosina."

Leaving Aldo's house, Susan and Rosina walk out into the murkiness of the day. The thought runs through Rosina's head that Nicola seems to be happier, more positive, with strangers.

Susan says, "I hate not being able to visit with you. I wish we could've gotten a comrade instead of that Wheeler lady." She seems tired.

"Of course, you come to the house. We won't talk about the case or the men." Taking a deep breath in, she says, "Maybe that would be better, anyway." Her taught face muscles release and she sighs. She smiles towards Susan.

"Yes, that would be nice. For a change," Susan says.

The day Susan visits, she brings a copy of the *Andover Townsmen*. Apparently, the case is the only thing they can talk about. Mary Vorse's article interviewing Nicola is on the second page. Aware of Letty tucked silently away in her room, they sit in the parlor, carefully choosing words and signing to one another. Susan nudges Rosina and points to the article and nods her approval. Rosina's face flushes as she reads:

> In interviewing Sacco's neighbors and the men he worked with, not one person had anything negative to say about him. They spoke of his gentleness, his smile always present, and his generosity to help others. His boss said he was a "highly skilled operative in a factory of over 600 workers."
>
> "I don't know what I did without him before he came here. He's my star worker."
>
> Sacco said he began to turn against government when he witnessed the squalor and poverty he saw amid so much wealth.
>
> "When I see conditions, the inequality of men, this is what drives me. It would be unethical if I couldn't help. Thanks to my father, my family, I always had something to eat, so why shouldn't I help?"
>
> Sacco has a friendly way about him, almost like a child. Life-loving that even after six months in jail, and without work, which seemed to be the base of his character, he is a vital, radiant little bundle of energy: passionate, alert, brimming with vitality. *Innamorato pazza.*

Innamorato pazzo, meaning "I'm madly in love with him."

"Yes," Rosina sighs. Gratitude fills her entire being. Everyone loves Nicola. She reads the last sentences:

> There is something about Nicola Sacco that made me think of swift happy things—jumping fish, a bird on the wing. This is a man who seems incapable of such an act of robbery or murder towards his fellow man.

Rosina stifles a sob before it can be heard and begins to pace it out—pacing back and forth, frantically—until she can only feel the wetness around her eyes.

29

On a cool autumn day, leaves circling outside her window, Rosina gives birth to a healthy, eight-pound baby girl. Looking beyond the glossy egg-white wash of mucus and blood, she is stunned by her daughter's dark thick hair and her full round face. "You have your father's look," she says with a lack of breath.

The doula, with her straight white hair hanging past her shoulders, washes the blood from Rosina's inner thighs. "A wonderful birth," she says, "You're a trooper," she tells Rosina, and the word "trooper" brings her back to the reality of mounted police, the law. Days later, the newspapers report of demonstrations all over Europe, including some scattered cities across the States to "free political prisoners." More and more people are taking interest in Nicola's and Bartolo's case.

The weeks following Ines's birth, Rosina receives gifts, through the committee, from people all over the world. Baskets of fruit, baby clothing, cash gifts, and even a mink coat which she refuses, and wants to return. Aldo says, "No. We'll sell it and use the money for the defense."

Passing through the parlor, Letty gawks and grunts inaudibly at the collected gifts on the floor near the window. "All this, and your *own* husband hasn't come home? Who has so many friends? Tell me another story..." she says in a low whisper, but loud enough for Rosina to hear before closing the bedroom door. Rosina speaks in the same low voice…*Well, I hope your house is almost finished. I can't wait to get you out of here.*

Each day someone from the committee stops by to see if she needs anything. They have become her determined, extended family. She sees them as links in a chain, all pulling together, one by one. *I will eventually embrace them all,* she thinks, and visualizes them around her dining table. Nicola sitting at the head, an Italian feast before them. *Oh, the lightness, the simplicity of such an ordinary moment.*

Not being able to visit Nicola, there are letters. Letters she is mostly happy to receive. And others, not:

> *My dear Rosa,*
>
> *I cannot wait to meet our new little bambina. I think of you and the children all by yourself, and it tortures me. I no longer want to live without my family. How will I make it?*

These are the letters she must put down. Prepare to read. She eventually teaches herself to skip over some of these words, to move deeper inside her shelter. The letters she finds more comforting to read are those where he speaks of his many visitors: Socially prominent women who champion progressive causes. Besides the "rebel girl," Elizabeth Gurley Flynn, another is Elizabeth Evans, a wealthy, sixty-something-year-old woman who is known as "Auntie Bee."

Nicola had written:

> *I recognized her right away from the Lawrence Strike, where she spoke and gave aid to the worker's families.*

* * *

A week later, while Dante is at school and Letty Wheeler out of the house, just as she is about to nurse Ines, there is a knock at her door.

"*Buongiorno, Rosina, come stai?*"

Luca takes up the doorway, clutching a large wooden box with a heavy brass handle. It is shaped like a physician's bag.

"*Allora*, May I come in? Something has come up." He glances over the room. His voice lowers, "Is your tenant here?"

Luca is tall with a square jawline and wide shoulders. A generous smile shows the whiteness of his teeth. Lowering the box to the floor, a button on his raincoat gets caught on the brass handle. Luca's face reddens as he struggles to release it.

"I've brought news of Letty Wheeler," he says.

"Letty Wheeler?"

In the bedroom, the baby begins to fuss.

"We've discovered she's a plant. She's an informer. The DA placed her here. *Hai capito?* Do you understand? She's the sister-in-law of Fred Katzmann, the District Attorney."

Ah, there had been so many misgivings, and it took only a few seconds for Rosina to digest the information. Rifling through her mind, she puts Letty's questions, her constant inquiries, to rest. "I knew it. I knew it. I had the feeling, and all along, I thought I was just being paranoid. I should've trusted my instincts more."

The baby's cry of hunger begins to escalate, and some drops of milk leak from her breast.

"*Ascolta. I'll* be happy to wait until she comes home and see her and her things to the door." Luca studies her face, inquiring. Rosina finds him open, unsettling—yet comforting. Her bitterness and anger gives way to a great relief. She'll no longer have Letty in her life.

"No," she says, "Throwing her out will be my pleasure."

Rosina's need for company, for her comrades, has grown more these last days. "If you like, wait until I finish feeding Ines, I will make you something to drink?"

Her light rose-cotton dress, well-suited for nursing, summons Luca. He gives off a slight shiver when his eyes rest on her breast. Her milk is plentiful, much more than it was with Dante. Sticky fluid seeps through her dress, darkens the nipple area. The rawness of childbirth still lurks, the smells, blood, fluids, the rock-hard breast, all mix into an unexpected carnal urge. Engulfed by it all, she feels a rush of heat on her face. Luca takes in the moment, flushed; he turns away quickly, the very air in the room seems to awaken, hushes between them as he moves towards the front door. "I have to go," he says, his back towards her. "Are you sure you're okay, throwing her out?" his drowning voice, more tender now. Dark hair curls near the up-turned collar of his raincoat. He closes the door behind him without turning to look at her, but not before saying, "a gift from the committee." She looks to the wooden box neither one had mentioned. *A gift from the committee…*one she will be forced to accept.

The timing could've not been better, having just finished nursing, she hears Letty coming into the house and rushes out to meet her in the parlor. "I'd like to see the key to the house," she tells Letty.

Letty still has it in her hand and gives it over to Rosina. "It works. I don't have a problem with it."

"Well," Rosina says, "I have a problem with it. Get your things. I want you out of my house immediately. You're nothing but a spy."

Letty seems to be at a loss for words. She stands there with her mouth open. "A spy?"

A short pause. "Oh…okay…so you now know." Her face is indignant, tight-lipped. "And what are you and your husband? Certainly, not innocents. If you were so innocent, why would you have to lie to me about who you really are? You think I don't know what you and your *so-called* friends are up to? You getting all those gifts of pity? Mrs. Nicola Sacco! Your husband, a murderer."

Rosina bites her fist, struggles to battle *Il Lupo*, but she feels it opening up inside of her. *La bocca del Lupo, the* mouth of the wolf soars: "Get the fuck out of my house. Now. Now!" she shouts, her pulses raging.

Letty struggles with her suitcase down the porch steps. "Terrorist! Communist!" she shouts. Rosina spits on the ground; it hits the back of Letty's great swinging jacket. "*Sei malvagia. Sei senza anima!*" Rosina curses and slams the door.

A half-hour later, Letty is still waiting at the end of the path. "*Fottuta puttana,*" Rosina fumes, then takes a deep breath and lifts the heavy wooden box onto the table. She unlatches the sewing machine cover. She doesn't turn to look, but she sees the shadow of an official looking black car pass the parlor window.

Rosina will sleep in her own bed tonight. She strips the linens that Letty had used and throws the blanket in the vat to scrub later. She carries the pillow that Letty used to the garbage pail. She will make a new one for herself. Moving through the house, she is unrestrained, no longer on edge; realizing now the degree to which Letty Wheeler added to her already stressful situation.

Later, in bed, she thinks of the sewing machine. Rosina remembers the remnants of material, old drapes, and the curtains stored in a cardboard box in the back of the hall closet. In her nightgown and flashlight in hand, she pulls the cardboard box out of the closet. Nicola's handwriting in black ink is on the top of the box: *Stoffe per Rosina. She* had almost forgotten the cotton voile curtains, a magnificent Copenhagen blue that when she first saw them at the Salvation Army, Nicola had said, "Why do you want curtains, we don't have a window." But she had been entranced by the fabric, by the joyful color. Now withdrawing the material, she visualizes a square neckline, three-quarter sleeves, clusters of delicate tucks, and narrow ruffles in a three-layer skirt. *A dress for Nicola's homecoming.*

The first thing Rosina does when she wakes in the morning is to place the sewing machine on the table. With a cushion on the kitchen chair, it will be the right height to work. She will send a word out to the comrade's wives, and surely, there will be orders for dresses in no time. Later, while sipping her coffee, she pauses to admire the black lacquered surface of the machine. She observes the green and gold scrolls with a red burst of color in the center. Her hand glides along the top of the machine, smooth and shapely, like a woman's body. She envisions beautiful, finished dresses, gowns, and of course, the money to feed her family. *Everything will be okay.*

* * *

It happens quickly. Was it because she had willed it for days? One of the daughters of a comrade was getting married. Rosina, commissioned to make a wedding dress, finds a young woman with a flat chest and narrow hips standing in her parlor. Rosina wraps the tape measure around her tiny waist. Reams of white satin and white tulle netting are spread across her settee. She senses the tension in this young woman. Sixteen? Seventeen years old, the most. "You must be very excited," she says, trying to make her relax. The girl gives her one-word answers, but Rosina is happy not to talk. There isn't enough time in a day between visiting Nicola, keeping up the house, and caring for the children to waste with small talk. The girl's mother brings French lace she wants inserted in the bodice of her daughter's wedding dress—a last-minute request which will have to be hand-sewn.

Soon she begins to welcome hand stitching because her right arm is sore from the constant turn of the wheel, and her pointer finger on her left hand, callused from rubbing against the needle where she guides the material. The parlor soon looks like a sweatshop, bulk fabrics from matron sisters who are too large to find evening dresses for a wedding bring in a bundle of shiny gray satin. The one problem she has is to keep reminding Dante not to touch or play near the materials.

* * *

"If you don't like Uncle Sammy"

If you don't like your Uncle Sammy,
Then go back to your home o'er the sea;
to the land from which you came,
whatever be its name,
But don't be ungrateful to me;
If you don't like the stars in old glory,
If you don't like the red, white and blue,
Then don't act like the cur in the story
don't bite the hand that feeds you!

When Rosina first finds the flyer in her mailbox, she's uncertain if it's targeted towards her. There were all sorts of political uprisings lately, how could she be sure? The weekly meeting at her home once again, she begins to feel she is actually participating, helping in some small way to bring Nicola home. When she shows the flyer to the group, Aldo and Luca pass it between them, catching each other's eye, then the other's glance at it and continue to forward it back to her. "What?" she asks Aldo.

"Has anyone seen this before?" He addresses the men.

Three days later, Rosina gets her answer. The flyer is again in her mailbox, but this time with a handwritten scribble at the bottom,
GO HOME YOU WOP.
This is my home. You *bastardi. O figli di puttana.* You will not terrorize me. She crumbles the paper and throws it into the wastebasket.

* * *

Rosina hates taking the children to the jailhouse. But there is no choice. Nicola wants to see his son and meet his new daughter. When the sound of the Iron Gate slams behind them, Dante grabs her by the leg.

"Mama, I don't like it here."

"I know, *mio caro*, but Papa wants to see you."

"Why can't he come home?"

"Soon," she says. "Here, help me hold your sister's blanket." Dante refuses to take it and lets it drop onto the concrete floor in the holding room. The weight of the baby, stiffness in her shoulders and lower back ache from feedings, the same way she felt when she nursed Dante.

"Please, be a good boy and help Mama. Don't you want to tell Papa that you're a big help with your sister?"

He frowns and bunches up the blanket in his arms, just as the female guard enters to frisk the three of them. Dante refuses the guard's touch. He hangs onto the back of his mother's dress. "Please...he has nothing. What kind of mother would I be to hide something on my child?"

Still clinging to Rosina's thigh, Dante cries as the guard runs her hands along the child's back, between his legs. She says over his crying,

"You never know these days. If you've seen what I've seen, you wouldn't say that."

When Nicola enters the room, he is upset he can't calm Dante. He looks over to the guard who stands by the door where he entered, and the guard nods at him. "It's okay, come to Papa," he says, and he throws his handcuffed arms over Dante's head and brings him to his chest. "My boy...my boy. Introduce me to your baby sister," he says, and Dante wipes his tears by rubbing his face into his father's shoulder.

Nicola's eyes glaze over when he sees his daughter. He looks at her in wonder. "Her hair is like mine. So much like me."

A knot hardens in Rosina's throat. "*I...I... know.*" she cannot speak for a moment. And some way, somehow, this particular guard allows them to all embrace one another. Rosina will never forget the familiar warmth, and yet the awkwardness of their embrace. *The invisible iron bars between them.* One of her arms wraps around Nicola, the other holds the baby, and Dante, caught in the middle of Nicola's handcuffs, is the only one who isn't crying. Minutes later, Rosina digs in her handbag for the small truck she brought along for Dante to play with and gives it to him. In no time, he amuses himself by rolling the truck towards Nicola.

"What is today?" Nicola asks as he pushes the truck towards Dante.

"Tuesday."

"No, the date."

Remembering the children who came to her door in costumes only yesterday afternoon, she says, "November 1st."

He shakes his head. "*La Festa di Ognissanti*, All Saints Day. All over Italy, they're celebrating."

"But we never celebrated," Rosina says.

"Maybe we should have."

"What do you mean?"

"Maybe, if we were believers, I wouldn't be here." He stares at his hands in his lap, "This can be a punishment. *Possibile*."

He doesn't mean this. Ines in her arms, she is worn and tired. It shouldn't be this way.

He mumbles under his breath.

"What?" she asks.

"*Niente. Niente,*" he turns in his chair, and in an unexpected, strange gesture, he sits up straight and smiles at the guard. She is surprised by the self-absorption she is witnessing.

"They moved me to another cell because the hinge on my door needs to be replaced. I'm basically in wire cage now. The guy next to me never stops talking. He's *Calabrese,* Domenic Carbonari. I don't trust him. He claims to be an anarchist."

Lowering his voice to a whisper, he says, "He keeps asking me where, where can he get some dynamite? When he gets out, he wants to blow up some buildings, people. *Pazzo,*" he taps his forefinger on his temple, "*completamente pazzo*, he's crazy."

"*Si,*" Rosina says, "don't trust him. I want to tell you about our boarder. It turned out she was...."

"*Lo so g'ia,*" Aldo told me. We can't trust anyone, not anymore." He rubs his thumbs together vigorously.

This is a betrayal. Why can't she have a private conversation with her husband? Desperate for any kind of intimacy, she needs to share the outrage, the indignation that took hold when she found out about Letty Wheeler. She is tired of trying to be positive, where is her consolation? No one else could possibly know what she's been going through!

Clutching his stomach, Nicola bends over in pain.

"What's wrong?"

"*Mi fa male lo stomaco.* Maybe I see a doctor."

30

The first time Rosina meets Elizabeth Glendower Evans, Luca introduces her as they step into her parlor. "No...no...she says, "Call me Auntie Bee. That's what I'm known as."

A tall, stoic grayed hair woman with small, delicate features, she wears a light blue tailored summer suit that compliments the gray in her eyes and a silk scarf draped around her neck. In Italian, she would be looked upon as *armoniosa* because of her harmonious look. Aldo had informed Rosina that in addition to financial support, Mrs. Evans is involved with the defense committee, bolstering their cause with Boston elites. He said, "She's a socially prominent champion of the underdog, besides being a journalist. We're so lucky to have her interest."

Since visiting Nicola in jail, she has also become a friend. Moving for the duration of the trial to her friend's home, the Justice Louis Brandeis of the Supreme Court. Brandeis is a liberal judge who sympathizes with the men and isn't afraid to make it known. The defense fund had counted on Brandeis' support, but now with all the publicity, he was forced to recuse himself.

"We are so disappointed about the Judge," Rosina tells Auntie Bee, as she pours tea.

"Let's not worry about that," Auntie Bee says, "Many powerful groups are backing us."

Rosina tries to numb herself to the up and down rollercoaster emotions she faces daily. She is happy to have met Auntie Bee, especially since Susan had to go home to Maine to care for her aging father. There is no way of knowing when Susan will be able to return. Frustrated and angry—the obligation before her, Susan had banged her fist on the table. "Of all the times now, when the trial begins."

Rosina felt her heart drop to her stomach, as though she were being abandoned—the never-ending flow of loss consuming her. Even so, she could only reassure Susan, "It's okay. Your father needs you now."

"God. What the fuck will I do there all day? I hate being a nurse. I'm not good at it. My aunt said it was my duty. Duty...crap. If I were a man, would it be my duty?"

They both knew the answer.

On the concrete steps of the courthouse, they wait for Nicola and Bartolo to arrive on foot from the jailhouse. Auntie Bee takes Rosina's elbow and guides her to a spot in the shade. The gawkers have already lined up...they too wait.

"Here they come," Auntie Bee says as they turn the corner. Suits, ties, and hats, even in this heat. Nicola and Bartolo are handcuffed to policemen and to each other. Surrounded by six or seven officers of the court, it gives the appearance of a parade. Rosina shakes her head at the irony. The gathered crowd begins to roar as they watch the men approach. They repeatedly clamor: "Justice for Sacco and Vanzetti! Justice for Sacco and Vanzetti!"

The men reach the steps and she and Nicola are eye to eye. He blows her a kiss. Rosina gasps with deep sadness. Auntie Bee puts her arm around her and says, "Come, dear, let's go in and sit." The care she offers makes her weepy, but she can no longer cry.

* * *

A heatwave struck the town of Dedham.

Three weeks into the trial, and each time she enters the courtroom, she hyperventilates, takes deep breathes over and over. The more air she tries to take in, the more panic rises in her. *Stay calm. Dante, and Ines. they need you. If you fall apart, they'll have no one. The children. Think of the children.*

An absurd stillness fills the courtroom. The only movement is the juror's fanning themselves. One massive fan oscillates over the sea of men's white shirts in the jury box, while another smaller one is set for the comfort of Judge Thayer. Rosina's angst towards this judge grows stronger each day. His smug expression. The stories she's heard about him. His overt favoritism to the white Anglo-Saxon men in the room.

When they're allowed to seat themselves back down, Auntie Bee whispers, "That Thayer is mad at the whole world. The latest leak is that the Judge, while in his 'private club,' bragged, *Did you see what I did to those anarchist bastards the other day?*"

Aldo, the committee, and their attorney had twice failed to remove the judge; there was no proof of his bias. Each time Rosina sees their attorney, Fred Moore, there is something about him, his appearance, or is it his choice of words that seem to harm the men. His long gray-haired ponytail and relaxed, informal Californian way of dressing get under the Judge's skin. Aldo said he heard Judge Thayer, while in his chambers, called him a communist: "A long-haired anarchist from the west coast."

"We have nearly one hundred witnesses who will vouch for Nicola and Bartolo's character," Rosina whispers into Auntie Bee's ear. "All will say they are good, hard-working men who care for others," she sighs, "I am writing their names in my notebook to thank them. *Yes, certo che lo sono, of* course they are, *she* repeats. Peaceful, loving men who have done good deeds for others." She needs to stay with these thoughts.

Auntie Bee makes her feel like a child the way she taps her hand says, "I know, dear. I know."

Seated in the steaming courtroom, witnessing Nicola boxed in an iron cage, hearing Auntie Bee's approval or disapproval in the background, Rosina struggles to keep positive. How lucky she is to have Margaret, a young friend of Auntie Bee's, who took the children swimming for the day. She tries desperately to focus on the children.

Judge Thayer asks, "Is the prosecution ready to present their case?" Thayer is like a very old man. Small built, white hair—partially balding, with a pointed goatee that reminds her of the convent goat, Louisa, who was half-blind. She may have laughed at such an image any other time, but this man is too dangerous to take lightly.

Fred Katzmann, the district attorney, says: "Yes, your honor, I first want to read a statement to the jurors.

The judge nods.

"The Commonwealth assents to the request," he reads, "of both of the defendants that all evidence heretofore offered in the course of this trial to the effect that either or both of said defendants bore the reputation of being peaceful, law-abiding citizens be stricken from the record...and ...entirely disregarded by the jury, so that as a result ...there is no evidence before the jury that either, or both of said defendants bore the reputation of being a peaceful and law-abiding citizen."

Aldo, the defense committee, and the entire courtroom roar in protest. Judge Thayer bangs his gavel over and over. "Quiet. I said, quiet. Or I'll clear the courtroom. If you I-talians want to stay in my court, you keep your mouths shut."

Fred Moore, is the only one seated in the courtroom, ruffling through papers. "Bastards. Why isn't Moore objecting?" Rosina turns to Auntie Bee, "that is such a bias statement. Is he allowed to say that?"

"We need a new attorney," Auntie Bee says.

"Yes, someone who will fight for my man," she says, "he doesn't fucking care what happens to them."

A long procession of witnesses for the prosecution follows. A hat was found near the body of one of the victims who was shot, and they said it was Nicola's. Nicola offers to try it on, and when he does, the courtroom breaks out in laughter. The hat is too small, too dirty, and stands up on top of his head. Another witness, Mary Splaine, a bookkeeper who works at Slater & Morrill, was on the second floor of the building where the murder and robbery took place. Through the grime of a closed window, she says she saw Nicola in the getaway car. "He stood up in the back of the car with his left hand on the front seat. He was slightly taller than I am, maybe weighed 145 pounds. He was muscular, a good-looking man, hair brushed back—clean-cut face with a high forehead. His hand was very wide and strong."

Fred Moore asks, "And you saw all of this from a dirty, greased filled window from the factory's second floor?" This is one of the times Judge Thayer does not reprimand him for speaking up.

Katzmann, the district attorney, consistently manages to bring up the fact that the men are anarchists, and when Moore objects, the Judge tells the court stenographer to strike it from the record. "The fact that they are anarchists shows their true character," Judge Thayer says. The battle between Moore and the Judge is constant.

During lunch break, the committee usually gathers on the courthouse steps, but the heat brings them to a tiny-grassed area in the back of the building. Aldo and Luca talk about the gun and the ballistic expert who is in charge of the investigation.

"He's convinced Nicola and Bartolo could not have committed the crime. He said it was clearly the work of professional criminals. We have to get him to take the stand after the DA is done. I'm preparing to get him on our list." Aldo says.

Rosina takes a deep breath. "I'm going back to see if I can talk with Nicola before the session begins."

As she starts to walk away, Luca calls to her, "Rosina, *un momento*. Can I come by on Saturday? I have a present for Dante?"

Before she has a chance to respond, Aldo approaches them. "I spoke with Nicola before court, Moore is definitely out. We've all had it with him. Nicola wants him fired." Aldo wipes the sweat from his forehead with a crumpled handkerchief.

The stifling air blows wisps of her hair onto her forehead. Her dress sticks to her back, and her underarms are soaked with perspiration. Can the men pick up her fetid odor? An odor born of fright, *la paura,* the wet air weighs on her.

* * *

On Saturday, Dante is a menace. Digging holes outside, right in the house's pathway to the front door. Not coming in when Rosina calls him for lunch. Rosina settles Ines in the highchair with pieces of corn flakes on the tray. She goes outside and takes Dante by his arm. "Inside now," she demands, and she drags him. Once inside, he runs at top speed to the bathroom and locks the door behind him. "Good," she shouts, "wash up." After ten minutes, Rosina bangs at the locked door. "Come out now, or I won't allow you play with Jimmy tomorrow." She waits, then hears the latch fall against the door, and when she opens it, he's sitting on the toilet—hands still filled with dirt. "Wash up," she says. "I made your favorite. *Fagioli.*"

"I don't want to eat," he frowns.

"Dante, why? Why are you like this today?" she kneels before him and feels his forehead for fever. He pushes her away. Ines begins to fuss in the highchair.

"Let me put bambina down for a nap, and you and I will have a talk, okay? Maybe if you hurry up, we can play a game. *Va bene?*"

He frowns. Rosina hands him the soap. "I'll be right back. Wash up."

Rosina is beginning to doubt her ability to raise children without Nicola. More than a year since Nicola was arrested. Fourteen months in jail, and finally, the trial has begun. Dante now eight years old. *I know nothing about being a boy.*

"Come," she says, "Let's talk. Just you and me." She is surprised he follows her into the kitchen without protest.

She sits on the kitchen chair and pulls him into her arms. He smells of earth and sweat and his hair, like wet dough. She combs back his mane with her hand. Head shaped hair parted, so like his fathers. "What is wrong, *ragazzo mio?*

He starts to cry. Rosina knows what's wrong. She too, begins to cry. "I, we, wanted so much to protect you, *amore.*" His tears wet her neck, "Please forgive us. Papa and I wanted to give you a better life than we had, so we stayed here, in America. We wanted you not to struggle. Now, I must tell you. Your father and I, we are people who don't believe in the government. The government is only for the rich, the powerful people. We fight for the poor, for the working class. Do you understand, Dante?" She takes a cloth napkin from the table and wipes his eyes and her own. "Papa is not what they say he is. He is a good man. He would never rob or hurt another person. Now, we must fight, really fight hard to save your father, to bring him home."

"Papa's hands are tie-tied together with iron rings." He breaks into heavy sobs. Has she done wrong by bringing him to the jailhouse?

"*No,*" she shouts, answering her own question. "*Figlio mio,* this is what they do. We live in a world that is not always fair. Good people sometimes get hurt. Bad people sometimes get away with doing wrong. You *must* learn this, Dante. You must learn that this *world is hard.* These people with power want to crush us. Aldo, Susan, Auntie Bee, and all our friends know this. That's why they fight for us."

There is a knock on the screen door. Rosina wipes her eyes with the napkin, kisses Dante on the forehead, who no longer is crying, but now looks a little fuzzy. "*Mangia,*" she says.

On the porch, Luca holds a giant white rabbit. The rabbit's ears lay horizontally and flutter like wings. "I hope this is okay. Dante told me he loved rabbits."

Dante comes running up, behind his mother, he clings to her dress.

"Where will he live? We don't know how to care for a rabbit," she says.

"You won't have to do anything. I'll show Dante."

"Come in," she says. *Thinking she doesn't need anything else to care for* and then feels guilty when she sees Dante's eyes light up.

"Allow me to get the cage. Dante, do you want to hold her?"

Dante's smile spreads across his face.

Luca hands the rabbit to him. "Be gentle, her bones are very tiny."

Dante holds the bunny close to his chest. He already loves her. "The cage is in the truck. *Un momento.*"

In the parlor, Luca kneels on the floor next to Dante and begins to teach him about the habits and care of rabbits. His deep voice, masculine yet gentle, brings a curious comfort to Rosina. "Here," he pulls something from a large sack he has brought along. "You must brush her at least every 2 or 3 days." He hands Dante a small brush.

"Can I put him down?" Dante asks.

"Yes, of course. It's a female, a girl."

The bunny begins to hop. Dante laughs excitedly, drops the brush, then quickly reaches for the rabbit once more. The bunny cowers against the wall in fear.

"Okay, Dante. When you want to pick her up, you must prepare her. First, pet her, like this." Luca runs his rough hand lightly along the rabbit's head and back. "Let her know she's safe, and then when she's calmed and no longer trembling, you slowly pick her up. Reach under her belly, like this." He demonstrates. "And never pull her by her ears."

He smiles up at Rosina. His heavily hooded eyes fix on her for a moment. She finds herself smiling at him—bemused and relieved by how natural this all seems. After setting up a cardboard box for the bunny to play in, and depositing hay, carrots and dark green lettuce in the cage, and while Dante is totally absorbed, they sit at the kitchen table.

"You have no idea how well-timed your visit is," Rosina says as she pours coffee into Luca's cup.

"I promised Nicola I'd look out for the boy. Besides, rabbits are lots of fun. Back home, we had a farm. Won't tell you how many of them ended up on the dinner table." His exuberant laugh seems to explode in the room. Tears of gratitude want to escape, but Rosina's tired the complicated emotions—shifting, settling in her brain like fog. She fears the kind of scars that change the soul. But there is Dante's smile, and she dissolves into it, letting herself be safely encapsulated in the moment.

"I can't thank you enough," she says.

"*Niente. Non é niente.* You have family here, Rosina. We're all doing our part." He scratches his day-old beard. "Oh, yes. I have a note here from Auntie Bee." He takes a cigarette from his pack and looks around for an ashtray. "Now, where did I put that letter?"

A summer storm is brewing. Thunder rolls in the distance, bringing Dante to her lap.

After searching his vest pockets, Luca finds the letter tucked into his inner shirt pocket. Hints of garlic and basil rise from the paper as she unfolds it, and she smiles to herself. So typical of a man who lives alone. She unfolds the note.

> *Dearest Rosina,*
>
> *My dear friend, Ann, Judge Brandeis's wife, and I had a talk about your daily trip to the courthouse and how difficult it is for you.*
>
> *She has offered to give you and the children two bedrooms in her house, as they're not here during the summer months. You and I will be able to go to the courthouse together.*
>
> *This is an excellent plan. You would benefit greatly by the move. We can arrange to put all your belongings in storage, and you'll save money for rent. Margaret can still babysit the children when you want to visit Nicola, and when we go to the courthouse.*
>
> *The trial looks like it will be a lot longer than we originally thought.*
> *—A.B.*

"I never expected this," Rosina says. "Do you know about her offer?"

"What is it, Mama?"

"*Dopo*, later. Dante, go see how your bunny is."

"Good idea. No?" Luca's face lights up with certainty. "You should leave here."

She is surprised by his frankness, yet once again feels cocooned by his concern.

"I don't know. I'll have to think."

Dante comes running into the kitchen. "Mama, I'm going to name my bunny Tootsie."

"Tootsie?" she cracks a smile, "Now how do you know such a name?"

Dante looks down at his shoes and smiles, timidly, "And Mama, you forgot to mention Mr. Luca. He fights for us, too." Then rushes back to Tootsie.

31

Rosina had never seen a home with such rich décor. The Brandeis home has a wide carpeted staircase which rises up from the center hall, leading to the bedroom where she and the children and Tootsie stay. The marble countertop in the bathroom, gold baroque framed mirrors over the double sink, and heavy velvet sea-green drapes keep the room dark so one can sleep late. The bedroom they stay in is three times the size of her parlor back at Mr. Kelley's farm. Gluttony and greed had always made her uncomfortable, but now she's wondering, is it also her own sense of unworthiness? These feelings aside, she decides to permit herself the luxury and hide her views from Auntie Bee. She doesn't want to seem ungrateful, after all, they were sharing their abundance of wealth with her: could she have asked for a more convenient way to get to the courthouse to visit with Nicola?

Each morning Auntie Bee has her car pick them up in the circular driveway and drives them twenty minutes to the court. The children have taken to Margaret, Auntie Bee's young friend. Beholden to these women, she will cook something for them, sew a dress or suit for them as soon as all this madness is over. Sitting in the back seat next to Auntie Bee in her high collared lace blouse and her finely textured skirt, she contemplates what could she possibly make for a woman who has so much?

Auntie Bee reads the newspaper in the car, as she does each morning. Today, their new lawyer, William Thompson, will be taking over the trial. He is a local lawyer who is much respected in the community.

"My, my, my," she says, and begins to read out loud. "Judge Thayer was once again overheard in his clubhouse saying, 'I'll fix those anarchists bastards. Those *wops* are going to hang for this. And that long-haired anarchist from the west, this will be his last job.'"

Rosina says, "Let me see that." She recognizes the reporter's name; he is at the trial each day. She had learned to trust his words. "Such an evil, evil, evil man. He'll be sorry for this, wait until he sees Thompson," she says. "I'd like to hear him call *him* a communist!"

"You have to understand," Auntie Bee says, "Thayer is not part of the old-world Boston aristocrats, who have loads of political and economic power..." as she speaks, she places her hand over Rosina's, who is suddenly alerted to the softness of auntie Bee's skin. "...he's constantly trying to prove that he's better than them." Removing her hand, she goes on, "Aw, the poor man comes to the bench tarnished and hostile," she says sarcastically.

Rosina closes her eyes and wants to sleep. She wishes the courthouse was miles and miles to go. Luca was right, the rabbit likes to play all night. She heard her chomping away on the hay and hopping about, the cage door jangling at every turn.

It's been twelve months since she's shared her bed with Nicola. One year of waiting for the trial to begin. It is like coming out of a darkened room onto a stark-bright stage, dissected, cut open for all to see. Hearing white, Anglo-Saxon witnesses say they saw Nicola and Bartolo during the murder and robbery, placing them at the crime scene. She can feel their hands around her neck, choking her. Even though some witnesses had stumbled, revealed themselves as liars, it didn't seem to matter. They were held as pristine citizens of Massachusetts, who were just doing their duty, while the District Attorney, Katzmann, kept pounding away about the men fleeing to Mexico. About their unpatriotic duty to the flag.

"Hear ye! Hear ye! God save the Commonwealth of Massachusetts." Judge Thayer snakes his way towards his bench. He looks around the courtroom. Thompson, already standing, nods to him. He pretends not to notice their new lawyer and says what he says each morning before court begins: "We should be reminded of our heroic veterans of Massachusetts who went to war for us... who keep our country safe. Not like the men who ran to Mexico."

Auntie Bee shakes her head in her dignified, condescending fashion. The light, mauve feathers on her straw hat, mirror her movements. "Do you have my binoculars?"

Rosina opens her purse and retrieves the binoculars.

Auntie Bee's own purse is large, more of a satchel, filled with her notes and papers for the magazine she writes for.

"My eyesight is getting on in years," she says.

A week of conflicting testimony against Nicola and Bartolo, and today there would be more. The defense had a hundred Italian witnesses take the stand to substantiate both men's character. Their last witness was to take the stand today. Their new lawyer, Thompson, was looking forward to her testimony. She was an eyewitness he had met with previously, showing her photos of the men, she said they were not the fellows she saw that awful day.

A petite woman dressed in a black straw hat and a black dress with white polka dots and ruffled trim takes the stand. Her name is recorded as Lola Andrews. She states, "Me and my friend, we're out looking for work, and we had just left Slater and Morrill and wanted to go to Rice and Hutchins because we heard they may have jobs." She is chewing tobacco or gum because her mouth keeps moving even when she stops talking.

"Go on, Mrs. Andrews," Thompson says.

"We don't know the way, but we see this shiny black car, maybe a Buick. Two men standing with the hood open looking inside. So, I stopped and asked if they knew where Rice and Hutchins was."

"Do you see those men here in the courtroom?"

Thayer bangs his gavel, and looks towards Auntie Bee and shouts, "Put those binoculars down. This is not a circus."

Everyone's heads turn towards them. There is a burst of muffled laughter in the courtroom. Auntie Bee smiles at him, and whispers to Rosina, "That's exactly what this is."

Thompson continues, "Let me ask you again, Mrs. Andrews, do you see those men here in the courtroom?"

"Yes, I do, yes sir. Right there in the cage. I know for sure one of them, the one on the right," she says, pointing to Nicola. "I remember him because he was so good looking."

Mumbling and movement from the committee echoes in the courtroom. Thompson is wholly puzzled, "You know...?"

Shouts from Nicola interrupt him. "I? Me?" Nicola jumps from the seat in the cage, his pointer finger poking at his face, "I am that man? You lie, take a look!" the guard reaches between the bars and shoves Nicola back down.

The gallery is now in an uproar. Judge Thayer bangs the gavel on its plate over and over.

Thompson's face is fuming red. "Your honor, may we have a ten-minute recess?"

"If you must," Thayer says. As he steps down from his bench, Rosina catches the familiar, cynical grin spread across the judge's face.

Thompson gathers the committee at the end of the court corridor. "She outfoxed us, fooled us. I'll fix this lying bitch. She'll be on the stand til she tells the truth." Reaching for his pocket, Thompson grabs his handkerchief shakes it open and wipes the sweat from his red face.

"Someone got to her. Puttana!" Aldo says.

"This is the woman who said she never saw Nicola and Bartolo before?" Rosina's voice cracks. "This is the woman who we hoped would release them from this nightmare?"

For a moment, everyone seems stunned, blinded by a new reality. Here she was in a coterie of close friends, yet each day she seems to take a step back, peeling away from them slowly. How could they truly understand what she and Nicola are going through? And Bartolo. At times she witnesses their laughter, the way they go about their "other" business. Their lives are not falling apart, not really. Can she blame them? Even she doesn't want to be here—but it is much too late. "*Quella puttana del cazzo*" slips from her lips. The men stare at her. They never heard her curse. "Don't look at me like that," she says with anger. "There's a lot more where that came from."

"Great, that's what we want. We need to be on fire," Luca says, with an approving smile.

"What we *need* is that man from the passport office. He's our only hope," Rosina says.

The hot, wet air follows Rosina back down the corridor. A glimpse of a black and white polka-dotted dress swaying towards the women's bathroom hurries her steps. Once inside the bathroom, Rosina turns the lock on the door. Lola Andrews appears very thin with big joints. Her large hands, bony knuckles, holds a mirrored compact. She smooths powder over her nose.

"Why are you lying about my husband? You know it wasn't my husband."

Lola Andrews takes a moment to close her powder case. She slips it back into her purse and faces Rosina.

"Oh, you are so pretty up close. You have amazingly large, round eyes. You should use kohl around them, you'd be twice as attractive."

Rosina is numb, dumbfounded taking a moment to understand what this woman is saying.

"Why? Why are you lying about seeing my husband that day?"

"I'm just doing my job. There is the law, you know."

"Do you have children?" she appeals to this woman who seems almost inebriated.

"Oh, kids, they take up a lot of time." She's again looking at herself in the mirror, pressing her thumb and forefinger to remove the caked lipstick that gathered in the corner of lips.

Rosina wants to claw at her with her bare hands. She grabs hold of the woman's shoulders, surprised by her large sharp bones. She shakes her. "You are destroying my family," she growls.

The woman pulls away from Rosina's grip. "It's not my fault," the woman hisses. "I see what I see. It's our duty to not lie. Do you want me to stand up and swear—then lie—and then have me go to prison?" She peers at Rosina, her eyes dark and glossy. Someone is urgently banging at the bathroom door.

"That's my husband," Rosina says. "He's a good man."

The woman softens. "It'll be okay," she says. She tries to pat Rosina on the shoulder as she goes to open the door, but Rosina backs away enough that Lola Andrews ends up patting the air.

"There's something wrong with her," Rosina tells the group. "She's...she's what is the word? *Mitomane?* A compulsive liar. Anything I said, didn't matter. Can't we prove she's lying?"

Thompson says, "I'm going to twist her around in that chair until she reveals herself, that's the best we can do for now."

32

Nicola is sick. Thanks to a few sympathetic prison guards, Rosina is allowed to visit him in his cell. Many of the guards are taken by Nicola's attitude and gentile nature, except for the one big red-haired Irish man. A quick, visual sweep of the colorless cell crawls over her skin as she enters. A smell of urine seems fused into the humid cement block walls.

"I've been dreaming of the dead. *Mia madre, mio fratello*, they bring me comfort, yet their expressions, so strange, in last night's dream." He faces the wall, doesn't want to look at her. "Sleep once was peaceful, *sereno*, well earned through my hard labor. But now there is no work, no sleep; and the judge's gavel wakes me every half hour." Rosina tries to get him to sit up, but he pushes her hand away. Feverish, he is not really there in the cell with her. She is alone.

* * *

When Rosina goes to sleep in the big bed that night, Dante is already asleep on one side, and Ines is next to him. She moves Ines to the middle. She falls asleep to the sound of her children breathing.

Rosina's dream is out of the ordinary; uncanny. She is on the ceiling of Nicola's cell, watching him: *He touches the cool stone wall of his cell and waits for his hand to absorb enough dampness to wipe it along his brow, his thinning neck. The heat, a prison cell of its own. He hears whispers: "Don't cry. You've cried enough. Basta. Basta." Is this the sound of his voice? In the darkness, he searches under his yellowed, flat pillow for the sacred heart medal Mr. Kelley gave him. He was embarrassed to refuse it for fear of hurting his feelings, and now he was embarrassed to let anyone see him with it. Yet, the night dense with searing desperation, he clutches the medal in his hand, rolls his fingers over the outer ridge of the tin heart, but cannot bring himself to talk to God. God has become the real enemy, whereas before, he was merely a fable. He cries out: think...think of it, amore mio. The days before the children, when love was new. Where, are you, Rosina? he moans.* At the sound of her name, her eyes pop open, and Ines is pulling at her nightgown to nurse.

* * *

When they arrive back at the home of Justice Brandeis each day after court, the white rocking chairs on the porch, with their floral cushions, invite Rosina to take a moment. Behind her, blue shutters from ceiling to floor hug the sides of the massive bubble-glass windows. Inside, sounds of innocence play through the screen door; Dante with his sister, her rolling belly-laughter at his silly peek-a-boos.

Rosina closes her eyes for a moment. She wants to drown her existence in the boring details of washing and ironing clothes, sewing, and cooking for the children. Reading a book. Books. How can she concentrate on reading? The only thing she can focus on is the newspapers—stories written about her husband and Bartolomeo. Lately she has found herself elated by the mass protests that have broken out in New York City, Chicago, and all over Europe. She sees the headlines: THE POOR SHOEMAKER AND POOR FISHMONGER NEED YOUR HELP.

Aldo and the committee have done a tremendous job exposing the broken system of bias against Italians. The hatred of immigrants who don't speak or look like Judge Thayer or the jurors. They came to the "free" country only to be persecuted, to be "locked up." The irony of it all lives inside of her day after day.

* * *

The ancient branches of wisteria, nodular and gnarled, are still able to produce drooping clusters of purple flowers zigzag against the side of the porch. Rosina's thoughts flee to the convent, those moments she helped the nuns pick the saffron from the flowers: it was always before dawn. They would rush to get to the gold red, the *oro rosso in* the dark.

"*Fate presto!* Hurry," Sister Cristina would chant, "before the petals wake up."

In the dark of the morning, they'd gather in the field to select the purple-silvery buds, and then later, back in the kitchen cellar; they'd gently pick the red pistils from the center of each flower and place them into wire baskets to be dried. Delicate, thin, crimson threads of saffron; the glorious *oro rosso,* brought much-needed lira to the Sisters.

Rosina's buttery vision is broken by the squeak of the porch-screen door.

Auntie Bee says, "You have a letter. From Europe."

Rosina takes the thin envelope, recognizing the Italian air mail postage stamps and her family name, Zambelli, on the back of the envelope. The paper, sheer cellophane, she gently tears it open. A round piece of felt with a rough-cut scalloped edging with a safety pin on its back, falls onto her lap. Glued to the center of the material she recognizes the image of Saint Agrippina, protector of all things.

Cara Rosina,

> *The news here is hard to read for your mother and me. To see photographs of Nicola and that other man in the newspapers is strange and upsetting.*
>
> *We don't believe your husband would do such a thing, even though I didn't like him. There are so many groups across Italia that believe in him. They say America is not a good justice system, but we pray they are wrong.*
>
> *Your mother and I go to church each morning and pray and hope that you've gone back to church and realize that we are nothing without the help of God. Tell Nicola to pray also. God cannot help him if he doesn't believe in Him.*

I've enclosed St. Michael, the Archangel for Nicola. Pin it to his undershirt when you see him. Your mother said she's making one for you, a particular saint, and will mail it. Please send us news about how you are getting along.

We are worried.

Con tutto il nostro amore,
Papa

She holds the pinned Saint Agrippina in her palm. *How little you know, Papa. Your sacred saint is not St. Michael after all.* She hastily takes the letter in both hands, twists the brooch in the center, that crumbles it all into a ball, and throws it into the kitchen waste can.

* * *

Two weeks later, Lola Andrews takes the stand. No longer in her polka-dot dress, she wears a deep purple satin rayon chemise which reminds Rosina of the purple fabric draped over the mirrors when her grandmother died. After three days of questioning, she is confused, no longer bubbly and pert. Andrew's ex-landlady is a witness and says Lola Andrews cannot be trusted. "She's known to lie. Not a truthful person," the friend she was with that day, says, "I don't remember us stopping to talk to any men." And then, it happens. Lola Andrews begins to babble. "They wouldn't leave me alone..." she breaks down, "they wanted me to recognize the men...to say I saw them there that day."

"Who?" Thompson presses.

"I don't know. Someone from the government."

"How much did they pay you to lie?"

The courtroom erupts with loud voices. The menacing gavel strikes and then the warning to clear the room.

Auntie Bee excitedly grips Rosina's forearm. "The link has been exposed," she says, "clear, and sharp."

Rosina makes eye contact with Nicola, and suddenly remembers what relief feels like. It seems to flow between them. Her ribcage opens; her breath like the flutter of a bird's wing in her chest. Hope lives again.

Nicola winks at her. For a moment, she flashes to him lying in bed, next to her, pulling the covers over them.

Mio Dio, he seems to be saying, with his eyes. *My God, this will be done. Finito.*

"Finished," she says, out loud, and blows a kiss to Nicola.

Outside, on the courthouse's steps, Thompson says, "We'll be wrapping up our defense on Monday. I have a written deposition from the fellow at the passport office who remembers Nicola being there. Also, we have all the corroborating witnesses who saw Nicola that day. We should be home free."

Lola Andrews was the prosecution's eyewitness, and now that she's a discredited witness, there is no choice but to allow Nicola's freedom. It is the first time in months that Rosina senses herself unwinding, and that night after waking to nurse the baby she is able to go right back to sleep.

* * *

Saturday. Rosina decides to make dinner for Auntie Bee, Aldo, and Luca. It has been so long since she's been in a mood to celebrate, not even after Ines was born. And now, surprisingly, in this unfamiliar setting, she isn't ill-at-ease. Once Rosina locates the kitchen tools, and the pots and pans, she finds cooking in a modern kitchen eases her labor. Early that morning, she prepares the *zabaione,* taking over twenty minutes to beat the egg yolks with the sugar, and finally adding the Marsala wine, then places the desert into six blue-glass goblets, and lastly into the deeply varnished oak icebox. Thankful that the iceman had arrived early that day, for the more chilled the *zabaione,* the better it will taste.

It will be a small group having a small celebration. Hope trickles over her the way the olive oil trickles over the eggplant crostini. The day is too hot to turn on the gas oven, so she tends to the chicken cacciatore on the stovetop, worried that a store-bought chicken will not taste as fresh.

Dante is excited about having company, especially Luca. Rosina finds herself smiling. Luca has managed to enter Dante's world with what seems like very little effort.

Auntie Bee's house slippers slap the wooden floor in the hall. She inhales deeply, "What smells so delectable?" She is still in her velvet embossed bathrobe.

"Margarite should be back soon," Auntie Bee says.

"*Bene.* I'll wait for Dante to help me set the table. He always wants to help when he knows we're getting company." As soon as Rosina says this, she feels guilty. Does she have the right to be so contented? Is she forgetting who and where she is?

"No…no, deary, I'm here, let me do it," Auntie Bee says, taking note of the cluttered cooktop.

"My, my, someone has been busy." Her remark pleases Rosina; yet when Auntie Bee quickly scans the kitchen, and sees the mess she's made while cooking, Rosina says, "Don't worry, I'll be sure to put everything back where it belongs."

Auntie Bee laughs, "Well I'm glad you know where they go, because I surely don't."

Once the table is set, Auntie Bee says, "I'm going upstairs to finish my column. This one is solely dedicated to our boy."

She knows Auntie Bee's way is only a term of affection. If someone else called Nicola a "boy," Rosina would find it belittling; after all, this was her man. Her husband, her lover. He was more "man" than most.

"You have time. Four o'clock we'll be ready to eat," Rosina says.

Auntie Bee goes to the cupboard, grabs a handful of shortbread cookies, places them in her robe pocket, and then takes up her cold cup of tea, that had been sitting out for an hour.

"Toodle-loo," she says.

Toot-a-loo, Rosina chuckles to herself, amused by the phrase.

Turning the chicken pieces in the sauce she thinks of Susan; how she'd want to be part of this tiny celebration. Remembering what Susan wrote in her last letter:

> *I'm interviewing nurses to be with Pops. I must get out of here, at least two days a week. I would love to go to Cambridge. Maybe we could meet there? I hear the police are still burning books.*
>
> *Our infamous Attorney General, Mitchell Palmer, continues to fill the streets with propaganda. The Red Conspiracy. The Communists will take your children. They'll kill you when you're asleep. Before you know it, he'll say we're going to eat their babies.*

What do you think, maybe we could go to Cambridge to put out some fires?

When she got the letter, Rosina was annoyed and upset by Susan's thoughtlessness. How could she possibly go to Cambridge, how could she go anywhere? Two children to care for, having to be in court every day. Her being so "out of touch" was deeply offensive. Yet now, several days later, slightly altered by good news, it no longer seems like such a far-fetched idea. She had forgotten what it is to actually live a life. *La vita è dolce*, she smiles to herself.

When the doorbell chimes, she rests the wooden spoon in the dish and goes to open the door.

Luca is freshly shaven. When he enters, she picks up his familiar scent of soap, or was it *Acqua di Parma colonia*?

"*Buonasera, Rosina. Mi sono fermato dal macellaio.*" He hands her a package wrapped in brown butcher paper. "I wanted to get this to you so you could put it in the icebox. With this heat, it will go bad in no time."

"You didn't have to bring anything." The door is still ajar. "Please come in."

"It's so quiet. Where's Dante? And the little one," he asks. He seems refreshed almost sparkling.

"The children are still out with Margarite. I expect them any minute. Actually, I thought you were them." Remembering the last time, when they were alone, she tries not to look into his eyes. The meat in the paper is thick and ropey. "*Salsiccia?*" she asks.

"Yes, both sweet and hot."

"*Grazie mille.*" She gestures towards the kitchen stool for him to sit and puts the sausage in the icebox.

"*Non è niente,*" he says.

Luca sits on the stool, his legs spread, one on the floor, the other hinged on the spoke. She watches longer than she should. How curious to see how a man sits, his legs boldly apart, so self-assured; for a moment, she is overcome by his masculinity. How long had it been since she witnessed this kind of confidence that once came so naturally to Nicola?

Luca places a small paper bag on the kitchen counter. "I bought something for the children."

"You are spoiling them," she smiles, still not wanting to look into his eyes. "Can I get you a drink? Auntie Bee is upstairs finishing her column."

"Do you have any *frizzante?*" he asks.

"I made some this morning."

Rosina siphons the sparkling water into a glass and hands it to him.

He quickly raises the glass, "*salute.*" And gulps it down in one shot.

Rosina prepares a salad of lettuce, her back towards Luca. "It's so hot outside," she says, as she tears the leaves into the salad bowl. His eyes are on her, and she is filled with a strange kind of heat.

"I want to say something to you, Rosina."

When he speaks her name, it seems alive with intimacy. A yearning of sorts? Or is this her own desperate need to be coddled?

"Oh…" she says.

"Before the others come." His voice is low, guttural. "Can you turn around?"

She nods, breathes deeply, and turns to look at him. Leaning over the slab of butcher block, he is closer to her. The pomade he uses on his hair doesn't keep all his waves in place, a tiny section, like stray feathers, skates over the right side of his forehead.

"I'm happy, glad that Nicola will be coming home. He doesn't deserve to be in prison. He's a good, honest man. And as you know I've been committed to seeing him home with you and the children."

"Yes, thank you, Luca. Of course, you are." She knows he's not done, so she continues to look at his mechanic hands, dark stains of grease under his short-clipped fingernails, and shamefully imagines them grasping, parting her.

"I Just want to say that Nicola is the luckiest man alive to have you as his wife. I realize that sounds like a dumb thing to say because of him being falsely accused and spending a year in prison, but if you ever need anything, anything at all, know that I'll come to you." He reaches out, brushes her cheek lightly with the back of his hand. There is a ruckus at the front door. Ines is crying for something Dante has taken from her. For a fraction of that second, she looks into Luca's eyes.

Aldo arrives a half-hour late, smelling of cigarettes but neatly dressed in his crisp white shirt and black slacks. "I've brought a guest, I hope you don't mind, Rosina. This is Felice Guadagni."

Rosina knows he is the editor of a newspaper but cannot remember the name of the paper. He was with Nicola the day of the murder and robbery. He offers his hand. "It's a pleasure to meet you Mrs. Sacco."

Another place setting at the table and they begin their meal. Rosina suggests the children sit with Margaret in the kitchen area, knowing the conversation will not be for Dante's ears.

"But can Luca sit with us?" Dante questions.

Luca places his hand on Dante's head and tousles his hair the same way Nicola does. "Later. I promise, we'll play together."

The conversation didn't take long to turn to witnesses that had been lined up for Monday's court day. "I've given Thompson all the witnesses names and he's corroborated their statements. We have Nicola's eye-witnesses from seven o'clock in the morning, when Dom Ricci saw him at the Stoughton railroad station," Aldo says, twirling the spaghetti into his tablespoon.

"And I ran into him in the North End about eleven-thirty outside of Boni's restaurant, and we had lunch together there," Guadagni says. "I left him around two o'clock. So, he's pretty well covered."

"I have a long list of Bartolo's alibis also. He was nowhere near the incident. He was selling his fish over in Plymouth," Aldo adds.

"Unfortunately, they are all Italians," Auntie Bee says, looking at Felice Guadagni, "Including you. Thayer keeps saying we can't trust Italians. Before I forget, Aldo and Felice, can you join me in the parlor after dinner? I'd like to go over some of my column with you. It's going out for print in the *New Republic* in the Monday morning edition."

Rosina hears Ines calling, "Mama...Mama...Mama."

Aldo wipes his mouth with the cloth napkin, "Of course, but can you trust us? We may throw you to the wolves," he jokes and everyone laughs.

"*Scusatemi,*" Rosina stands, "I'll leave all you editors to battle it out."

Dante comes running into the dining room, clasping his new metal cowboy and Indian figures. "Mama, Ines wants you."

"I'm going, *caro,*" she says.

Dante taps the cowboy at Luca's shoulder, "Can you play with me now...please."

"In a minute. I'm almost done eating," he tells Dante. Moments later, he wipes his mouth and takes his last slug of wine and says, "Wish I could help you guys. But you'll be okay. I have a job to get done. Looks like a tough one, too."

In the butler's pantry, Rosina sits in a chair she fetched from the kitchen. Ines's dark brown eyes with their thick lashes, gaze up at her; a look of innocent love that only a baby can convey. She emits soothing, calm even breaths as she nurses. Her chubby hand with its deep wrist folds pats Rosina's chest and breast. The muddled voices in the dining room bring back the days when she and Nicola had meetings at their home. She closes her eyes, pretends she is back at Kelley's farm and for a moment she is untroubled, carried off by waves of the past.

33

Rosina returns to her company, who have settled in the parlor. They toss compliments at her. "The meal was superb," Auntie Bee says, "I've never had eggplant before. Was afraid to try it. It was marvelous."

Felice adds, "Could I please have your chicken recipe for my wife? It was amazing."

"Oh, you're married. I just assumed you weren't," Rosina says. "It seems that all the men, most of our compatriots, are single. Now, why is that, Aldo?" she lowers herself into a club chair, and the swoosh of the soft cushion sighs beneath her.

Just then, Luca steps down into the parlor, his arm around Dante's shoulder. "Mama, we have something to show you," he says.

Dante looks up at him with a smile, "Go ahead," Luca says.

He rushes to his mother, tells her to open her hand, and when she does, he deposits a smooth, shiny, tooth into her palm. For a moment, they both marvel at the sight of his first baby tooth. "I shall keep it forever," Rosina says, hugging Dante. "Now, go put it in a cup, and I will find a safe place for it later."

Auntie Bee says, "Dante, don't forget to put it under your pillow for the tooth fairy."

For a moment, Dante looks at his mother bewildered, "Silly," he says, there is no tooth fairy." He chuckles.

"Why do you say that?" Auntie Bee asks, surprised.

"Mama told me," he says, and rushes out to the kitchen to find a cup to rest his tooth in.

Luca looks around for a place to sit and settles into a club chair across from Auntie Bee. "So, what have we interrupted?" he says, lighting up a cigarette.

Aldo with his quick wit, "Luca, now that you're here, you answer Rosina's question. Why aren't we married?"

"What? You want to marry me?" he smirks.

These light-hearted moments Rosina had ceased to remember.

Auntie Bee says, "Okay, my children, it's getting late, let me read what I've got so far. I don't want a lawsuit." She reads:

> Tomorrow, the State of Massachusetts will learn of the jurors' decision whether or not to find Nicola Sacco and Bart Vanzetti guilty of murder and robbery. The $15,000.00 or so that was robbed was never found. Witnesses claimed there were five men present when the incident occurred.
>
> No one has questioned who or sought the whereabouts of these other men. Both Sacco and Vanzetti have no criminal records, and there were eyewitnesses that put them elsewhere when the crime was committed. There were witnesses for the prosecution who proved to be false; committing perjury but not being charged.
>
> This trial has been tarnished and biased from its inception. Judge Webster Thayer told the jurors at the onset of this trial: Although these men (Sacco & Vanzetti) may not have committed the crime attributed to them, they are nonetheless culpable because they are the enemy of our existing institutions. I am aware the jurors will not have access to my writings, but the rest of the world may.
>
> They must know that these men are innocent of such crimes. Yes, they are guilty, but only of being

socialist. Of wanting to spread the wealth of our land to the poor, of trying to help the working man obtain better working conditions, better living conditions.

These are not the kind of men that steal and murder for the payroll of the working poor. I pray that Nicola Sacco and Bart Vanzetti will have a fair and unprejudiced trial, such as is guaranteed by the Constitution of the United States of America.

Auntie Bee lowers the papers onto her lap.

A mountain of gratitude lifts Rosina from her chair, "*Brava, brava. Grazie, grazie.*" There is a desire to hug Auntie Bee, and when she does, a hint of her gardenia soap drifts to her nostrils.

"*Semplicemente perfetto,*" the men say, almost in unison.

"Nothing to worry over," Aldo tells Auntie Bee. "*Allora,* I still have much to do. I'm off and running, like a racehorse."

His remark prompts everyone to stand and prepare to leave. "One thing," Rosina says to Auntie Bee.

"Yes, deary."

"Can you please use Bartolomeo instead of Bart? He deserves to have his full name recorded."

* * *

Having put the finishing touches on her dress, Rosina worries she may appear out of place. She's captivated by the bright color, *Copenhagen blue.* Lakes and canals come to mind. The Adriatic sea and sky—*the colore la libertà.* Her own unspoken symbol of freedom.

She arrives at the jail early so she can speak with Nicola before court commences. Nicola, ready for the day, is awkward in his baggy suit; even the tie seems too long. His hair is combed back neatly. She only now notices the shirt collar gaping from his shrinking neck. His cuffed hands lean on the table, and he looks at her with surprise. "*Sei così bella.*" He brightens, "You are my blue morning glory—a true sign of merriment."

Merriment? Rosina thinks, *where did that come from?* She runs her hand along the three-quartered sleeve fabric as if she only now recognizes it. "Nicola, remember the curtains we bought at the Salvation Army, and you had asked what I will do with them, because at that time, we only had one small window?"

"*'Si, si.*" He says, but she knows he's not listening. "I'm so happy this is coming to an end. I need to get out of here. I need to work." When she touches his hands, besides being sweaty, they are smooth, so soft that she must look down at them to be sure they are his. Where are the rough calloused fingers? She looks at her own yellowish pointer finger, the one that guides the needle pass the material, hardened like the outer skin of popped corn.

"I cannot sit another week or month in this place being so idle. I know I will die. So, whatever happens today, it almost doesn't matter. Either way I'll work, I'll do something."

"We must be positive, *Caro.* I feel so strong they will know you are innocent."

He nods to her words. "How are my children?"

"They are good. Dante is waiting for you to be home."

Again, not listening, he says, "Thompson was with me last night. We had a long talk, and I told him I'm taking the stand today."

It takes Rosina a moment to understand. "Why? Why would you do that?"

"I must speak the truth. They will know after I tell them, they will know we are innocent."

Rosina pictures him on the stand, his commitment to *the cause.* She cringes.

"No, they won't. Please, Nicola," she urges, "Just let the lawyer and the witnesses speak. You're going to tell the truth about our ideals? That's nonsense."

"They will know after I speak." He says more sternly.

"What will they know? That we're against the system? You can't, Nicola. They will never understand."

He pulls his hands away from her in a rough manner. "I must."

She is overcome with dread and starts to rattle off some of the witnesses' names and stops when she reaches Barbara Liscomb. "Nicola," she pleads, "this woman was looking out of the second-floor window of the factory. She's testifying that neither one of you are the men she saw that day. She's positive. She says she will never forget the face of the killer because after he fired his pistol, he looked right up at her window and pointed his gun at her."

"I know, I know all that, *questo è fantastico*. But this is our chance to open the eyes of the people. To let them see how government is controlling them."

"I no longer care about people. I just want you and our family to be safe."

"Please, Rosina, understand I will never have such a platform again. They can't hang us for being anarchists," he snickers, "*Dov'è la mia donna forte?*"

"*Donna forte*? Your woman is no longer strong. Just tired. Tired of this fight. I just want it to end peacefully."

"It will, *amore mio*. It will."

"How does Bartolo feel about this? You could be jeopardizing his case also."

"*Sta bene, bene*," he dismisses.

"I just want you to come home. That's all, my love. Nothing more." She swallows hard against the lump that has been in her throat for months.

The guard calls, "It's time Nick. We have to go."

They both stand, and Nicola looks at the guard for approval to hug his wife.

"Yeah, go on," the guard waves.

Although Nicola's body has shrunk, he still possesses an eagerness, that unrelenting mysterious aura surrounds him, alive, *even now*.

His arms around her, she whispers, "*Buona fortuna, mio caro.*"

"No luck is needed. *Truth* is our window, and Thompson is a good ol' Harvard man. Massachusetts loves him. He's part of the Mayflower family. Did you know that?" He half-smiles, his lips touch her ear. "*Ti amo amore mio.*"

She adjusts the brim of her hat. "I still say your father must've been a mule."

Standing in the middle of the courtroom, William Thompson is a far more imposing conservative figure than Fred Moore was. A tall, confident man with a barrel chest and a voice that is precise and measured.

"We should've had him at the beginning," Auntie Bee says. Harvard Club, Harvard Law School, vice president of the Boston Bar Association, all the labels that Judge Thayer could never touch."

An uncanny stillness pervades in the courtroom, yet the whir of the fans over her own brain chatter makes the courtroom seem noisy.

Thompson says, "If it pleases the court, your honor, I have before me a written deposition from *Giuseppe Andrower,* the former passport clerk at the Italian consulate in Boston, who was with Nicola Sacco during the hours of when the crimes of murder and robbery were committed. Because of illness, he was forced to return to Italy, where he now lives. We offered to pay his fare here, but he's too ill to travel."

Judge Thayer can be heard ruffling with his robe.

Thompson continues. "If it pleases the court?"

Thayer nods, yes. "Go on," he says impatiently.

Thompson walks in front of the Juror's box and begins to read. "Mr. Andrower states,

'I remember Mr. Sacco showing me a large family photograph. I told him it was too big, and he needed to return with a smaller one if he wanted to get their passports. It was around 2:00 o'clock on April 15th. I remember the time and the date because I just returned from my lunch break where I had to go and mail my tax return. I had gotten a one month extension to file my taxes.'"

Thompson moves to hand the court clerk the document. "This document was notarized and signed by two witnesses."

"Now I call the journalist and educator, Felice Guadagni."

Judge Thayer mocks, *"Journalist? Educator?"*

"Yes, your honor. He is a fine citizen of Massachusetts." He refuses to allow Thayer to get under his skin.

Thayer waves him off, "Go on. Go on, I don't need your added remarks."

Felice Guadagni takes the stand and states: "I ran into Nicola around 11:30 outside of Boni's restaurant on April 15th, and we ended up having lunch together. While there, we also saw and talked with *Albert Bosco,* a newspaper editor, and *John William,* his ad manager, who were also having lunch at Boni's. I know they will also testify if necessary." Felice twirls the tip of his mustache.

When Felice steps down, Thompson says, "Now I'd like to call Carlos Affe to the witness stand.

Carlos Affe is a small man with a receding hairline and a massive forehead. Rosina had never been to his grocery store, but Nicola always spoke of what a kind person he was.

"Mr. Affe," Thompson says," Tell us why you're here today."

"I'm an Italian grocer. My store is very popular in the Northa Enda."

The judge mumbles under his breath.

"How do you know the defendant, Nicola Sacco?"

"He's been-a buying my products for a long-a time-a."

"And on April 15th, did Mr. Sacco come into your store?"

"Sure, he did. Nic...I mean-a Mr. Sacco come-a into my store-r around 3:30 or 4 PM to pay-a his bill for the groceries he buys. He pay-a me every two-a week. He give-a me $15.50." Affe holds up a paid receipt.

"What was that money for? Thompson asks.

Reading from the receipt still in his hand, he says, "For-a-pasta, salami, cheese-a, olive oil, lard-a, whatever he bought-a."

Fred Katzmann examines the paid receipt and says, "The court should note that there is no date on this receipt."

"Who dates a grocery receipt?" Auntie bee's voice wavers.

Watching Carlos Affe walk from the witness stand, Rosina writes his name in her small notebook. When this is over, she will take the children and go with Nicola to his grocery store. She wants to live a larger life, to do more with her husband. A downpour of summer rain suddenly pounds against the roof and the windows of the courthouse. Rosina smells the rain through the opened court room windows, and a puzzling memory breaks through: her mother has her by the hand, they're walking through a fog, or is it a light sprinkle of rain? her mother presses her fingers together so tightly that it hurts. Dragging, lifting her off the cobblestone pavement to keep up with her own urgent steps. She remembers her mother's face, the tears running down her cheeks.

"I thought she never cried," Rosina says out loud.

"Are you okay?" Auntie bee grasps her hand and offers her handkerchief. Rosina is baffled by the laced-edged offering, but realizes her cheeks are wet. She takes it into the palm of her hand and dabs at the wetness.

33

Word has spread that Nicola is going to take the stand. In the afternoon, the courtroom is thick with encouraging comrades chanting, *la verità verrà fuori!* Truth will be spoken.

The air is buzzing with excitement and burning tension. Judge Thayer shouts over his persistent banging of the gavel. "Everyone sit down and be quiet or you'll all be thrown out."

The courtroom is packed with journalists. Auntie Bee points out another Elizabeth sitting next to Aldo. Elizabeth Gurley Flynn.

"Oh yes, she's the woman who visits Nicola."

"She's such a vibrant young woman. From New York, she's the lover of Carlo Tresca," she says, her voice cracking, halting from an onset of what appears to be laryngitis that began last evening. "She is known as the 'Rebel girl.' Next to her is Alice Stone Blackwell, she's a dear friend who helped to organize the suffrage movement." Auntie Bee smiles and nods at her across the room. "Elizabeth helped to start the Industrial Workers of the World, along with Eugene Deb and Tresca. We're in great company." Auntie Bee squeezes Rosina's knee-a sign of motherly care.

Silence befalls the courtroom as Nicola walks to the witness box.

District Attorney, Frederick Katzmann, is always dressed to perfection. Now in his pin-striped navy-blue suit with vest and maroon tie, he approaches the witness stand. "Good afternoon, Mr. Sacco."

"Good afternoon, sir."

Si' amore, be polite, Rosina thinks.

"Tell me, Mr. Sacco, do you love this country?"

Nicola rubs his chin, "I can't say."

"You can't say?" He looks at the jurors. "I want you to tell the jury if you loved this country in May of 1917."

"I will answer that later, when I can explain."

"All you need is a yes or a no. Which is it?"

"Answer the question," Judge Thayer says.

"Your honor, I want to explain how I feel about this question."

"Did you run away to Mexico?" Katzmann shouts, facing the jury.

"Si. No. I did not *run* to Mexico. I went to Mexico."

Low laughter in the back of the courtroom. The gavel strikes twice.

Rosina tries to catch Nicola's gaze, to signal him to not be "smart," but his eyes are still directed at the jurors.

Katzmann says, "So, we now know. You do *not* love this country. This is how you showed your love for this country by running to Mexico."

Thompson objects, "Your honor, this questioning about Mexico has nothing to do with this trial."

"I'm trying to show the character of the witness, your honor."

Katzmann continues, "Mr. Sacco, don't you understand that going away from your country is a vulgar thing when your country needs you and is at war?"

Rosina watches him, knows Nicola's body language. He sits taller in his seat, "I do not believe in war," he says.

"You do not believe in war?"

"Yes, sir."

"So, you don't believe it was cowardly of you to run?"

"No, sir. I was brave."

"Brave?" he asks, as though it were the most absurd thing he's heard.

"So, you came back to this country. Is it because of your love of money or was it to prove your bravery?"

"I don't love money."

Katzmann turns his back to Nicola and addresses the jurors, "You're the first person I met that doesn't love money." There is more laughter.

Thompson keeps interrupting, but the court ignores his pleas.

"Money never satisfied me. Just for food, clothes. What we need to survive and have a good life."

"So, you came back to the United States of America for the "good life" for money.

"No. For my wife and son. For my better job that I love."

"You love your job, and don't love this country?"

"I love this country because my home is here. My work. A man is nothing without his work."

"Well, Mr. Sacco that is honorable. So, Mexico did not give you what America does."

"More opportunity here."

"So, it is money that you really love."

"Opportunity is not about money. It's about satisfaction. And inner tranquility."

"Tranquility?" Katzmann laughs.

"Why is that funny?" Nicola's face heats up. "You're not happy with your work?"

Again, laughter erupts in the back of the courtroom. Judge Thayer says, "Okay, this is my last warning. If this happens again, you're all out."

"Your honor, may I approach the bench?" Thompson says.

Rosina, unaware she had been biting the inside of her cheek, tastes the smooth, sticky blood on her tongue.

Thompson argues that this line of questioning has nothing whatsoever to do with the murder and robbery that the men are being accused of.

Luca and Aldo, and the rest of the committee sit across the room from Rosina, apparently able to pick up some of Thompson's words; they nod their heads in approval. Auntie Bee, whose laryngitis seems worse, coughs, and shakes her head in disapproval.

Fred Katzmann begins again, "So you don't love this country, you don't love money, but you love your work. Mister Sacco, do you love your wife and child?"

Thompson erupts, "Your honor, I once again object to this waste of time, this line of questioning...."

Nicola interrupts him, face red, he shouts. Rosina can tell he wants to hurl himself at this man. "Of course, I love my wife and my children."

"So how could you leave them knowing our country was at war?"

"The war, Mr. Katzmann, was not here in Massachusetts."

The judge ignores the low hum of giggles that resonates from the back of the room.

"Good for him," Auntie Bee speaks in a scratchy, deep baritone.

Earlier that morning, Auntie Bee had applied a menthol rub to her chest—or was it a mustard paste? Now the irritating aroma catches in Rosina's throat, blocking the air to her lungs, making the bureaucratic walls around her feel more like the cage where the men sit.

Thayer, the law lord, in his black robe, sits upon his throne, clawing at his thin, gray goatee, while the rest live in fear of rules. Rules made for the lackeys of society. *Why* she thinks, *why couldn't we be plain? Not be driven by such a need to claim the truth of what we saw before our eyes. The Lawrence textile strike, the molasses massacre, the propaganda and hate we witnessed day after day. To be driven by such idealism made us happy, a purpose for good, yet now it seems we have squandered our happiness, and it may well destroy us.*

The molasses massacre. Nicola had been part of the rescue committee, and the day after the explosion of the mammoth tank, he had come home with his pants and shoes laden with the sticky substance. The fifty-foot tank was situated in the North End of Boston, near the freight yard where the Italian children tended to play. Only a small group of laborers knew of the poor construction of the tank and the ongoing leaks. Leaks large enough that children would fill their pots with molasses and bring them home. When the workers complained about the defect, the company fixed it by covering up the holes with paint. Painting the entire tank deep brown, the exact color of the molasses. A few weeks before the explosion, Nicola and a few others tried to speak to the authorities about the leaks and were told to mind their own business. Days later, after informing Eugene Deb's newly formed organization, IWW, the tank exploded, and thirty-foot waves of molasses carried workers in the freight yard and children playing nearby to their death. A week later, Rosina went along with Nicola. It was a shockingly grisly scene: Crushed buildings; the elevated railway was on the ground; automobiles, trucks, and dead horses lined the streets. It took many days to complete the rescue efforts and many months to clear the debris.

The sound of the gavel hitting the wooden block brings Rosina back to the oppressive heat in the courtroom. The movement of hot air from the fans brings little relief. The jurors ask for permission to remove their suit jackets, and Judge Thayer reluctantly allows it.

"So why Mr. Sacco did you lie when you were arrested?"

"Lie?"

"When asked by the Police Chief if you were an anarchist, you lied and said 'no'."

"Is that why I am here? Am I being tried because I am a socialist?"

Murmurs and low groans of protest muffle through the courtroom.

"Answer the question," the judge demands.

"We were never told why we were arrested." He looks at the judge. "I, we, lied because we know you are against our ideas. You do not believe as we do." Nicola then turns around to look at Bartolomeo, and Bartolo nods his head in agreement.

Rosina realizes at this moment she has developed a kind of kindred love for Bartolo. His heart is open and *puro*, more than anyone else she's ever met. *Puro*. It's as though he were a saint. There is something so peaceful about him, something she wishes she could somehow sew into her own fabric, in addition to Nicola's sometimes fiery character.

"We will allow the court to hear about your beliefs. This is important for your defense," Katzmann says.

Judge Thayer bangs the gavel. "When we return. The court will take a half-hour break."

Everyone rushes to be outside. The double doors into the hallway are eight feet wide, with spectators funneling to get out. Nicola and Bartolo are removed from the courtroom and taken to a cooler area in the basement where they would be allowed to remove their jackets. Rosina waits with Auntie Bee for the crowd to disperse. The image of Nicola and Bartolo sitting together talking, brings a flash of calm. Alice Blackwell and Elizabeth Gurley Flynn make their way towards her and auntie Bee. A brief introduction and Auntie Bee and Alice Blackwell are well on their way to exchanging memories.

Elizabeth extends her hand to Rosina and holds onto it longer than Rosina is accustomed. "*Buongiorna, Signora,*" she says, "Your husband is a very courageous man to speak up for the cause." Her hand is soft and smooth, a woman who doesn't cook or sew or have children. Rosina smiles at her, yet a bit uncomfortable by what seems like near perfection. Her skirt is a shorter length, and the heels on her shoes, are noticeably higher. Even her voice seems graced, as though her vocal cords were dipped in the nectar of sweet figs.

"This case has drawn lots of positive attention, people are listening." Elizabeth says with a smile. She has deep brown, thick wavy hair, parted off-center and piled loosely with a few combs. Her youth surprises

Rosina. "The prosecution hasn't even mentioned the murder or robbery! We can see where this is going." She speaks quickly, like Aldo.

"I don't know if you know but I've visited Nicola. He is a fine, gentle person. He showed me his hands, and said, 'These hands, shoemaker's hands, they're made for labor, for working. Not for killing or robbing. My philosophy on life would never allow me to kill another man or rob a worker's payroll.'"

Rosina nods her head in acknowledgement.

Elizabeth continues, "He knows who he is and faces the reality of why he and Bartolomeo are here. *È un uomo buono*," she laughs, "Forgive me for practicing my Italian on you. Carlo has taught me. I hope I said it right."

Rosina sees Luca standing by the opened door, searching for her. "Yes, they are both very good men. You said it perfectly."

She cannot deal with this kind of perfection now when her own life is so fragile, so undone. The growing nightmare if they find Nicola guilty. The fear of where and how she will live. Will she have the strength to go on alone?

"Excuse me," Rosina says, feeling the sweat between her breasts and the back of her neck, "I must go to the restroom before court returns." She hurries towards the doors where Luca is standing.

35

In the corridor, the old marble floor and tin ceiling seem to cool the panic in her chest, or is it the way Luca calmly takes her by the elbow, *"Come stai oggi?"* He disperses over her like a cloud of tranquility; even the C scar, a mock half-moon at the corner of his eye, seems to glow. She responds, *"Nervosa. Molto nervosa,"* and quickly becomes aware of his body as he moves closer to her; now a narrow space between them, their breath is as if one. She ought to cry out, *don't, don't be like this with me,* but shamefully craves the attention, the care, and desire he radiates. A blunt distraction of these agonizing days.

"S'i, era previsto. Nervosa, it's expected," he says. His hand still on her elbow, ushers her to the far end of the corridor where the others are in conversation. She is surprised to see Gino, the weary pharmacist, the man with the starburst scar on his half-open eyelid, talking with Felice. *"Buona giornata, signora Sacco,"* he says, looking down at the floor; just as she remembered him in her kitchen. The men chatter on in the background. *If we're blessed, we're born without any scars,* she thinks, *but in time life mocks you, offers you a crust of bread, and if you innocently share it with the hungry, wild dog, you draw back a bloody hand, thus the first scar.*

"What do you think, Rosina?" Felice says, "Rosina?"

"Rosina?" Aldo calls to her.

"Sorry," she says, "*che cosa?*"

"What are your thoughts about Nicola taking the stand? Do you think it will make things worse or better?"

It takes her a moment to understand this absurd question. "It doesn't matter what any of us think or feel. Nicola is doing his best."

Only one door to the courtroom is open, forcing people to funnel into the room, pushing through with their elbows, rushing to get a seat up front. Auntie Bee, who had never left her seat, says, "It was so wonderful to speak with my old friend. I had forgotten how much fun we used to have together."

Rosina attempts a smile and sits next to her. "Your voice sounds better, less scratchy."

"Ahh...perhaps with all the talking, I lubricated it," she laughs. "I hear there are hundreds of people outside of the courthouse carrying signs. And just look how many reporters are here too, today." Auntie Bee pats Rosina's arm. "It's proof... this case is about social injustice, and not about robbery or murder."

Rosina, exhausted by the circulating heat, the buzz of the courtroom, and the anticipation of Nicola's statement racing through her. She tries to calm herself by envisioning Dante playing with Ines on the deep blue and gold pattern rug in their bedroom, but instead, she sees herself the day after the police pillaged their home, chopping ice from the block in the icebox: the ice pick in her hand, she was chipping away as small crystals fell into a glass, when something terrifying had gripped her. The sharp point of the pick and the sound it made, gashing, slashing; the more pressure she applied, the deeper the carving, the wider the deformity. The ice block, which had been smooth as glass, was absurdly butchered. It was only ice. Yet she looked at her hand, dropped the pick, and was crazed by something so illogical, so senseless, yet now, here in the courtroom, she identifies it as fear. Fear at its deepest level crawls over her. She reaches for the fatty part of her thigh that had become black and blue from her pinches. She cannot help herself; it has become her safe place to vanquish her from hell, and she pinches herself hard.

The guard unlocks the cage gate and Nicola steps down and calmly walks to the witness box. He stands proudly as the attendant swears him in. His words are strong, filled with conviction. He is in his element.

Having his soapbox, he no longer looks like that shrunken man she'd been visiting for more than a year.

"Dante had lost all his earthly possessions, including his wife and home."

The name Dante alarms her. It takes Rosina a moment to realize he's not speaking of their "Dante" but of the poet Dante Alighieri.

"It was six-hundred years ago when he was in political exile. He had to depend on the kindness of strangers."

"We are not here for history lessons, Mr. Sacco. Stop it, now," Judge Thayer growls.

"Your honor, I just wanted to make a point of how political differences…"

"No more about your so-called heroes or you're back in the cage."

Nicola's stares toward the cage and says, "I'd like to ask the court why when the law states, we are presumed innocent until proven guilty, then why are we held in those bars?" His finger points to where Bartolo is seated.

Thompson approaches Nicola, and whispers something to him, then states, "Now, Mr. Sacco, can you tell the court why on the night you were arrested with Mr. Vanzetti, you lied about being anarchists?"

"We lied because we didn't want to be deported. So many of our comrades were being deported without cause." He stops for a moment and looks at Thompson. "Can I…?"

"Yes, go on," Thompson says.

"Our only crime is our loyalty to labor. You call us communists. I don't know what a communist is! My dearest friend and comrade could explain much better than me. He is a gifted orator. But he doesn't want to speak." He looks over to Bartolo, and both their expressions seem woven into the same thoughts. "I want to tell the court of my," he again stops and looks over at Bartolo, "of our philosophy. I would like to begin back in Italy but know I cannot." Nicola sits taller in his seat. "I believe that men should be free."

A snickering sound comes from the bench.

Nicola turns to the jurors, "My English is not good, but I try. Men are born free, and yet as he grows, he grows into chains. In a free society, men have the chance to profess their ideas. In education, free speech, literature. Some of the best intelligent men are sent to prison to die there. One of the great men of this country is Eugene Debs and he is in prison now as we sit here because he is a socialist. He only wants the laboring class to have better conditions, to provide his son better conditions. But they put him in prison because the capitalist class are against us. They don't want our child to go to high school or to Harvard college. They don't want the working class educated, they want us to be low at all times, to be under their foot, not to have us think with our head.

"Society says the great men are the Rockefellers and the Morgans. They give fifty—no, five hundred thousand dollars to Harvard College, and maybe a million to another school. Everybody says, 'What a great man this Rockefeller is, the best in the country.' But I ask you, who gets the benefit of those dollars? Not the poor. If a man gets twenty-two dollars a week and has a family of four, his children will never go to Harvard or any college. He is lucky if his family eats.

"There is no education for the poor. I want all men to have the same chance. And it begins with their work. It is the Rockefellers, the people with money that buy this world. They decide about war. War is money in their pocket. They start it and the low class must go and kill for them. I love all people. I worked for Irish, Polish, German, many people and I love them all. What right do we have to kill each other? Government gives you the right! They tell you *who* and *when* to kill. So, isn't government the real enemy here? Shouldn't they be the ones on trial?"

Muffled approvals can be heard from the back of the courtroom.

"I want to destroy all guns."

"Okay, is this over?" Judge Thayer bangs his gavel.

"Yes, your Honor," Thompson says. "We request one more minute." He nods to Nicola to finish.

"I want to say so much more," Nicola continues, "but now I say, I'd like all lives to be with nature. Nature is here for all of us. We are all the same. We all want the same for ourselves and our families. We don't want or need man-made borders. Nature is what will make us free. Those of you here, my friends, in this courtroom, remember that even the poor are allowed the fragrance of the frangipani tree."

A hush of silence layers the air. *Like angels passing*, Rosina thinks. Then without warning, the heavy wooden doors to the courtroom burst open, and a scuttle of more reporters enter the room.

Judge Thayer shouts, "Guards, keep those doors closed. No one else is allowed in." He then turns to Mr. Thompson and says, "Why is your client still sitting there?"

"Your honor, Mr. Vanzetti has asked that Nicola Sacco read a short statement that he has written."

"Haven't we had enough?" he blurts out. His face heats up, even his scalp looks red.

"Your honor, I believe it's important to show the code these men live by, which will show that they could not have committed such crimes that they're being tried for."

"Mr. Katzmann? You have no objection?"

Katzmann stands, "I have no problem with this, your honor."

"Go on, go on," he says, pouring himself a glass of water and turning his back to the witness stand in one full swivel.

Mr. Thompson nods at Nicola.

"I read the words now of Bartolomeo Vanzetti," Nicola reads:

> I champion the weak, the poor, the oppressed, the simple and persecuted. I maintain that whosoever benefits or hurts one man, benefits or hurts all species. I fight for my liberty and the liberty of all, my happiness and the happiness of all. I want a roof for every family, bread for every mouth, education for every heart, and light for every intellect. I am convinced that human history has not yet begun. That we find ourselves in the last period of prehistoric times. I see with the eyes of my soul how the sky is diffused with the rays of this new millennium. I say this to allow you to know that my dear comrade, Nicola Sacco and myself, could never commit such a crime of murder and robbery. We both live by this code of honor.

Nicola rests the paper on his lap and looks around the courtroom. In that small, still, second, even though tears have sprung from his eyes, Rosina sees his radiant self. Auntie Bee lets out a cry and grasps Rosina's hand tightly. And the ruckus of applause and stamping of feet causes the walls of the courtroom to quiver. Judge Thayer bangs his gavel over and over, shouting, "Enough. Enough, I say."

In the moments it takes to quiet, there seems to be a sense of relief hovering over the crowd.

Once Nicola is back in the cage, Judge Thayer states, "Now that we're done with all the *flowery* language, has the prosecution rested its case?"

Mr. Katzmann walks in front of the jurors. "Yes, your honor."

He clears his throat. "Gentlemen of the jury, I ask you to do your duty. Stand together like men who fight for Massachusetts' honor, men who love their country. Do your duty."

Judge Thayer runs his hand through his thinning goatee. "Thank you, Mr. Katzmann, now I will speak to the Jurors." His chair squeaks louder than usual as he turns towards them. "As Mr. Katzmann has said, you men are model citizens of this country, and you must do your duty. Although these men may not have committed the crime attributed to them, they are nonetheless culpable because, as they have stated, they are enemies of our existing institutions."

Clamorous boos drown out Thayer's voice. The judge stands and shouts, "Guards, lead the jurors out. Court dismissed."

* * *

A long Baroque mirror leans on a carved easel near the foyer entrance at the Brandeis home. Positioned so one can see themselves, checking on one's appearance as they come and go. Auntie Bee says Mrs. Brandeis is an impeccable dresser. "If there is a door to go out of, be assured there will be a mirror there too."

Rosina hopes to one day have such a mirror in her own home. Easier to put your hat off and on when you can see it. Placing her hat on the hook, she notices a letter addressed to her on the small mahogany table. A notecard from Susan. On the front of the card is a drawing of a goldfinch perched on a tiny branch. Inside, just a few lines:

> *You and Nicola are in my thoughts every day.*
> *I've written to him and Bartolomeo. My father has*
> *become more dependent on me. I've met a man. He is*
> *a new neighbor. He drew the bird on this card.*
> *More later.*
>
> *Love,*
> *Susan*

Margarite comes through the front door with the children. Dante runs to his mother. Margarite keeps his hair combed back smoothly. His face brightens when he sees his mother. "Is Papa coming home today?"

She picks up Ines, who is sucking on her finger and draws the thumb from her mouth. "We don't know yet, sweetheart, but soon, I hope."

"Mama, what a beautiful dress." He runs his hand near her waist, "it's so soft, too." She puts her arm around Dante's shoulder and squeezes him towards her. She glances at their reflection in the mirror; the aura surrounding the three of them stuns her, *how, how can they be so beautiful, yet so exhaustively tormented.*

* * *

Margarite knocks at the bedroom door in the late afternoon. The call has come to return to court. Rosina had fallen asleep with the children on the bed. When she sees Margarite, small, slight of build, both shy and energetic at the same time, Rosina says, "Thank you, Margarite. Thank you for everything. You've made so much possible for me by being here."

Margarite says in her soft tone, "I love the children. They are so much fun."

Smoothing her hands over the bodice and sleeves of her dress, Rosina says, "Let's hope after today we can go home, and they'll be out of your hair."

Downstairs, Auntie Bee walks into the foyer just as Rosina is putting on her hat. In the mirror, she adjusts her hat and catches the puffiness of sleep around her eyes. It is six o'clock in the afternoon, and the sun is so jarringly fierce that when she bends to step onto the running board of the car, she becomes dizzy. Auntie Bee sucks on some medicinal lozenge, filling the vehicle with menthol. The odor, the heat, the bright sun, the butterflies in her stomach, all disorienting, her skin prickling with *I don't...I don't want to be here.*

Aldo, Felice, Luca, and all the other men are already seated in the courtroom. To her right, the other Elizabeth nods to her, while Alice and few other sympatico young women take seats next to them.

Fans blow humid air. Hats and newspapers wave, creating a breeze in a disorderly fashion. Additional armed guards are stationed outside and all around the courtroom. Nicola and Bartolo enter through the side door, looking wilted and deathly pale. Nicola doesn't look at her; his eyes are fixed on the floor, she is glad. This moment is not about their love or their eagerness to be together; it's a moment suspended in a world they never thought to be part of. When the jurors enter and take their seats, the tension escalates.

The court clerk calls, "All Stand. The Honorable Judge Thayer."

As was decided, Rosina and everyone in the committee, remembering the Judge's remarks earlier that morning, remain seated. She wishes for Nicola to look up to see their defiance.

At first Judge Thayer pretends not to notice, then waves them off in a dissenting fashion. He says, "Gentlemen of the jury, have you agreed upon your verdict?"

"We have, your honor."

Judge Thayer nods to the clerk.

The clerk stands and says, "Nicola Sacco, please rise and raise your right hand."

A low murmur. "*Qui,*" Nicola stands, raises his hand, but now looks directly at the Judge.

"What say you, Mr. Foreman? Is this prisoner guilty or not guilty?"

The foreman stands. Black suspenders over a white shirt, white hair, and pale-skinned with eyes the color of the Adriatic Sea. His hands shaking, he says, "We find this prisoner, Nicola Sacco, guilty."

Silence. No one moves. Bartolomeo stands and raises his right hand, and when the word "guilty" echo's once again, Bartolo's arm is frozen in place.

Judge Thayer states, "Gentlemen, of the jury, I again offer you thanks for the services you have rendered."

Then the crack of the gavel and Nicola's voice rings out, "*Sono innocente.* You kill two innocent men." His words cut into Rosina. She bursts from her seat, races towards him. Pushing aside a guard, she hurls herself into his arms. Her hat falls onto the floor as they grapple to hold one another. Rosina's sobs echo through the room, evoking the cries of mourning doves captured in the eaves of the clay convent roof. She knew their wail, a moaning hollowed-out sound that reaches inside the jurors, the spectators, and brings tears to William Thompson, who tries desperately to comfort her and Nicola. Her knees buckle, and she hears Nicola's words wet against her neck and face "*Ecco il nostro purgatorio,*" his words echoing the cries of the doves caught up in the steeple, *here, here is our purgatory.*

* * *

Rosina refills their suitcase later that evening. It's a moment of intense private stillness; the case open on a French chaise, her children asleep in the huge bed. She must leave in the morning to go back home. And as painful as it will be, she must work. This must be what mourning is. It is as though he is dead. She shakes the thought from her head. *Nicola is here. Still alive.*

Folding Ines's pink floral dress with its puffed sleeves, she regrets how Nicola has missed so much of the children. She had tried so hard not to cry in front of Dante, but he saw her eyes were all bloodshot and swollen. She managed to tell him there will be another trial. "An appeal," she said. Auntie Bee was there. It seemed no one wanted to leave her by herself. She had to fake sleep to be alone. She is tired of being polite and of conversations. She wants a room to scream in, to make the walls shatter. It was only when Dante replied, "Like the peel of the apple, Mama?" did she break down weeping, and Auntie Bee and Margarite had to explain what an appeal was. When she put him to sleep, he said, "Don't cry, Mama, we have the app-peals."

* * *

The next morning before leaving the Brandeis house, she is holding Ines in her arms. The child kicks against her bruised thigh. Auntie Bee is reading the newspapers and wants to say something but waits until Dante leaves for the car with Tootsie in his arms.

"Take a look at this, Rosina. The world is outraged by this conviction. France, Italy, Germany, there are protests everywhere."

She glances at the pages and what catches her eye is a description of herself in the courtroom.

> A streak of red hair surged towards the cage, bursting past startled guards; Mrs. Rosina Sacco flung herself at her husband, screaming out, "*Mio marito. You kill my man.*"

* * *

When the car drops them off at Kelley's farm, Rosina notices the garden; the wilted, lifeless stems have turned brown. She'd tried to keep Nicola's crops up, but now they're not suitable, not even for rabbit food. The house is stifling with its closed windows. The old hardwood floors and practically bare walls seem undesirable, inhospitable as if she'd never lived here before. Dante is happy to be in his room with Tootsie. He is busy looking and playing with the toys he'd missed. Moments later, Dante wants to go out and see Pinocchio. She places Ines in her highchair and gives her a biscotti and the rubber cow she always wants to chew on. After putting their clothes in the drawers and closets, she knows she must prepare something for the children to eat, but there seems to be so much grief inside her. *I was here without him for more than a year, so why now do I feel such a vacancy within these walls? Another stage? Lessons. What more could we learn?* Her thoughts ramble on to her mother in Italy, to her father, to their sacrosanct God, then back to what to give the children for dinner.

In the closet, she pulls her brown dress off the hanger and changes into it. Her blue dress on the bed, it is now a bad omen. She moves to the sewing room and reaches for a scissor, then goes back to the bedroom.

On her dresser, she sees Susan's card. Such a detailed drawing of a goldfinch and starts to cut around the edges of the bird. When done, she gently places the bird on top of her dresser as though it were something precious and reads the card once more, then tears it into pieces.

Moving to her bed, she lifts the bodice of the blue dress and begins to cut. The collar, sleeves, the part where her breast was is still warm. The long chemise skirt takes a while—she praises her decision to not have made a full skirt. *As if she had known.* She hears Ines babbling from her highchair. When Rosina is done and the blue pieces lay scattered at her feet, she takes the comb from her hair. There is a familiar tickle on her shoulders as she snip-snip-snips until the floor is covered in her tresses. From the kitchen comes Ines' shrieking call for attention.

36

Rosina finds it more and more difficult to visit Nicola. The fifty-minute drive to Norfolk County Jail and having to ask someone to watch the children, plus hours of work lost at the sewing machine, but mostly it's her heavy heart, the fear, and anticipation of not knowing how she'll find him. After three years and four rejected appeals, he is broken, and each visit seems to unearth a more damaged man than the time before.

The committee is inundated with letters of support from around the world. Some addressed to Rosina. She reluctantly accepts them and piles them in the woven basket in her bedroom. The letters are encouraging, yet they bring so many questions. Things she wants to forget, questions she cannot answer: *What happened to the stolen money? Who and where are the other three men who were there when the crime was committed? Why weren't they acquitted when witnesses, such as Lola Andrews, had signed an affidavit saying that police, and the assistant district attorney, had intimidated her into giving false testimony?* There are days that she cannot read them. Today is one of those days. She must hurry because Luca will be coming to take her to the jailhouse.

In her sewing room, the bridesmaid dress hangs on the back of the door. She had been musing about the convent lately; how serene it was.

That day the dried flowers in the tall vase had attached to Sister Cristina's habit. She had asked Rosina to gently peel them from her so as not to harm the buds, and the way she couldn't stop tee-heeing covering her mouth with her petite hand. Why had she wasted all that time, closing herself down, hating her parents for bringing her to such a forgiving environment. And now, the shade of blue-egg wash garment reminds her not only of the dress she had destroyed but also of the only painting hanging in the convent: an oil painting of the Virgin Mother's hooded blue cape with folds of varying blues. She had recently opened a used book of Italian painters Nicola had bought at the Salvation Army. There she found the same painting of a Botticelli that hung in the Mother Superior's room.

Rosina spends some evenings sitting together with Dante to teach him about his heritage, determined to inform him of their culture. To prove to him that Italians are not the lowest form of humans: *We are not guineas, wops, and dagos. Murderers or thieves. We are mostly good people.* She is looking forward to taking him to the Boston Museum of Fine Arts. They will go on a voyage together...dream and learn. Luca had already offered to take them, but she wants to be alone with her children. This much she can do. She will look for other books on architecture and science. She will teach him and Ines about the great men Galileo, Puccini, Michelangelo, about opera and Enrico Caruso and Arturo Toscanini. *Will she continue to have the strength?* Thoughts sink into her belly. These moments of weakness, of self-doubt consume her daily. She's already forgotten Leonardo DaVinci.

At the sewing machine are the beginnings of a bridal gown. Folds of white voile cascade over onto the sheeted floor. Just as she hears Ines running down the hall, she quickly closes the door behind her. Ines loves to go into the room to play with the material, especially the voiles and organza, their airy lightness layers just so over her head: the child marvels at her veiled existence. Earlier, she had found her sitting in the middle of the pile, softly giggling, playing hide-n-seek. Guarding the sewing room door, she catches and enfolds Ines in her arms, jiggles her into a chuckle. "Oh no, you don't. Carmela is coming to play with you."

Carmela is Rosina's newfound friend. She is the wife of Romeo, who came up with the idea of wearing armbands. He has become an integral part of the committee. Carmela, unable to have children, savors the time spent with Ines and Dante.

"Mama is going out for a while." Ines struggles to get down. Rosina manages to plant a quick kiss on her cheek as she slides from her arms, and at the same time, a knock at the door is heard.

Ines scurries to the door and, capriciously fickle, jumps into Carmela's arms, comfortably settling herself on her wide hip. Carmela has a broad open face with such transparent skin that she appears younger. She is also a large woman with ample proportions. She tells Rosina she fills her baron womb with pasta and pastries, "And now," she once said, her clear hazel eyes gleaming, "also, I fill up with your children."

Luca hands Rosina a batch of letters secured with a rubber band. On his right arm, she sees the word, *Sacco*. Such an odd peculiarity to see her name displayed this way!

"So, we already have the armbands? she asks.

Luca turns around slightly for her to see: *Free Sacco & Vanzetti*.

"Would you like to put one on?" he asks.

"Later," she says, "Let me get the *carciofi* I made for Nicola." She rushes to the icebox. She had stayed up late in the evening to cut the artichokes and stuff them with cheese and bread and garlic. He must eat. There was no money for prosciutto, but she hopes he will savor it as he used to do. Since last month's hunger strike, he still has not gained back any weight.

Before closing the front door, she calls out to Carmela, "Dante will be home from school the usual time."

In the automobile, Rosina strains her neck to watch the great flock of Canada geese flying in synchronous movement. She had read they mate for life. The car engine is so loud she cannot hear their honking, but she knows it's what they do, as well as she knows the touch of Luca's hand that searches across the cracked leather to grasp hers.

"Can you come and put a slide lock on the door to my sewing room? Ines wants to constantly go in and play with the spools of thread and the material."

"*Si*," he says, "I'll go to the hardware store and pick one up."

"*Grazie mille*," she sighs.

"No, *grazie mille. Piacere mio*. Always my pleasure."

She again murmurs a sigh.

"What is this heavy breath?" he asks.

"You help to make my life easier."

"I wish I really could," Luca says, tightening his grip on her hand.

Even with Luca's touch, she must prepare to conjure up good memories of her and Nicola. With each visit, she must remind Nicola and give him hope. Remind him that life could be the way it once was. And she reminded herself, too. Oh, the early days when he called himself Ferdinando; their first date at the restaurant. How they laughed about political prisoners, his brother and friends calling jail "the altar." The times he would sneak her into his boarding house. That first time they made love on his lumpy mattress. The early morning when Dante was born. All truths, even as they are frayed; dangling threads from the past that can no longer be mended.

Luca's voice rises over the loud pistons of the engine. "He probably won't eat the artichoke. He still isn't eating. Aldino is sending the doctor to see him. Nick is insisting someone is trying to poison him."

"I know," she says, "that's why I bring him food from the house."

Shivers run down Rosina's spine and arms every time she enters the jail. She is the only one in the waiting room. The guard has disappeared. Cold, steel table and benches. Concrete walls and floor. She had forgotten to take her shawl. Fifteen minutes pass before the guard returns. He holds onto Nicola, taking him by the arm. Nicola drags his feet, the chains around his ankles scratch persistently against the concrete floor to where she is seated. After all these years, she is allowed to touch him, to caress him if she chooses. When she puts her arms around him, he repels, thrusting his chest towards her, arching his back from her touch. "Oooh..." Nicola wails.

"What's wrong?" Rosina says

"Bites. The bugs!" He says, "They bite at night when I try to sleep."

"Bites?" Rosina's inquiring eyes look to the guard, but he's reading the newspaper.

"What kind of bugs are they?" she says, not really expecting an answer. "Let me see your back."

"It's the roaches. I know it's them." Nicola turns around, and she lifts the prison shirt to look at his back.

"Roaches are not known to bite," she says.

His back is smooth and clear of any blemishes except for what appears to be his own scratch marks. "I don't see anything," she says.

"Every time I close my eyes to sleep, they begin to gnaw at me. "Roaches, bedbugs." He trembles. "I'm afraid one will get into my ears. And my ears are already buzzing." He probes his finger in his ear.

Rosina opens the paper bag, feeble-mindedly she offers him the *carciofi*. "I made you your favorite."

He looks at the artichoke, but his eyes are glazed with something so foreign and uncanny, it prevents him from seeing what is before him.

"Someone is poisoning me. My legs become numb at night. At nighttime they knock at the walls, and sometimes I see them watching me. They want to make me crazy." He pushes the dish with the artichoke onto the floor. "Poison," his lips curl in disgust.

The guard who wasn't looking says, "What happened?"

"I'm sorry," Rosina says, kneeling to gather the broken dish and wipe up the breadcrumbs and garlic. "It slipped. Can I get a rag to clean it?"

Nicola sits with a vacant stare, and Rosina tries to comfort him by embracing him. "No more food," he says, pushing her off.

"*Amore mio*, you must eat, or you die. Please, for me and the children."

He struggles to release himself from her embrace, "Maybe it's your food that is poisoning me!"

The guard returns with a large, stained towel and hands it to Rosina. She once again kneels to clean up the floor. *This is not my man. Something so frightening, something worse than death, seems to be happening. How can he believe I would poison him?*

She must leave. She tells Nicola she will ask the authorities to find work for him. Appeals or not, there has to be some way to help him. She finishes wiping the breadcrumbs from her shoe, then waits for the guard to open the steel door. Nicola's elbows are on the table and his head in his hands. He looks up, and suddenly more coherent, he asks, "Who drove you here today?"

She can hardly look at him. "Romeo," she says.

<h1 style="text-align:center">37</h1>

Rosina hears Lucas struggling to loosen the lugs on the rusted pipes of the toilet bowl, occasionally cursing at it, *"rompicoglioni,"* he snaps. Lately, Ines has had the habit of throwing things into the toilet bowl and watching them swirl in the water until they disappear. This time it was Dante's tin whistle, and he screamed and cried at his sister, "I hate you, I hate you." Then Ines had begun to cry, not knowing what he meant, but whenever he cried, she also would. Luca berated him for saying he hated his sister and reminded him that she was blood, and blood was the most important thing. Dante ran off, saying, "You're not my father."

"You're not my father." A phrase Rosina had been hearing since she asked Luca to stop spoiling him.

Luca is stretched across the floor in the bathroom, twisting the pipe behind the toilet seat. "When can we turn the water back on?" she asks. Struggling to get the nut off, he turns his head to look up at her, *"Quel cazzo di dado,"* he curses.

"Thank you, Luca."

Wrestling with the bolt, he says, "Stop th-ank-ing me."

Rosina likes watching him work. His movements are rugged, sensual, the way his back expands, the muscles in his arms show themselves. And the sounds he makes. Moans, groans—perhaps sounds he would make when making love.

Last evening, before he left for home, he cornered her against the closed door. Kissing her neck and face, she felt him swollen and stiff against her stomach. A larger man than Nicola in all ways. Later in bed, she places her hand on her stomach where she felt him earlier and pushing aside the incessant guilt that grips her day after day, she knows the time for them to be together is near. These stirring moments, the arousal she feels, seems to be her only joy. Shamefully she looks forward to them—the only time she comes alive and remembers her own needs.

* * *

The letters from Susan are insistent, full of pleas for Rosina to respond. She knew Bartolomeo was corresponding with her, so Susan knew of the five failed motions for a new trial. Rosina had thought long and hard about why she was so angry with Susan and could only resolve it as her own shortcomings. Outrage deep in her core—misplaced and targeted at Susan had revealed itself over the last few months. After a year and a half of no communication with her friend, Rosina's resentment and jealousy was like an itch that came and went. *Yes*, she hungered for that open free life that Susan lived, a life she knew would never be hers. It wasn't Susan's fault, not anyone's fault. *You go where your blood takes you. We have no way to choose—imposed upon us and dictated while still cradled in the womb—there is no choice.*

The children are asleep. Rosina gets into bed. The blanket twists around her foot and as she unwinds it, a fleeting thought of Nicola spreading the blanket over them surfaces, but she leaves it as quickly as it came. With her legs crossed under her, and two pillows behind her back, the bed, since Nicola is gone, has become her own tiny fortress. Books, magazines, newspapers, and a small basket filled with pins and needles so she can do her hand finishing work on a garment before going to sleep are all scattered on the bed. Tonight, she brings paper and a fountain pen and begins to write.

Dear Susan,

> *Although I haven't answered your letters, as you*
> *might have wanted, I was happy to receive them. I*
> *know you keep up with all that is happening with*

Nicola and Bartolo in the newspapers, including the letters from Bartolo, but there is so much more.

Words have no meaning for what we've been through. (You know my English is not perfect, but sure you will understand me.) It's more than three weeks that Nicola is not eating. He is delirante, I don't know the word in English, but he is seeing and experiencing things that are not there. Three alienists examined him and found him in a ...she reads from the scrape paper on her nightstand...psychotic state.

One doctor argued it was because of starvation, while the others said he was mentally ill. Suffering from chronic paranoia. (I know these words because I asked them to write it down for me.) They believe he is incurable, and as you know, he was admitted into the Bridgewater Psychiatric Hospital for the Criminally Insane. Such an awful name for a hospital; the word psychiatric should be enough, but they had to add criminally insane.

Ahh...I have so much to say to you. I have been so moody, lunatic, crazy pazzo, we say. I knew Nicola should've never stood in court to speak, but he was so confident, so stubborn, he would prove his innocence. He kept telling me, "They will see my character, that I'm not capable of such crimes."

A week ago, our blessed Auntie Bee visited him, and he told her he heard my voice in the room next to them. He said, "They are convincing my wife to poison my food. They're using her to spy on me."

When I saw him last, he talked about un magnetismo—o una forza magnetica, strange physical feelings around his heart, buzzing in his head and ears, and at night when he tries to sleep, he says someone tries to inject his legs with a liquid to keep him from walking. "But I'm smarter than they are," he told me, his teeth were chattering. He said, "I stay awake so they can't touch me. Their petty tyranny will not get to me."

Susan, when he talks to me, I must turn away from the fear in his eyes. I swear his eyes never blink. He is so thin, so small. The doctors have told me that he seems to get worse when I visit him, so it would be better if I stay away for a while. I am okay with this because so many people see him each day.

His visitors are what one of the papers has the nervo to call the "sob sisters." They are all wonderful, kind, educated women that choose to help Nicola and Bartolo. One of them, an English tutor, Cerise Carman Jack. Mrs. Jack is trying to convince Nicola to start eating, and she will begin to teach him English. It seems the whole world knows what good men they are except the authorities.

Yesterday, Luca brought me news that Nicola would be force-fed with a tube in his vein, so thankfully, he has finally agreed to begin eating. Luca. That is another incredible story perhaps I will speak of at a later day.

All my love to you and your Gordon, and I hope your father is doing well.

You should see Ines. She is the image of her father.

Multi Baci,
Rosina

Susan's reply came quickly.

Dear Rosina,

Thank you, thank you, for finally answering my letter.

I know how hard it's been for you and how very busy the children and your work must keep you. And you're right, I do know what is going on with the men.

You may not realize, but I'm active here in Maine protesting. I head up a group of like-minded people who have joined me at rallies, holding up signs, FREE POLITICAL PRISONERS. I wouldn't know what to do without this work.

Gordon spends most of his days working as a draftsman (A person who draws illustrations for the newspapers, magazines, etc.), and then in the evening, he is in his studio. His studio is located about four hundred feet from the house in the middle of the forest that surrounds our property. Although he can no longer speak or walk without assistance, my father seems to be happy here.

You have dozens of my letters to answer. I am thinking maybe we can meet in New York and have a grand time protesting and passing out flyers to help the men.

I look forward to hearing from you again.

Oh, and now you have piqued my curiosity about Luca.

All my love,
Susan

It doesn't take long for Rosina to realize she no longer wants to be connected to Susan's world. Susan did have a way of making her feel less empty, but now she realizes she no longer wants to be a part of this world. The cost has been so high. How unrealistic, meeting her in New York, *completely out of touch with reality*, Rosina thinks. She brings Susan's letter to the dictionary and looks up the word "piqued."

Dear Susan,

Nicola received special permission to work in the hospital ward. He felt great happiness to be able to work again, and I am so relieved.

When I visited him, he was filled with a sense of joy. It was two weeks of gladness for us. I brought the children, and he played with them and told Dante about his work. He was praised as an excellent worker.

Then on Saturday, thankful I had left the children home, I found him on his cot too ill to meet me in the visitors' room. He said, "They throw the tools at me, too dangerous for me to work." He is no longer the man I married. He has not been the man I married for such a long time.

I feel like we are on that rollercoaster people talk about in Coney Island. Me hanging off the side, dangling like a kite string at the mercy of the wind, anchored by Nicola's hand.

The newspapers predict he will begin another hunger strike, so once again, they are setting up their charts, recording his days without food, his fever, drawing out the demons and spooks who suck blood from the weak.

You can see I am constantly fighting anger. Rage wins most of the time. I must finish this letter later. It's time for lunch.

Rosina finishes washing up the lunch dishes, and says, "Let's go water Papa's tree." Ines takes her make-believe watering can and they head out to the side of the house where the wooden rain barrel stands. Rosina pretends to scoop up water for Ines, then lowers the pot handle to fill her can with water. They walk a few feet to where she had planted a fig tree over a year ago. She had named it *L'albero della vittoria*: Nicola's Victory tree. The fig tree is already as tall as Dante. When Dante helped her dig into the soil, she thoughtlessly told him when the tree gets to be his height, his father will be home.

She's seen Dante watch the tree from the corner of his eye. He doesn't want to talk about his father. In the same way, she is so tired of talking and hearing about the case. Her heart hurts so deeply for her boy. *He didn't ask to be born. He doesn't deserve to suffer.* Children at school have bullied him. "Your father is crazy. A murderer." She is sick and worn from seeing him come home with a sad face. His anger at her for sending him to school has silenced him. She wants to keep him home, but there is no time to teach him. She must work at her dressmaking. She must care for Ines and try to keep the home for them.

She sees in the newspaper that *The Phantom of the Opera* is playing in the theater. She had been dreaming of going. Maybe she could ask Luca to take her. An escape. To be thrown into such a fantasy would be a blessing, but her mounting guilt surfaces once again. *Mio marito che soffre;* my poor suffering husband. They were in this together from the start. Their *ideals* have brought them to this hell, and she must pay along with him.

Rosina begins to write again.

> *Susan, it's taken me two days to return to this letter. You might already know the news that after six months in the psychiatric hospital, Nicola is being released and will be back in his cell in Dedham Jail.*
>
> *The alienist has recommended he work. He said he found Nicola to be an intelligent, sensitive man whose basic needs are healthy and normal. He needs to have a purpose of allowing him to be productive.*

She stops writing. *What am I doing?* she folds the letter in three and slips it into the nightstand drawer.

38

In November, an early snowstorm closes down Boston and its surrounding areas. Rosina is happy to have Dante at home. The schools will be closed through the Thanksgiving holiday. Rosina's heart beats happily as she watches Dante play with his sister. All his anger seems to have disappeared as he stacks the building blocks that Luca had bought for him. He makes a tall building on the floor and says, "Mama, do you like my church?"

"Church? How do you know about churches?" she says as she's hand-sewing darts into a bridesmaid's bodice.

"It's the one at the corner of the school."

"Oh," she says and smirks at her overdefensive ways. "It's wonderful. But you shouldn't build on the floor. Ines will knock them over."

The moment Ines hears her name, she looks up from her half-dressed doll and begins to run to the building blocks, and *boom*, they all scatter. Ines rollicks in laughter. Dante grabs hold of her around her waist and tickles her to the floor.

Later, by the dinner table, Rosina stands over Dante with a bowl of mashed potatoes, ready to scoop some into his dish. "You were so sweet to your sister today." she says, "How is it you weren't angry when she knocked over your church?"

Dante looks directly up at her with his bright, clear gaze and says, "I'm happy I don't have to go to school these days."

Unexpectedly, she tears up. *How can she have a child who is so aware, so truthful, and has suffered so, and she not help him?* Maybe she could take him out of school. She could try to find a tutor. At least for math, since it is her own most inadequate subject. She enfolds Dante in an embrace, forgetting to lower the bowl of potatoes, some fall onto his shoulder roll onto his lap, but it doesn't matter. *Oh God, we should've been better parents*, she thinks. "I'm sorry, so sorry...." her words mix with her tears and come out jumbled, but Dante understands.

"Don't cry, Mama."

"I should've never sent you to *that* school. No more." Stronger now, she stands straight, "You will learn at home."

Rosina's son flings his arms around her waist. "Thank you, Mama. I promise I'll learn."

And then Ines's small hands holding onto her thigh, she demands, "Me too, Mama."

* * *

Nicola has been exercising outdoors and is allowed to polish floors and sometimes work in the prison kitchen. His physical condition improves and he is gaining weight. Having decided that eating meat is what makes men aggressive, he eats potatoes and beans only.

The New England Civil Liberties Committee, which supported the men throughout the trial, has become more active personally. Mrs. Cerise Carman Jack and her daughter Betty visit the men weekly. Mrs. Jack keeps her word meeting with Nicola twice weekly to work on his English.

When Rosina sees Nicola, he is brighter than he's been in years. His feet and wrists unchained, he sits across from her. "Mrs. Jack talks to me about their farm. Her husband is a professor." He reaches for a piece of paper and hands it to her, "Here, she wrote this down for me."

Rosina reads: *John Jack is a professor of dendrology.* "What is this den-dro-logy?" They chuckle at the sound. "*E un dentista?*" she asks.

"No, *dentista,* he studies trees. Such a big word." He laughs again, "Why can't they just call it *botanico?*"

These small moments where he seems renewed and Rosina feels a lightness she hasn't felt in a long time.

"They named their farm Folly Farm," he says. "It seems like a place of freedom and happiness, some kind of mystical enchanting place." He holds that dreamy look. "Mrs. Jack said comes spring they will be bringing flowers and fruits, whatever their farm produces."

"Oh, Nicola," she says. "Remember the old days. When we were free. Together."

Nicola holds her gaze. He clears his throat. "You don't have to visit me so often" he says, measured. "Stay home with the children."

Rosina smiles. This is what she wanted to hear, and she is glad. But then, her emotions recoil. She's lost. Tears spring to her eyes. Such dread: the upcoming court appeal, the way it devastates them each time.

* * *

Weeks pass since she last saw Nicola. Aldo was the one to tell Nicola the court appeal was denied once again. "Nick took it in stride; he was expecting it. He said, if we keep going to the same people, the same judge, presenting the same false evidence against us, why should we expect anything different?"

Rosina has prepared biscotti and packed sweet tangerines they found at the market. "Good vitamin C," Luca said as he put them in a paper bag for weighing. When Luca and Felice visited Nicola, he had mentioned he missed the smell of tangerine skins. "It's the small things you appreciate," his expression, capturing a memory of the past.

Luca, later that evening, saunters into Rosina's sewing room and leans against the door jamb.

"I'm going to go now, but I want to tell you something."

"Yes," she says, without taking her eyes off the pulsing needle of the machine.

"He knows. Nicola knows about us."

Startled by his words, she forgets to take her foot off the sewing machine pedal fast enough, and the material bunches into knots under the needle. "What are you saying?"

Yards of lace across her lap, she trips over the material as she stands.

Luca catches her by her shoulders before she falls.

"What do you mean? He knows?" she glares into Luca's reflection.

"I didn't want to tell you. The last time I was there and each time before, he always says as I'm leaving, "Luca, take care of my Rosina.""

"That doesn't mean he knows! He's just looking out for me." She says it, but she doesn't really believe it. "Why wouldn't he have asked me. Talked to me about it?"

"*E' strano*, it's strange. But he doesn't want you to be uncomfortable. Nicola is a good man. He's not stupid, Rosina."

"I know he's good, and that he's not stupid," she says more angrily than she meant. She turns her back towards him. "You should've have never told me this." She gathers up the material from the floor, piling it all on top of the machine.

Luca seems dumbfounded, "I thought you'd feel some relief. Not guilt."

An expression of disbelief is on his face. Suddenly, a scalding shame grips her. She begins to shake. "Can you leave, please!"

He goes to touch her arm, but she backs away.

"Rosina, I'm sorry if I upset you."

"Not now. Please, I need to be alone."

* * *

The jailhouse is cold and damp, as expected. Rosina is happy to see Nicola wearing the green woolen cardigan with deep front pockets and gold embossed buttons. When she places the tangerines and biscotti on the table before him, she remembers when they bought the sweater. It was before they married. In the tiny shop his Jewish friend Morris owned, Nicola was modeling the sweater, and when he turned to ask her how she liked it, she was struck by the twinkle in his eyes and knew that as one of the moments she had fallen in love with him.

"I have great news, my Rosina," he says as he opens the paper bag and sees the fruit. "Oh," he smiles, "Someone must've told you about my craving for tangerines."

"As if I don't know my own husband," she says. Although it's true, he has become part stranger. The years apart, no matter how hard she has tried, have robbed them of their intimacy. Their companionship strained, pulled apart by the system, the very rules they've fought against have brought them to their knees. Living estranged lives, each afraid to speak of their pain, fearing they will cause more pain to the other. *Perhaps I should confess about Luca*, she thinks. *Possibly our ability to connect to each other will return, and this gnawing cold sensation I have when I'm with him will wither. But what will I confess to? She hadn't made love with Luca. Not yet. Should I tell him of my desires to lay with this man? Never. It will only hurt.*

She returns to the moment. "What news?"

"I cannot believe it. It's still stirring inside of me." He shivers with delight. "Aldo wanted to tell you, but I said no, I want to be the one."

"What is it?" Rosina had seen this glow, this expression of joy on Nicola before, but not in the six years since imprisoned.

"Early this morning, the guard slipped me a note from the Portuguese, Celestino Madeiros. The young man who is on death row."

Nicola takes his time.

"Yes?" Rosina asks impatiently.

"In his note he confessed to being a member of the gang that killed Parmenter and Berardelli. He confessed he was one of the men who took part in the robbery. It was the Morelli brother's gang who committed the murders and robbery."

Rosina, in total disbelief, covers her mouth with her hands. "Where? *Where* is this note?"

"Aldo has taken it to Thompson, and they will get a typed, written confession from Madeiros to hand deliver to the courts."

Rosina's fingers, as if stunned into position, are still pressed over her mouth until she sees Nicola begin to shake. His whole body vibrates into heavy sobs. Rushing to embrace him, she realizes she feels no *real gioia*; despair has won so many times that it seems impossible to allow happiness in only to have it taken once again. Yet, she manages a few words, "There is hope. *Verità Verità*, the truth will win, *amore mio*."

39

The first week in December, Thompson had a typewriten, fully detailed confession from Madeiros. It took nearly two days to get Madeiros to name the men who were involved. After the District Attorney saw the statement, Thompson planned to file a motion for a new trial based on the confession. By March there was still no response, so Thompson decided to go to the Supreme Court. The newspapers printed Judge Thayer's remark— "Let them go to the Supreme Court and see where it gets them." The judge added that under Massachusetts law, the original judge on the case would be the one to rule on the motion.

Still, waiting on a word for a new trial allows a fragment of hope. Enough for Rosina to be grateful for what she has. Especially when the work at the sewing machine is monotonous: six bridesmaids' dresses, all the same color and style. Cerise Jack and her daughter, Betty, and Auntie Bee, Elizabeth Gurley Flynn, Alice Stone Blackwell, Virginia MacMechan, and Mary Donovan; they surround Nick, as they like to call him, and Bart, and herself with their time, gifts, dependency, and support. All of them deserve sainthood, Rosina thinks, but then discards the thought, wondering if she will ever be free of the Church's persuasion. Thanks to the women's generosity, Nicola can offer her, and the children gifts he receives from them: apples, berries, peaches, cherries, homemade honey, chocolates, and early spring flowers. She thinks of Nicola, his eyes pools of light, when she visits with the children, "When I see little Ines run to me for kisses and hugs and then asks me if I have something for her, it makes me so happy. She knows I always offer some little thing from what my friends bring. And the best part, she kisses and hugs me some more." He laughs.

On Saturday, Rosina is rushing to finish the bridal party dresses. Carmela had packed a lunch for the children and herself and had made their way to the picnic grounds, when Rosina hears footsteps on the creaking floorboards of the porch. Auntie Bee is standing there, attorney Thompson walking up the path behind her. A shiver runs through.

"I... I thought you were Carmela," Rosina says. "She always forgets something." *If she keeps talking everything will be okay. She doesn't want anyone else to say anything.* "Can I make you a cup of tea, coffee, something to eat."

Auntie Bee touches her forearm and says, "Let's sit, my dear."

"No. I don't have time to sit." She points to the billowing fabric at the sewing machine; even though from where they stand, they cannot see it. "See all the work I have."

Thompson says, "I'm here at the request of Nick, he wants me to explain the way the law works and..."

"Please. I know how the law works. Why would my husband send you here?"

"Nicola is worried about you. He wants to be certain you're cared for."

When they both sit on the settee, Rosina paces in front of them, "Go ahead, tell me, even though I already know.

"Rosina, I'm sorry but the Supreme Judicial Court has handed down its decision to not have a new trial. They say it rests with the judicial discretion of the trial judge, and we all know that Thayer from the first moment had decided the men are guilty."

Auntie Bee bewildered, shakes her head back and forth. "It seems to me that Judge Thayer is the only one who has the right to be wrong. The man believes that he's God."

"So, Madeiro's confession means nothing?" Rosina makes her way to the parlor window. A stone's throw away, a few stems of crocus push their way above the ground. What defiant little plants they are. "I think it's time to unwrap the fig tree," she says. "I'll have to ask Nicola."

"The word of a thief and murderer is just not strong enough to reopen the case." Thompson clears his throat, a sound she has gotten accustomed to hearing. "Nicola has asked that you not be in court for the sentencing."

"Sentencing? Hasn't he already been sentenced? Almost seven years now?"

In the silence of the moment, Rosina makes her way to the chair across from her visitors who are beaten, both looking downward as though in prayer. Images of the nuns comes to her. She closes her eyes.

"When?"

"Most likely in a few weeks. Thompson says, "It's up to the courts."

"Rosina, darling," Auntie Bee, starts, "We've got at least one hundred petitions out there against the death sentence, reporters like Gardner Jackson are doing all they can. Hopefully it will help."

Thompson joins in, "Our strategy now will be to get life sentencing. We have Felix Frankfurter, a Harvard Law School graduate who is extremely influential with intellectuals all over the world. He has agreed to review the case and is going to help in any way he can."

Hating the sound of all these "official" names and words, she looks at both of them with cold determination. "Do you really suppose it will matter!" Her heart is a stone in her chest. "I must get back to work."

The silence in the room cuts into them—swallows them—something has shifted, something it seems no one can or will identify.

40

Two weeks later, on a Saturday evening, Nicola and Bartolomeo face Judge Thayer. Police surround the courthouse. Spectators line the streets. When the clerk of the court asks Nicola why the sentence of death should not be passed upon him, he first pleads in his true passionate style for Bartolomeo, praising him as a kind, gentle man who is loved by all people. A man who could never commit such crimes. Then he says, "I know this sentence is between two classes. The oppressed class and the rich class. That is why I am here today on this bench, for I am the oppressed class, and you sir, Judge Thayer, you are the oppressor. I have never been guilty of such crimes of murder or robbery, not yesterday, nor today, nor forever."

If Rosina were in the courtroom and not locked away in her home with the electrical cord pulled from the radio, she would've heard about the onlookers weeping, and the enormous crowds outside the courthouse.

When Bartolomeo is asked the same question, he speaks for forty-five minutes. His words bring tears to everyone in the room.

"I am innocent," he says. "I have never stolen, nor have I ever killed anyone or even spilled another man's blood. I have struggled all my life to eliminate crime from this Earth. I have struggled to eliminate the exploitation and the oppression of Man by Man, and yes, this is the reason I am here today, for this reason and non-else. Some of the greatest thinkers of the world, in Europe, here in America, writers, scientists, the best and greatest statesmen, they see the injustice here and know. I wonder how it is that the men on your jury believe they are right, while the whole world knows they are wrong. I do not wish on a dog or a snake the misfortune I've experienced. I have suffered for things I am not guilty of. I am suffering because I am Italian, and indeed I am an Italian. I am suffering because I am a radical. Indeed, I am a radical. I am convinced that I am right. If I were reborn again, I would live again to do what I've had done already."

It was reported that Judge Thayer in his chair was looking out the window at the flowering trees—turned away from the men when they spoke. It was further noted in the newspapers for weeks after, that Judge Thayer when pronouncing their sentence; "To suffer the punishment of death by the passage of a current of electricity through your body" neglected to say, "And may the Lord have mercy on your soul."

* * *

The day after sentencing, entering the jail, the guards seem humble, almost reverent: *Sit Mrs. Sacco—Nick will be right out—Hot out there today—Can I get you some water?* Rosina needs to cry but cannot. How comforting it would be if the red-headed guard that stands with her would embrace her. Then she might be able to wail, and caterwaul like a street cat and empty herself of this agony.

Nicola seems resigned. His suffering will now come to an end. Relieved and uplifted, wrapped in some kind of deranged lunacy he whispers to Rosina, *"Our torment will finally end. Don't let this ruin your days, pretend we're in a play. Yes, pretend, we'll be fine."* He *whispers into her ear, moistening strands of her hair with tears that flow down his cheeks.* "You must dig the fig tree up in the early winter and cover it in burlap and bury it in a trench and then cover it with mulch or bring it into the house."

Rosina leaves the jailhouse confused, diminished, and dull. Refusing Auntie Bee's car, she walks in a dream-state. She walks for hours. Numb. She walks through an unforgiving wild rain shower. Hard rain bounces off the sidewalks and steam rises from the concrete.

Moments later, the sun breaks through and, in the distance, she sees an *arcobaleno*, a rainbow of blue, green, and gold. The world will still be here. The world, still lush and beautiful. All will still be here. Except for her Nick. Wearily, she remembers her idea to visit the Governor. She could plead for the men. Save them, she would say. She recalls her visit to Galleani—*it had worked*. And like the unexpected appearance of the *arcobaleno*, she feels an unexpected spark of hope.

Weeks pass and Nicola seems happier now that he and his friend, Bartolo, were moved to Charleston State Prison. Aldo was cleared for a bocce ball set and he and Bartolo played together twice a day.

"I want to play ball with my son," he tells Rosina. Not remembering that Dante is being home schooled, he says, "Now that the summer is here, he has no school. You can bring him when I have yard time."

How can she tell him, a man on death row, that she must work? She is not only there to serve him and his needs; she has her own needs.

"I don't want Dante to be inside the jail—it will not be good for him."

"No...no," he shakes his head, "I don't want him in here. He can stand outside of the prison wall, maybe. And I'll be on the other side and we can throw the ball over the wall to each other."

When Rosina tells Dante of her father's request, he is sitting on the floor with Tootsie on his lap, his hand filled with rabbit hair from brushing her coat. "That will be better, Mama. I don't want to go inside that jail. I don't want to see what the death row looks like."

Ines, a few feet away from him has her cloth doll in the shoebox, a make-shift cradle Rosina has lined with a gingham quilted material. She scolds the doll, "I will send you to dead row, if you don't sleep."

Rosina is stunned that her children even know these words. The way Dante says *death row* as easily as he asks to play outside.

* * *

Three stays of execution have passed, and on the day before what is said to be the final scheduled execution, Rosina is able to get an appointment to see Governor Alvan Fuller. She prepares by reading the hundreds of letters and articles printed in the newspapers supporting the men. Elegantly written letters by known writers here and abroad that her own words seem so unimpressive. She will speak from the heart. She will flood his chambers with truths. If needed, she will be Machiavellian, cunning, flattering him, for what good has come from their honesty? She is full of passion for correcting the evils that have taken over their lives. In spite of all this, her legs are heavy concrete blocks. It's as if some kind of gargoyle is sitting on her shoulders. In the pocket of her dress, she touches the soft petals of a pink lily Ines had given her. *This,* she thinks. *This...*and she holds the petals lightly in the folds of her fingers.

Luca escorts her into the Statehouse building. In her handbag, she has a copy of a petition the committee delivered to Alvan Fuller the day before. Seven hundred and fifty thousand signatures for a stay of execution. She will beg for life imprisonment. This is the best she could hope for. The Statehouse is overwhelming; the Brandeis house looks like a cottage compared to the hallway with its round columns. Luca had dressed in a suit and tie, hoping they would allow him to go in with Rosina, but the young man in his blue navy suit says he must wait for Rosina in the hallway. Rosina doesn't look at Luca. She wants to stay focused, so she follows the back of the navy-blue suit into a room where there are two sofas facing one another. The young man directs Rosina to sit on one of the sofas and says, "Governor Fuller will be with you shortly." Rosina is faint. She realizes she's been holding her breath.

When he walks into the room, she hears his heels clicking on the wooden floor, then his voice. "Well, Mrs. Sacco, what can I do for you?"

Rosina recognizes him from the newspapers. Hair parted on the side, clean-shaven man with his shirt collar so starched it pinches his jowls. "I've come to plea for my husband." Her voice sounds weak and trembly. "I have a petition here with 750,000 signatures." She draws the paper from her purse. "Please help these men. They are both innocent."

He moves to his large mahogany desk under a huge arched window.

"Come, sit here," he says, pointing to a leather chair across from his desk. He doesn't wait for her to sit but continues to speak. "A few days ago, I went to see the men. I saw Mr. Vanzetti, but your husband, Mrs. Sacco, refused to meet with me."

"Your eminence," she says, this word she had been practicing. "Please try to understand he is angry. He's been imprisoned for seven years already. His spirit is destroyed."

"Mrs. Sacco, I have the Harvard committee looking into their trial. I will have an answer soon. There is nothing more I can do, Mrs. Sacco. I'm sorry." He pulls the chain on his pocket watch; "I have another meeting."

That's all?

"Please, Mr. Fuller, your eminence, I know you are a man of God, and rightfully so. I know you've received thousands of letters and telegrams asking not to execute the men. My husband is innocent. He could never hurt any man." The governor puts his hand out to assist her out of her chair. She rises on her own. "Please, your honor."

He turns his back and starts to walk towards the door. Rosina has the urge to beat him, to pound on his back continuously until he breaks, but instead, she drops to her knees, "I beg of you," she cries. "Be that great man that everyone says you are. The best Governor Massachusetts has ever had. Listen to God. Massachusetts needs that great man tonight. Please, your eminence."

When he sees her kneeling on the floor, "Please, get up. There is no need to be on your knees." He pushes a button on his desk. "Come on, up now," he scowls.

"Governor Fuller, you are a man who can be a god. You can be God. You have the power to change the lives of two children." These words summon deep sobs. Sobs she cannot control.

The young man in the navy suit is lifting her by the arms, "Please, madam," he says.

The Governor turns and says, "I'm sorry." And closes the door behind him.

Rosina takes a handkerchief from her purse and wipes her eyes and face. She looks at the young man and asks, "How...how can one man have such power? Shaking her head in disbelief, "How can human beings do such things to each other?"

The young man holding her up is not only pale, but silent.

* * *

That evening Rosina fixes the settee with a blanket, sheet, and pillow so Luca can sleep. Luca will drive her in the morning to say goodbye once again to Nicola and Bartolo. Then along with Aldo, Auntie Bee, Cerise Jack and Betty, and all the other supporters, they will be staying at the rooming house across from the prison.

Carmela and Romeo will be with the children through the night. The very thing Rosina wishes she could do.

In the morning, she feels paralyzed— not wanting to feel or think or talk. She doesn't answer when someone speaks to her. Later that evening, when she finds herself in the boarding house, she doesn't know how she got there. The walls in her room are unsubstantial, chiffony-thin. She hears a low murmuring of voices. Like the calls of mourning doves. But there is nothing spiritual here. They wait for the Governor to call to stop the execution. She sees their shadows under her door, pacing, gathering in the hallway. Would anyone understand that she doesn't want him to call, that *this* has to be over? They have been in this wretched place for too long. She allows her tears to drip from the corner of her eyes onto the pillow. The clock on the bedstand is eleven-forty-five at night. She will pray to Sister Cristina: this reticent nun, her only link to a possible God. *Pray to your Virgin Mary, my beloved Suora, per favore, release Nicola from agony, set him free, please...hail Mary full of grace, the Lord is with you; blessed are you among women, and.... The* chant doesn't reach within. It is the quiet repetition of the words that bring a calm. *Repeat...repeat.*

Auntie Bee knocks at the door. "Are you okay, sweetheart?"

She swallows hard, "Give me a few minutes." The clock hands have almost reached midnight. She hears church bells ringing. Why? she nods off for a few moments and wakes to the sound of more church bells...an unsuitable sound here in warehouse row, on this bitter, grave night. The clock hands have moved past midnight. *What is happening? Has the Governor come through? Have they allowed her to sleep through the phone call?* The lamp on the night table begins to tremble. Rosina moves to the window and, just across the way, sees the lights from the prison flicker off and on, then all turns dark, except for the shooting zaps of electricity escaping from the power poles within the prison grounds. Spent currents of electrical static have settled Massachusetts into darkness. Sparks fly through the night sky, speak to Rosina; fast and furious, they move through her body and leave through her gaping mouth in shrieks.

Auntie Bee screams, "Someone help." Luca lifts Rosina off the floor as she howls. He carries her in the sparse room to the rocking chair, cradles her in his lap, and rocks back and forth, weeping, "I know. I know." The cries from the rooming house are piercing. They are heard all over Charlestown.

* * *

The funeral saw a downpour of rain that Boston hadn't seen in years. Aldo had arranged an eight-mile procession from the funeral home to the cemetery, with a stop in front of the State House to disgrace the murderers. Aldo, who sits across from Rosina in the funeral car, says, "Katherine Ann Porter, Edna St. Vincent Millay, telegrams from Mussolini, LaGuardia, so many dignitaries. Fifty-thousand mourners passed their coffins at the funeral home." Teary-eyed for three days now, he continues, "We've done a good job of exposing the crimes committed by the government," but looks ahead at the side-by-side funeral cars that carry the men. "Apparently, not good enough."

She wants Aldo to stop talking. She doesn't respond. A numbness, the finality of death carries Rosina. It's as if she were dead, just moving from place to place to get things done. When they reach the Statehouse, they find the street has been broken, jackhammered during the early morning hours. They cannot pass. There are police on horses and wooden horses. Rosina gazes at the thousands upon thousands of mourners through the car window, then steps onto the car's running board. A voice inside her is screaming, *No, No.* The policeman yells at her to get back in the car and to turn the car around. Rosina feels rage, as if she were pierced with a hot iron poker. The procession has moved up behind her, arm in arm, shoulder to shoulder, a solid wall of black armbands, unbroken. They march through the fractured sidewalks and streets, forcing the policemen to move aside. They stop in front of the Statehouse in the pouring rain and chant,

"Justice is crucified. Justice is crucified," repeatedly until the thunder in the distance signals them to move on.

EPILOGUE

Rosina hears Luca in the old barn, trying to remove a fender from the old-rusted truck they had found there when they bought the small farm in Watertown over a year ago. She and Ines are watering the vegetable garden. It is a clear, sunny day with fast-moving clouds.

"Looks like we'll be getting lots of figs this year. We've kept it very warm through the winter months. Look how big the tree is," Rosina says.

"Mama, why can't we see the trees growing?"

Rosina is delighted by her questions. "For the same reason, we can't see you growing. It has to do with time, lightyears? And maybe math, I don't understand myself."

"Papa could see the trees growing. He told me."

"Well, *bambina mia*, Papa was gifted. He had a special imagination."

"I want to be like him."

"*No. No*, you are much better the way you are. You will never be fooled." Rosina drops the weeds in the growing pile and moves the sweaty hairs off Ines's forehead, "You see things the way they really are, and that's what's important."

Ines's energy is boundless, "Look, look up, Mama," she points to the skies, "See Tootsie there with a baby rabbit. They're kissing." She jiggles Rosina's shoulder, "Hurry, look."

Rosina looks up at the cloud shapes and stretches her imagination; all she sees is a vulture attacking a squirrel.

Luca walks from the barn to the house, shouting, "Who wants lunch?" And Ines runs in, "I do, I do."

Rosina kicks off her rubber boots in the mudroom and quickly rinses her hands in the bowl of water waiting on the bench. She removes her towel from the hook and sees Ines's towel hasn't been touched.

She shouts, "Ines, did you wash your hands?"

Luca shouts back, "She washed them in here. Are you coming for lunch?" Luca's bachelor days have trained him well. He enjoys working in the kitchen and always helps.

Framed on the wall above the towel hooks are Bartolomeo's last words. She will take it down one day, pack it away, but for now she needs to see it. Well known, it has been printed over and over in newspapers and books, cut into metal planks, and carved on wooden plaques, and although she knows it by heart, she reads it once again, her daily prayer.

> *If it had not been for these things, I might have lived out my life talking at street corners to scorned men. I might have died, unmarked, unknown, a failure. Now, we are not a failure. This is our career and our triumph. Never in our full life can we hope to do such work for tolerance, for justice, for man's understanding of man, as now we do by accident. Our lives—our words—our pain—nothing. The taking of our lives—lives of a good shoemaker and poor fish peddler—all—this moment belongs to us-— this agony is our triumph.*

Rosina puts her soiled towel back on the hook. Dante comes bicycling up the path with an empty canvas sack hanging off the handlebar. Newspapers delivered; he rushes past his mother bursting with that same kind of pleasant accomplishment that oozed from his father after completing a job.

"I'm starving," he says.

Humidity sticks to his short-sleeved buttoned-down shirt—revealing his bony elbows and flattened chest. The sight of him, vibrant, and filled with life doesn't distract Rosina's searing notion of what will take hold of him in the end. At times she finds herself wrapped in irony. She laughs deep and low, all their work in vain—how foolish—a handful of agitators trying to change the world for the better. But now she sighs with relief—*this* is no longer her burden. Her family, Luca, and the children, this tiny farm, this is her glory. Even when she stirs in the middle of the night—and wonders how *L'idea* affected the children, she's galvanized by the truth. When Dante, so much like his father, turns his head a certain way, her heart thumps. Or, when she hears his laughter drifting in from another room, it brings her to her knees. Yet she accepts this grief with a grace she had unknowingly learned while in the convent. There is no other way.

Rosina Zambelli Bianchini died at the age of 94 in 1989 in a nursing home in Massachusetts.

ACKNOWLEDGMENTS

As a child of Italian immigrant parents, the names "Sacco and Vanzetti" resonated throughout my childhood. My father, a self-proclaimed anarchist, who championed the underdog, renounced institutions and was aware of the bias against foreigners. My loving, Sicilian mother, paralyzed by the strength of social injustice, related to Sacco's wife, a mother of two children. Their discussions reeked of how immigrants were poorly treated.

I researched books and articles about Nicola Sacco and Bartolomeo Vanzetti and found little information about Rosina, Nicola Sacco's wife. The more I read, the more I felt and imagined her life. E. L. Doctorow once said, "The Historian will tell you what happened. The Novelist will tell you what it felt like." Hence, I took his words and ran with them.

This work of fiction is based wholly on the imagined life of Rosina Sacco, I chose to write this story through her eyes. A sad, frightening tale, and through my research and reading the writings and letters of those involved; I found a desperation so deep and daunting to mankind, yet so human that I felt compelled to write this story.

Any writer of historical fiction owes a great deal to the exhausted research documented by the non-fiction writer. The authors who went through the pains of gathering facts and reporting them to the best of their ability. While there are many books written on the Sacco and Vanzetti case, here are the few I chose to read and found to stir my imagination. *The Sacco and Vanzetti case by Michael M. Topp, Sacco and Vanzetti, The Men, the Murders, and the judgment of Mankind by Bruce Watson, Howard Zinn's* collected speeches, and *Susan Tejada's, In Search of Sacco and Vanzetti*. Tejada's unbiased account and intimate narrative was more than enough to continue to light my imagination and spur on the story that had been lying dormant within me for many years. I want to thank Susan Tejada and all these authors who worked so hard to try and set the record straight.

Since this work is the total imagination of this author. I did not allow history to hem me in. I've included some characters of that period, and invented others.

I'd like to thank my husband Jim, and my daughters Laurie, Suzann, and Alexandra for their continued encouragement and for always being by my side. My beautiful grandchildren William, Joseph, Emily, Antonio, Christopher, Andrew, Dimitri, Isabella, Gabriella, Lachlan, and Holden, plus the greats, Cristiano, Landon, Olivia, Aurora, and Dream who make me happy each day. My sister Millie who loves all things Italian read an early version and joyfully inspired me to continue. *Molte grazie* to Sonia Bartoli and Linda Lappin for correcting and fine-tuning my Italian. Lastly, gratitude to Dr. Bill for doing all that he does in the literary world.

MIRIAM POLLI
2024

ABOUT THE AUTHOR

Miriam Polli's debut novel *In a Vertigo of Silence* was named one of the Best Indie Books of 2015 by Kirkus Reviews. Her stories and poems have been published in commercial and literary magazines and are included in two anthologies. She received recognition from the Italian American Writers Association for her story "Gifts of Grief" and an honorable mention for the World's Greatest Short Short Story Competition, where there were several thousand entries. Her poem "First Born" won the 11th Annual Robert Frost Poetry Contest. She is also a recipient of a PEN Syndicated Fiction Award. A native New Yorker, Miriam now lives in Virginia.

www.ingramcontent.com/pod-product-compliance
Lightning Source LLC
Chambersburg PA
CBHW061810190726

48289CB00007B/2147